THE
SUMMER
AFTER JUNE

THE
SUMMER
AFTER JUNE

Ashley Warlick

HOUGHTON MIFFLIN COMPANY

BOSTON · NEW YORK

2000

For information about permission to reproduce
selections from this book, write to
Permissions, Houghton Mifflin Company,
215 Park Avenue South, New York,
New York 10003.

Library of Congress Cataloging-in-Publication Data

Warlick, Ashley.
The summer after June / Ashley Warlick.
p.   cm.
ISBN 0-395-92690-4
I. Title.
PS3573.A7617S86   2000
813'.54—dc21   99-40638
CIP

Printed in the United States of America

Book design by Robert Overholtzer

QUM 10 9 8 7 6 5 4 3 2 1

For Moo-Moo,
Mom,
Piper,
and Sophie

Coming east we left the animals
pelican beaver osprey muskrat and snake
their hair and skin and feathers
their eyes in the dark: red and green.
Your finger drawing my mouth.

Blessed are they who remember
that what they now have they once longed for.

A day a year ago last summer
God filled me with himself, like gold, inside,
deeper inside than marrow.

This close to God this close to you:
walking into the river at Wolf with
the animals. The snake's
green skin, lit from inside. Our second life.

— "The River at Wolf," by Jean Valentine

THE
SUMMER
AFTER JUNE

THEIR LAST NIGHT, he told her how leavings have several virtues.

This is the way it will be, he said.

Come morning and her driving, the sun will warm her fingertips on the wheel of that big car and it'll be as if he's there, inside that sun, inside her fingertips. He'll take up in the thinnest parts of her, and he told her to name those parts: the beds of her nails, the roots of her hairs, the vessels, the bones. He told her he'd run that space like it was all his own, and he'd keep running until she felt it, until she shivered and swelled just a bit bigger to be full with him.

Their last night, he told her he would always be with her, whether she was here or there or not.

I'll make it easy for you, he said. *This is for keeps.*

Orrin has come to her this way every morning since she left him, every morning for three in a row. He's steadfast about his promises, and she's been made to feel it, made to be grateful and trusting in sweeter, higher things. She drives I-10 with the sun rising in her windows, trimming the Gulf Coast deltas, she and the baby. This is the last span of highway they'll need to be on for a while, and she wonders how Orrin will come to her when she's not behind the wheel of this car, when she has no need for travel in the early hours of the day.

In Galveston he said, *You'll think of me in morning times most often*, and she said, *Yes, I will*, but that's not been true. She thinks of him all the time, or not at all, the way your brain thinks to beat your heart or breathe air into your lungs without your knowing it. There's the feather he tucked beneath the visor in her car, a green feather, from one of his birds. So many little things bring Orrin.

They still talk inside her head, conversations quiet and simple in the coolness. It's enough to keep her driving long into the distance so as to listen and to speak.

He'll say, *I know how it would be if you hit the water from a height, like if you fell, or dove from a cliff.*

Then she'll say, *How would that be*, and she'll whisper, as if he's just so close to her, as if he could hear her think those words, and maybe back in Galveston he can.

He'll say, *You'd be falling and falling and all drawn up in yourself and ready to hit that water like it was a brick wall, and then you'd just keep falling, your skin stinging and crawling off your bones, and you just falling, your lungs filled up with water instead of air.*

And she'll say, *That's what you think?*

And he'll answer, *That's how it would happen to you. Me, I'm a different story.*

She'll laugh to herself, and maybe later they'll talk about another thing. There are moments she can feel his hand in hers, along her thigh and at the hollow where her neck becomes her shoulders. She hears his voice; feels his touch. She does not miss him yet, and this is why.

She has always had a high threshold for pain. Sometimes it may be hours before she realizes she's hurt herself. She has learned there is no pain out there that could bring her to her knees, that could cut her or bruise her, so she would stop what she was doing and lie down and not get up again. Pain is always loose and free and available. It will wait until she wants it.

She drives with the window of her big car rolled down, an old Loretta Lynn song turned up on the radio. The breeze is warm and sugared with early Alabama fall. She sings for the baby, his silent, sleeping company, and she thinks how soon he'll be waking up, wanting her. That's what she'll fix on until he goes to sleep again.

She is twenty-five, a quarter of something she has yet to figure out. She has been to college. She's had scientific training and knows the chemistry of common things. She moved from her parents' house when it still belonged to both of them, had a job back in Charlotte in a medical center, held a place in the solid, everyday world. Her life was coarse and complicated to her, beginning and ending so much.

These things about her have not changed since she left home. She still knows what she's always known, but added to that is Orrin, what he told her about herself. He had young, awkward things to say at first, how she was smart and strong and good and pretty, but from him she wanted to hear what she'd never heard before. So then he told her how she had a woven step, the inside of her calf brushing the back of the other like her steps were plaiting themselves to the ground, and they began walking everywhere together. He loved her. She knew it. But he said it would be just once upon a time when she went home again.

She's been gone from Charlotte since the spring, west to the Gulf of Mexico. She has not seen her fiancé, Cott, her parents, her job, or anyone she knows from home since March, and now it's fall. They all think her to be missing, to have been taken or murdered or hit over the head so hard she may not be herself anymore, but she is fine and well, and has been for the longest time. She didn't believe she would ever go back, but Orrin told her differently. Now she treasures all the things Orrin said as tiny nascent truths, waiting for the space to become full, to become themselves.

She drives through the night so that the baby will sleep. During the day, they take rooms in pink hotels with swimming pools and ceiling fans and laundered sheets cool from the air conditioner. She remembers the time she and Orrin brought air conditioners to her grandmother's house so they could be lovers in winter times and colder places, December, Montreal, Juneau. Now she thinks that if she reached out, he would be beside her, his head on the pillow, his body in the sheets. It's only a spell they've chosen not to break.

This carefulness with spells is the way they've always been with each other, but what they call *always* is just the stretch of summer out behind them. Time has passed differently. She often forgets they knew each other as children, forgets they knew each other before they were lovers, when Orrin was polite and she was desperate. Now the thing between them has grown up. She has the feeling it will be okay without her.

She takes the baby to the pool when the maid comes around. They float, she on her back and the baby pulled up on her chest, his cheek to her lips. She whispers to him how she and her sister loved their lake back home, and he trails his long toes in the water. There are often other children in the pool, boys in striped trunks with beach balls and rafts and pails they fill with water and dump on the concrete. There are women with books and sunglasses perched beneath lone umbrellas. The baby sees all this, and she's almost sure he feels no part of it. That's fine. He will be different from other boys, other men, and such is life. Such is what she's made for him.

Night comes, and they drive again. When she gets tired, she makes a point to find water — the ocean, a lake, a slow thin river good for swimming. She does it like an animal tucking in for winter, an insect spinning its cocoon. She straps the baby into his seat on the shore, skins off her clothes to pile on the sand. Distant headlights catch her whiteness, the crown of her head, the spread of her bare shoulders in the otherwise dark.

She takes to the water all at once. There is breathlessness and late summer cold, but she dives and surfaces, swims out and back. She sees Orrin in the ghosts of things beneath the surface, just beyond her reach in that spellbound way. It's in the water she feels closest to him, because it's true that all water is connected and flows around the earth in circles, and someday, she thinks, he could have this water on himself. Then, in her mind, she's connected to all the water she ever swam in, all the people she ever loved and was a part of. It is enough to make her do this every night.

When she returns to the shore and the baby, she dresses wet, wrings the water from her hair into her T-shirt, and lets her skirt cling to her legs. She takes her time. She's waiting for Orrin's sunlight to rise and take up in her the way strength might, or goodness or beauty. Then she'll gather the two of them back into the car and continue on her way.

Her name is Lindy Jain. She has left the Gulf Coast for the city of Charlotte, where she grew up, left one man she loves for another who came before him. It is not an easy thing to explain. She knows there are parts of her mind that don't necessarily meet, one thing not always leading to another. She trusts this, that our means need no present end, that sometimes you can do only for yourself. It is how she can love the man she is leaving and still leave, how she could once leave the man she was to marry and still go back now.

THE NIGHT SISTER

WHEN JUNE DIED, they let Lindy prepare the body. It's like that sometimes in hospitals. They're just other places where you can talk people into allowing things that aren't quite ethical, that maybe you aren't really qualified to do. When death comes to one of your own, there's so little that can ever be done anyway.

June was Lindy's sister. Lindy was a nurse at the big medical center and a tissue technician in her off hours. She was trained in the possibilities of life, of death, of any kind of being. She was very good at what she did.

But by the time June's body got to the morgue, the coroner had been all over her, and there wasn't much good to be done. June had been dead too long for her eyes or any of her soft tissue to be usable, and there were issues of contamination to consider. She'd been murdered. Her body had lain open for hours.

Lindy did not touch the autopsy marks. She stitched June's eyelids, washed her skin, kissed the center of her chest, where her heart had been. There were people waiting for Lindy, for the body, right outside the doors. She cut June from hipbone to hipbone, held back the flesh, slipped off her engagement ring, and let it fall inside. She'd forgotten her gloves, wore no gown.

What did things like that matter when it was your sister on the table? She cut the palm of her own hand and bled, as bright and red as ever. It felt like an accident, that cutting, even as she meant to do it.

She stitched her sister closed, and for Lindy a lot of things were over then.

Some months passed. Spring came. Lindy gave up her job at the hospital, and she and Cott stopped sleeping together in the night. They made love, but there was no sleep, no rest. She did not miss it and could not understand how she had ever slept so much before June was murdered.

Endings are beginnings. She knew that, but to hear other people say it about her sister's death made her angry. It was like hearing something out loud she'd been whispering to herself because she thought the trick was in the whispering. She'd get angry, and then she'd want to start over with her sadness, and find a way to feel that no one could describe in passing. She was a stubborn woman. She wanted always to be original.

She still lived in her hometown, in a pretty little bungalow on the east side, where there were restaurants and bars and good bookstores and stationers. The hospital was close by, and ancient oaks canopied the streets. In her kitchen was a pale pink Coolerator stove, and in her parlor were riffles of cards and letters and expensive wedding gifts. Down the hallway, as Cott liked to say, Lindy kept a good bed, a warm bed heaped with feather quilts and coverlets, flannel and mohair and chenille blankets like pine boughs in winter, thick with scent. She kept herself there as often as she could.

It was late March and warming. Lindy lay in her well-kept bed with her eyes closed but her mind like a battering ram at her skull. Her body ached with being awake. She'd been awake all night long. Beside her, Cott had slept soundly, and now he was dressed and gone. He probably thought she was sleeping when he left, so he hadn't disturbed her with a kiss. She would have liked a kiss, though. Maybe it would have made the difference in her head.

She had spent the night with a single thought. She wanted to break her heart for good.

She'd been months at trying to figure a way to care for herself, to return to what her life had been before June died, but she was a bad patient. Nurses always were. There were two kinds: the nurse who couldn't be bothered with pain, and the one who had it far worse than anybody else. Lindy believed she was becoming both. She was dividing inside, multiplying, like a cancer. There were days she could not stand to be with herself.

And so last night she reached the end of something, and her mind hammered out this thought for a solution. She would break her heart for good, for the last and the best. It was common sense. What did everyone say at the clinic? There were no wheelchairs in heaven. You had to have a heart for it to hurt you. She was coming apart anyway. Well, then, she thought, let's get on with it.

She pushed the bedthings from her legs and started water in the bath, as hot as hot could be.

There had been only bad days since the winter, days of waiting to forget or remember, to move in any direction. Lindy was a nurse, soon to be a wife, and yet she wasn't working at either one. She stood in her bathroom and gazed out at the gravel alleyway, swayed slightly in her joints. She was already late for work. How much of the morning did she have to get through? The paper was folded open beside the sink to the weather, weighted with a half-empty cup of coffee. There would be storms, brought north to Charlotte from those brewing in the Gulf of Mexico. She stood at the window and knew she could stand and gaze and do nothing else for the longest time.

*

June had been found dead in her dining room on a January evening gone balmy and out of season, as if it wasn't really winter, wasn't really anything at all. Lindy stood on the gravel of June's driveway, her shoes thick with clay, her stockings spotted, the air spiked with the smell of fresh-turned earth. She heard a girl squeal and call out laughing, as if it were summertime. Her skin was cold as metal. She shivered, and her jaw ached up into her skull from how she held it tight.

They had called her at the hospital, where she was watching over a seventeen-year-old boy with his heart out of time, arrhythmic. She was standing at his bedside holding his hand, evening her own breaths to even her own heart and teach him how. She couldn't say it didn't work, but the boy had been defibrillated twice already, and that hadn't worked for sure, so she did the only other thing she knew to do, which was like deep wishing. While Lindy held his hand, he woke from his Demerol and smiled a glass smile at her. She pressed his palm to her chestbones.

"See?" she said. "It's like this."

And then she was standing in June's driveway and June was dead, and Lindy was cold in a warm night, and there was nothing else.

It was June's husband who had found her in their dining room, their baby son wailing from upstairs. Beyond that, the details were hazy gray. There was blood; it was on Jimmy White's shoes. He'd been at work since eight in the morning, when he kissed June's cheek going out the door and she called something to him that he couldn't hear or couldn't remember hearing. When Lindy arrived that evening, he sat on a car fender in the driveway, crossed his arms, crossed his bare feet at the ankles, and watched the baby put rocks in his mouth, each time reaching down and taking the baby's hand in his own, taking the rocks and setting them neatly in a row on the fender. He whispered to the baby, *Don't do that, son,* but he didn't pick him up.

Lindy had spent three suspended months since that night, waiting for something to happen. She never had the dreams in which men came to her door and said it was all a mistake, they'd been wrong, June was safe and sound and cooking dinner in her kitchen downtown. Lindy had cut June open herself; she knew, in her heart, she was dead. She felt that ought to be worth something.

She listened to the water running in her bathtub and felt its steam gathering in the house. Since June died, she seemed to be living through flood or famine, a disaster brought on by too much or too little. She had tried being angry about that, then sorry for herself, then just sorry. She tried all her old tricks for grief, but they were only tricks. The grief in her was smarter than that. She drew her finger through the condensation on the windowpane, bubbled out the shape of a heart. It was a tight house, Cott once told her, built like a drum. Nothing got out of there.

She rested the newspaper on the edge of the tub, stripped off her T-shirt, and eased into the steaming water.

She knew the human body held twelve pints of blood. She knew the average bathtub held two hundred pints of water. She knew where Cott kept his razors and where the blade should cut to be fastest at its work. A heart without blood seized, then stopped, and that was a broken heart.

She turned the tap with her foot and let the cold water rush onto her skin. There were other ways of undoing herself. She could do better than dying.

She dipped her head beneath the water, opened her eyes and watched the ceiling. She could see everything clear and perfect under water without her contact lenses, and she'd always loved that, the way the light refracted and healed her vision. It was a small trick, something the doctors wouldn't tell you, that water cured most everything. It made sense; we are most all water inside our skins anyway.

June had told her that a woman's parts were water-loving things; their bodies were shot through with canals, their organs seafaring. Lindy believed it. She believed, too, in spirits and tinctures and sugars of lead, in Epsom salts and castor oil; that a bad burn could be chanted out with a verse from the Bible, that going barefoot was good for you, and that soaking your feet would stop a headache. She believed this the way she believed a surgeon could start a heart that had decided to stop, that a person could be made to breathe if his body didn't want to anymore, that skin could grow again after it was peeled off, that bones could mend, that blood could thin. She'd watched those things happen with her own eyes, as many times as she'd watched them not happen, and no one could tell her why one and not the other. She'd learned not to rule out the possibility of miracles and the capacity of a person's will. She had a kind of faith. She believed the right thought could change your life.

She thought to take the baby for her own.

The baby was June's, a little boy like a ring around the moon. He had June's dimpled chin, her concerned expression and backward ideas about what should go where. He was eleven months old, and June had been dead for three of those.

As Jimmy White was not one to be counted on, the baby stayed with Lindy's mother, and Lindy saw him every day she could. She brought him plastic cups and cardboard books, as if he were a tiny shrine she kept because he reminded her of June. He reminded her so much of June that sometimes she pretended he was June, and that somehow, the way it was in movies, June was passed into her baby and she and Lindy could be together still, only as aunt and nephew instead of sisters. It was just something to pretend. But she did tell the baby everything when there was no one else around. He would lay his head on her shoulder, and she would talk and talk until she could think of nothing else to say. Sometimes, he would pat her back.

Her mind was made up.

She would get the baby and leave directly. They would go south, back against the storm that was coming their way. She would take nothing with her and tell no one she was going. She'd leave behind being a daughter, a wife, a nurse, a good person who would not steal a baby, and her life here in Charlotte would be shattered. She would miss it. She would feel horrible. She would stretch her heart like a rubber band until it snapped, and she'd start over, all the way over, from the bottom up.

She would leave today from the clinic. It wasn't much of a job, and it gave her little to do. She was a phone nurse, and she called patients even when they had no questions for her, called her mother and daddy and Cott sometimes on his mobile phone and checked up on them, made certain they were well and fine, and she was paid for that too. A phone call was a phone call. The clinic wouldn't miss her when she was gone.

She had loved working at the medical center. She was accustomed to the nights on call, the beeper she wore even to bed, the way her time hung from her to be taken up at any hour. But she lost that job. A month back, she was floating for ER when they paged her and paged her stat with no response. They found her on the curb with a burned woman they'd just discharged, sharing a cigarette. Lindy told the head nurse they were waiting for the bus. The head nurse found her a leave of absence until after the wedding, at least, and this job doing phone consults at the clinic across the street.

It was too easy for her. People would call to talk about their back pain or their cluster headaches, and she could chart it for them. They lifted things carelessly. They worked too hard. She'd say, *Think about it like this,* and they'd say, *I never would have thought of that,* but for Lindy, it was a straight shot. She couldn't understand a brain that worked another way. She relied on the straight shot, the snap decision, the gut feeling that told her the only course to take.

It was that kind of feeling she'd had about Cott, years ago. Now, the wedding was to be in three months. She had a dress at the seamstress, and hanging beside it was the dress for June to wear. June had tried it on at Christmastime, and they'd laughed because the fabric was sheer enough to show the small tattoo she'd got after the baby was born. It was on her hipbone, a seashell, fluted and blue. She'd got it because while the baby was growing in her belly, June dreamed of the ocean floor in the most vivid way, and she was a woman, after all, who liked to be marked.

Jimmy White had hit her once, but that was months ago,

and not an instance anyone would mention now that she was dead. June had come to Lindy afterward and talked about how very hard it was to love someone, love him as if he's a season you stretch to make a whole year, and Lindy had loved her then for saying so. How strange, to love someone because she can stand what maybe she shouldn't. But all the reasons for true love were strange.

Lindy fell in love with Cott the way people drink too much, eat too much, run too far. Something inside her that she trusted pushed her to do it. When she was a girl, she'd watched a man at the country club drown because he'd made himself swim twice the length of the pool, under water, without coming up for air. She watched the lifeguards pull him out at the shallow end, his skin already blue. Lindy understood how such a thing could happen. She remembered being out to dinner with Cott when they first began dating. She had things she thought to say to him, but she was shy about it, chose instead to raise her chin and act as if they'd been together for years. Soon, it felt that way. A decision was a powerful thing.

There was a pair of Cott's shoes beside the tub. They'd been there for weeks, discarded before a shower and never picked up and put away. Lindy let her hand float in the air above them, the water coming off her fingertips like a rainy day. The night before, his feet were bare when he stepped across her threshold. He'd left his work boots on the porch. They ate in the kitchen what they'd found in the cupboards, Lindy sitting on the black countertop, Cott between her knees. He tried to feed her with a spoon.

He said, "I talked to you on the phone today, and nothing you said made any sense."

"I feel sick," she said. "Hot. I'm full to the top of my chest."

"You don't want to eat?"

"I don't want to eat."

She slipped her thumbs along his hips, her nails nicking at his jeans. There were so many spaces on his body that fit her hand.

Cott was a construction foreman. He built things, raised up the steel skeletons that held stories and towers and penthouses high in the air. He had first come to her one midnight at the hospital, a knot on his elbow the size of a tennis ball from a fall on site. He had to tell Lindy twice what he did for a living, because she had it in her head that he was an actor, that he made falls on cue, on command, or when someone snapped his fingers at him, like a person under hypnosis. It was that way sometimes in Emergency; her brain could be that literal. He told her he'd been fine after falling but now he couldn't straighten his arm, which in the end was his own fat fault. He'd done the same thing before and hurt his knees. He'd had a problem after that with painkillers, so there wasn't much the doctor could do for him, was there? He'd just be going. He asked her for her name, even though it was printed on her tag.

She fell in love, maybe then, maybe a while later, and there had been years of nights since then, and in some weeks they were to be married, even with all that had gone badly in the past months.

But last night, making love on the countertop, Lindy couldn't bring herself around. She had wanted transport more than anything, but she never left her kitchen, the plate of food pushed aside, Cott's jeans around his knees, his belt buckle tapping coolly on the tile. Her kiss on his cheek was stone-sweet, like late peaches or a good night's rest, and it was over. He pulled away from her, and her hands slipped down his hips. She looked right through him, her face dusting over with sadness and loneliness. She had no idea what to do with him next.

She reached from her bath and caught his shoes by their throats; they shed cuts of grass, slurries of red clay. She slipped them on her feet, crossed her ankles on the neck of the faucet like a coffee table. Used to be, she'd take a bath and tie her hair up in ribbons while it was wet, and she'd get out of the tub, walk past Cott in some thin threadbare towel, and he'd reach for her. She'd leave her hair tied up so that when it was dry, it

17

would come down thick as haystacks, with a curl and a sweet smell to it, the way hair can smell like the best of you.

But they'd not been like that this year, not since the winter. Might not ever be that way again. Cott didn't know how to help her, and she didn't know what to tell him. Sometimes the easiness between people gets lost, she thought. Something happens, and that easiness is left blindfolded in the woods, twenty miles from home.

She opened the newspaper and let it leaf into the water.

She knew that sometimes you did things you weren't proud of, for reasons that you were. She trusted the path of a plan a long time in the coming. She thought, We will forever be hurting ourselves, our own selves and the others we cross into. It was how she'd made her living at the hospital, on other people's hurts. The hurts would always be with us. It was the hovering of pain she wanted free of.

She hung over the tub, her legs balled against her chest. Water streamed from her shoulders and hips down to the shoes on her feet. She was strong when she wanted to be, and right now she wanted strength, determination, enough to get her through the day. She tried to remember what it was like to be happy, comfortable, light. She tried to remember the last time she'd truly been kissed, but that wasn't fair. When was the last time she paid attention? She didn't have that long to hang there.

She put the shoes in the water, left the water in the tub, dark with newsprint and mud and blades of grass, and she liked the look of it, like a tiny suicide. She kicked over her coffee cup, because it too seemed a possibility, but it only slivered across the tile into countless, disappointing pieces.

She sighed and sat heavily on the lip of the tub. Glue is useless, she thought. Throw it all away.

*

Lindy heard the porter say it was the season of comets. It was the time of year when they come from behind the sun as if from out of hibernation. *Eating up the sky,* he said. *Like they was made of hungry fire.* He was bent across the row of seats in front of her, looking for a light bigger than a full moon, a tail longer than the Big Dipper, talking to himself and loud enough to wake the dead.

She and the baby had taken the train because nobody took the train anymore. Its ride was rocking, not rhythmic but side to side, strung with power lines and freight stations, clattering into the soft dark of dawn. Lindy realized it was the sound of a train that was rhythmic, not the motion. A train slowed down when it went over a bridge, because if it reached the same frequency as the bridge, the bridge would shatter, like a wine glass. She wondered, why the bridge and not the train? Why the wine glass and not the person holding it? The stiff weight of her leaving rested in her stomach and beat against her ribcage when she let it, as if she was the wrongest thing alive.

They were peeling through a new Alabama daybreak, headed for Mobile, for the Deep South, the Gulf of Mexico. She held the baby in her lap, her uniform open and his cheek warm against her chest. Lulled by the motion beneath them and the heat of Lindy's body, he was near sleep. She could feel the change in his weight against her. It took so little to soothe him. Less than nothing. June had been dead for near a quarter of his life.

She laid her cheek on the back of the seat. Now she was the gone sister. She didn't want to imagine the scene back at her mother's house, or what Cott must be feeling. Instead, she thought of Jimmy White. She'd decided he did not deserve his son, this part of June still on earth, so she didn't have to care how he was worried now that they were gone.

Before he and June were married, Jimmy White ran bingo parlors and adult bookstores, and there was a lot of his business he didn't talk about. He kept loose money in the house, tucked away in strange places. He once shot a man on their back porch when he was followed home with a night's take. He held ten thousand dollars' cash in one hand and a gun in the other. It was the start of big troubles between him and June.

"Some advice for your married life," their mother offered Lindy one day shortly after. "Your grandmother told me this at your age, and I'd say it's about dead-on proven fact. You know how to tell a true man?"

Lindy shook her head.

"You ask him if he could shoot somebody. That simple. In the end, a man who'd be true to you never could."

"But, then, he'd never shoot somebody for me, either," Lindy said.

"There's your choice. I know, it's not an easy one." Her mother took a long look out the kitchen window. "Lord knows," she said, "I've lived with mine."

June and Jimmy White were married seven years in all, the last two of them bad. Each fight started with his leaving home and saying he'd never be back, and each ended with a sigh, a shrug, a few days of sleeping on the couch. In the beginning, June would be frantic. After one of the last fights, she'd called for Lindy at the hospital, sobbing and eight months pregnant.

"I should have known," she said. "He's always been a sorry son of a bitch."

"Well, then, you knew," Lindy said, "and you married him anyway."

But a sister thing broke in Lindy's heart to hear June so beside herself; she should never have been made to feel that way. Also, she was carrying a baby, and Lindy could catalogue the effects of sorrow on expectant mothers, from superstition to fact. It was said that pregnant women had to be careful with their eyes, that they could ruin their children if they stared too long at something ugly or dead. And it was true that a baby listened to the mother's voice from the inside, not hearing the words but sensing the feelings in them. June sounded so awful.

Lindy got somebody to cover her shift and found Jimmy White at the Sardine, which is where he always went when he was never coming back. She still liked him then, the way she supposed most women liked their brothers-in-law, because they wanted to. She sat with him in the Sardine, matched his drinks, and shot some pool. They did not mention June but once. Jimmy White said, *She's the last person I'll ever love.* The last one, because if he left her, she'd keep the baby, and he couldn't live with that.

He did say things about women in general: how they were all changelings, all manipulative; how he'd always hated women and could only now bring himself to admit as much. Lindy took offense where appropriate. She was affectionate and prodding when she could be, but he kept on talking, his eyes shifted down the cusp of her blouse. It made her feel like a tease.

"June's pregnant," Lindy finally said, laying a flat hand to her collar. "And you did kill a man."

"Months ago." He spun his bottle on the bar top. And then, "Miles to go."

He nodded to a couple sitting on stools at the end of the bar. She was blonde and candied-looking, and the man's tongue was in her ear, his hand slipping below the waist of her jeans and back up her spine again to her hair, blonde and sweet and short. She laughed. The man laughed. Jimmy White laughed.

"That sort of shit makes me uncomfortable," he said. "And I know a lot of men who'd kill for less than I did."

Lindy went back to June and promised herself it was the last time she'd make it all seem better. She'd only meant for June to have what she wanted, the three of them being a family. So Lindy said what could be said in that direction, true and not. But she knew, too, when Jimmy White got home, June would be mean to him the quiet way that hurt people get mean, speaking when spoken to, and keeping her clothes on as much as possible. At the time, Lindy figured he deserved it. They had their ways with each other. Her meddling helped or hurt only as far as they allowed it. Now, it didn't matter one way or the other, because June was gone.

When the police searched the house after she was murdered, they found Jimmy White's safe busted, a trail of bills out the sliding glass doors into the yard and beyond, but it was money

Jimmy White ought not to have had, and by the time people stopped worrying about that, the trail had long gone cold.

"Jimmy White will go to hell," Lindy whispered, and that was the last time she spoke his name.

⚘

The porter clipped her knee as he passed by for a better window to see his comet. His touch sent a shock through her skin, just static, but it made her gasp. How silly, she thought. Her body got scared before she knew to tell it better. She felt hollow about that, and then just stupid to herself. Tears came up the back of her throat, and she hated them. She wanted to rest, to go home, someone else's home, to be clear of feeling selfish and sour and wrong.

She'd abandoned her car on the west side of town, a window busted and the baby's car seat empty. It will look bad, she thought. It will look as if we've been stolen.

She had three thousand dollars' cash wedding money, the clothes on her back, the weight in her stomach, and her mind set to stone. She had the train, the coming light, and her sister's baby asleep on her chest. She listed it in her head as if writing it on a chart, the signs or symptoms of what ailed her. She would continue that, as if following orders for herself, and hoped she'd begin to feel as though she knew what she was doing.

She stroked the baby's back. She would have slept too, on that train, but she hadn't slept soundly in months and knew better than to expect it this night. The morning was already gathering outside her window; back in Charlotte, she knew, rain came up by way of a hurricane and kept coming. While she was driving across town to dump the car, two kittens dashed into the road, one black, one white, both so soaked that she'd had to decide they were kittens and not trash caught on the wind. She'd pumped her brakes, but the car one lane over did not. The white cat was hit, and it stayed with her still, the back legs rabbiting, the spray of red beneath the tires. It made her grit her teeth, if she let it, even all this time later. Why was she like that? Why did she care, when there was so much more she could have been regretting? She knew only that the kitten had nothing to do with her and she did not want to think about herself.

Outside her window, the dawn light was like a fire in the hearth, so gold as to make everything seem cast of metal. Lindy found herself wishing for a storm, something like what was brewing in Charlotte when she left, something to continue. In Alabama, she'd heard, frogs could rain from the sky, fishes, blood, winds that could whisk you away. She had always loved storms. There were times at Cott's when she'd sit out on his patio in the summer storms and let them wet her down, the cement she sat on, the magazine she held, filling up the glass by her side. She'd drink that rain when it reached the top and hold out her glass for more. He'd watch her. She knew his eyes were on her all the time.

She wished she'd left a letter, a word for Cott, something to hold in his hand and read over. She wanted something written down between them. But a note would have been too black and white, and in her heart she was against the idea of telling the whole truth. It was something she'd learned at the hospital, learned again when June died, and kept learning in the months leading to this moment. Sometimes it was better to parcel out only what was necessary and keep the rest to yourself.

But then, she thought, you were left with yourself. That was the thing about lying: the darkness, the footlessness of it. Lindy felt as if the inside of her went all the way to nowhere.

◈

When the train stopped in Birmingham, the baby twisted in her arms, awake and hungry and needing a fresh diaper. He wailed out, and it was sharp. She had the impulse to cover his mouth. She made her hands fast around him and wished she knew better what to do; she lay her cool fingers over his skin like slow, clumsy feathers. He was the loudest thing she'd heard in days, and, just as quickly, was quiet again.

23

He watched the passengers getting on and off, the porter calling out connections. The trains were named — the Pan American, the Azalean, the Hummingbird, the South Wind — beautiful names, but the people were tired and moved as if their bodies were tender, as if their skins were too full, their bones swollen. Lindy curled herself into the seat, held the baby tighter to keep them both small and tight together.

When the woman passed, Lindy thought she knew her from somewhere. She looked like someone she'd gone to church with when she was a child. Lindy turned quickly toward the windows, sank down into the red of her seat, and pulled the baby even closer. It was too soon to be discovered; she found herself getting angry. It flushed up warm in her neck and cheeks. Nothing but a little girl caught, she thought. Nothing but a sneak and a thief. What could she say to someone who knew she had no business here?

The woman sat down with a girlfriend across the aisle from Lindy, and they chatted in slow tones. They did not stare, made no move to say hello. But Lindy couldn't shake the feeling that she knew her from home. She kept her back turned and listened for her name in their talk, but they weren't concerned with her at all.

Later, when the seizure hit, the woman turned pale in the lips and her girlfriend called out for help in a high, watery voice. The porter came with a man, a doctor, from the back of the car, and they pulled the woman into the aisle so that her head rested at Lindy's feet. When the color came to her face, red and hot, she lifted her arm to Lindy and her eyes so locked with Lindy's that she trembled. She'd not known the woman after all, not from home. The woman had reached for her because she still wore her whites from the clinic. She still looked like a nurse, even though she did not act like one.

Lindy did not take the woman's hand. Afterward, she would tell herself it was because she'd been surprised and her arms were full of the baby. She told herself she was not a nurse anymore and could not be responsible for the health of others, that she was in a slow seam of forgetting all those things she knew and, in truth, could not be trusted. Still, she called out in her head, *Check her airway, her pulse, loosen her clothes, get a blanket. Check her tongue and make sure she doesn't swallow it.* She heard herself whisper, *Shhh. Shhh, now.* The words fell on the baby's neck, but that was all she offered. It was a hard seizure, and the woman fought it out from inside.

The woman lay in the aisle for some time, a swath of sunlight passing across her unlaced shoes. The doctor asked her about epilepsy and brain trauma, possible cause and effect. When Lindy was little, June had read to her from a book about a girl who was epileptic. She'd liked especially the parts about the disease's curious powers — clairvoyance, intense hearing. June had told Lindy she wanted to be an epileptic for a time after reading the book, but she was always wanting things like that when they were little: to be an angel, to wear a cast, to commune with dead relatives, to eat what grew in the yard. Lindy missed June the way she was when she was little. Even if June had been alive, Lindy would have missed her the way she was when she was younger, as if the two Junes were separate sisters, younger and older, daytime and night, one easier to miss than the other because June had grown up, the little girl of her ending as all little girls end. Lindy didn't want to think about the rest.

The woman had wet herself in her seizure, and the smell lingered faintly in the car, even as the spectacle was past and the passengers had returned to their seats. Lindy had the urge to tell the woman she was glad she was okay, because that's what she felt for her, relief, but the woman would not meet her eyes. She stared out the train window as the scenery dominoed, and Lindy could see the edge of shame in her profile. It was the desperate, cornered look that came from being in the place where it all happened. She knew what the woman was thinking: this would be all right if she could just get up and go away. It made Lindy feel not so crazy for what she herself was doing. It was the way a normal person's mind went, too, and on smaller pains, on embarrassment, on fear.

In her hospital service, when Lindy had seen a patient return from a seizure, she'd been fast with comfort and moving on, so fast her head spun when it was over and she stopped to think how that person's life had been briefly in her hands and briefly in the hands of something worse. In her old life, with her old whole heart, she would have crossed the aisle to the woman and laid a hand over hers, would have said something to make her smile. She would have needed to do that, but she didn't anymore. She could be relieved, and nothing else, and later they would go their separate ways.

The baby turned in Lindy's lap, and she tucked them back into the ride of the train. There would be so much to accustom herself to in the coming days, so much she'd have to think about before taking a step. It was not as much as a stroke victim's having to learn to walk again, or to speak. And it was not as much as a baby's having to learn those things for the first ever. But Lindy could tell it would be a long time before the natural thing to do was the right one. She would move slowly, she thought. She would treat herself as if she was new.

ↈ

The afternoon was painfully bright, and Lindy felt dirty, as if she'd spent too long with her mouth closed. She stood on the platform in Mobile, the baby in her arms and his hands in her hair. They could have been on a platform in Mobile or Tallahassee or Charleston, but Mobile was the destination she'd bought the tickets for, because that was where the line ended. She watched the train until it was no more than a glint in the distance on its way back up the tracks, and even after that, because she wasn't sure what came next. It was better to stand still than do something she'd later wish she'd thought about.

The baby whispered air into her ear, and it made Lindy

shiver. She wanted to be the one carried on somebody's hip. She wanted to be fed and clothed and picked up and held close.

She reached out and grabbed his hand. "You're okay," she said, and he cooed and rapped his heels against her thigh.

"Now say it back to me." But he laughed and leaned away.

Lindy became methodical about their needs, as was her habit when she had habits to be counted on. She was good at nipping panic before it fanned too high. She could make order; divide and list what needed to be done. That's what had made her a good nurse, would have made her a good wife, a good mother.

"Hungry?" she asked, and they were off.

She found a lunch counter on Royal. Inside, there were cigars for sale and dirty magazines, glass-front coolers, counter stools. It was noon, and the place was full. She bought a newspaper, took a stool with the baby on her lap, ordered them grilled cheese sandwiches and milkshakes.

Although Lindy read the paper every morning, she'd never read it for her own name before. She scanned column by column, checking the national pages for a picture of the baby. Newspapers thrived on tragedy breeding tragedy, and she imagined it would not be long before someone reported the story of her disappearance, her poor parents and their lost daughters. The baby squirmed in her lap. He batted at the folded pages and liked the sound, so he batted some more. She held the paper higher, and higher still, until she couldn't read it.

Fuck tragedy, she thought. She folded the paper and pushed it off the counter's edge to the floor.

She spun a quarter on the countertop. They couldn't stay in Mobile. She knew the more steps between herself and home, the less likely she was to be found, and one long train trip wasn't enough. She watched the quarter make its way beyond the baby's reach. Heads, they would jump a bus. But for where? Her fingertips pressed the bridge of her nose. She hadn't thought this through, not for herself and him, too. She spun the quarter again. Tails, she'd just start swimming.

By the time the food came, she was sick to her stomach, but the baby ate with both fists. He held a french fry aloft and sang to it, a high reeling song. Then he laughed and ate some sandwich. Lindy liked that about him. He'd always been quick to take care of himself, all his little life.

When June was pregnant, Jimmy White had looked forward to getting up with a baby at night. He talked about walking the floor, rocking the cradle, about how he didn't need sleep himself and so would be a natural at fatherhood. It was a matter of pride. But the baby, home from the hospital, slept through the night, except for feedings, and did so forever after. Jimmy White was disappointed. Some nights he'd linger at the nursery door and curl up on the floor, like a dog. June said she'd trip over him in the morning.

Jimmy White wanted a houseful of children. When June wanted to get married, he told her that was the only good reason to get married, to have a houseful of children, all he could afford. It took them a long time to get started. And then, once June was pregnant, Jimmy White turned nervous. He'd come home from the stores with bagfuls of locks for the cabinets, stoppers and bumpers, devices to keep babies from falling in, slipping up. When he started installing shatterproof windows, June made him go to the beach for the weekend with his friends.

It only got worse once the baby was born. Lindy wandered into conversations with him that began with questions about parenting and petered out into nowhere comfortable. There was an afternoon she dropped by to check the baby's umbilical cord. She brought a soufflé cake and found June in the shower, Jimmy White bent over the baby's crib.

"I could break him so easy," he said. "Just by not thinking. Like his neck wobbles so much, I think I'm going to turn around and it'll be broken. You know what I mean?"

"New parents always think things like that," she said. "Babies really aren't fragile. Just think of what they go through to be born."

It was as if Jimmy White hadn't heard her. He looked tired and gray, paunchy, as if he'd been the one in labor. He reached into the crib and laid a finger on the baby's soft, rising chest. Then he hummed something in his throat that was far from soothing.

"We all fall down," he whispered, and the baby stirred, raised his little fists, and tumbled back to sleep.

ॐ

At the lunch counter, an old woman sitting next to Lindy tried to play games with the baby. She was trying to explain something about chicken hatch, and her greased fingers crossed and uncrossed in the air before his face. The woman wouldn't stop, wouldn't leave him alone. Her lipstick ran a perfect circle around her mouth.

The baby squirmed in Lindy's lap to get away. His eyes went big and pooled and he reached for Lindy's chest, sucking at his thumb, at handfuls of her hair. He banged the heel of his shoe against her thigh. The old woman asked his name.

Lindy said, "He isn't mine."

It was a stupid thing to say; it had flown from Lindy's mouth like a slap from her hand. The woman had assumed Lindy would be pleasant, because women with babies are pleasant, conversational. They have stories about their children. Lindy didn't want even the action of speaking, let alone a conversation, but she'd gone too far, and now the woman was staring at her.

She put some money on the counter and left the restaurant for the street. The baby had been named for his father, but Lindy wouldn't call him that. She had names she liked, but they were all color names and feeling names and names that sounded like things other than names: Mason and Hale and Webb and Bud, and place names like Jackson and Dallas, but it was hard to name something right; she'd have to take her time. She had, she thought, all the time in the world for the baby. Her nephew. Hers.

She stopped on the corner. Her breath was knocking in her chest, her mouth pasty, her stomach shy. She closed her eyes, felt the baby's weight sway in her arms, the moist pat of his hand on her cheek, and his teeth at her shoulder. She could crumple to the sidewalk, she thought, melt into a puddle of white uniform. When she opened her eyes, the baby squealed like a stiff hinge.

"You," she said. "What are you squealing at?"

He leaned into her ear and squealed again.

From the rise of Government and Royal, Lindy saw freight ships on the water armed with the great booms of cranes, wrought iron and red clay and leaves of interstate highway curling into each other. A wind came up under her skirt in the most gracious way, and she had the thought that she could live here if she had to. It was the first of many times she'd think such of the place she landed, and it was comforting. It meant she was adaptable, and that was good.

But in her mind, she was nearly married, and so did not do things all her own, would not live here without Cott. She missed him, and a wave of nerves passed across her hipbones. Now that she was gone, she worried where he would turn with whatever he was feeling. Men like Cott weren't very good at handling themselves, outside of bar fights and reckless driving. Lindy knew he had once taken pills, although they'd never talked about it. She thought she'd often kept him safe from the things they didn't talk about.

There had been jobs that turned on him, like bare, flipping wires, jobs where he flew the steel and tied it all in place, tens of stories in the air. He carried his weight in re-bar and belt, carried a measuring tape that would not measure how far he had to fall or to climb. She remembered a day he'd been tying hold-down corners way out on the perimeter of a tall, tall building. He had to slide the bar over Tryon Street, had to keep the weight down, shoot the rod out, and wait to get the bounce right to feed it back in. Something happened. It was hairy, he said, and he laughed, and that was all he'd tell her.

But when he sat to take off his boots beside the door, Lindy guessed what had happened. He'd stumbled. She watched something pass over his face like a determination not to be sick, and then a fear that he might be anyway, now that he could, now that he was home. He leaned back into the ladder of the chair and let his head hit the wall.

It scared her, but she'd known enough not to show it. She drew him to her on the couch, took his head in her lap, and pulled at his earlobes with the pads of her thumb and knuckle. She whispered how she'd been waiting for him to get home, to get her hands on him, just like so. It was big talk, but once she'd said it, it became what she had been waiting for. He smelled like metal and machines, clear as drilled teeth. Her shoes came off, and she turned beneath him so that her legs wrapped around his waist, her bare feet finding the fly of his jeans. They lay like that until the sun went down, and when she touched him, he felt like a man again. It was a significant moment for them, and Lindy had been proud of herself for it.

When she worked in Emergency, she'd seen construction men cut, crushed, spiked through with rusty things, more meat than feature. She would check their uninjured parts for whatever of Cott's she might recognize: his long eyelashes, the port wine birthmark on his thigh, his jammed, fat ring finger. More than once, she'd have her hands on a warm body going cold and she would call up Cott in her head just to see him on his feet, to know that he was okay. It was as if he worked the high wire without nets, was at war, at sea, and she wanted her letters in his pockets. She trusted it was the small things she did that kept him safe. Small things were what she knew to do.

She and the baby would need a change of clothes.

She found a secondhand shop, a tea-stained woman humming behind the counter. Her song found words in Lindy's ears, something old-fashioned and hymnlike. The baby pulled dresses down from the racks and laid them atop Lindy's head so that he could reach for more. She had her arms full. Clothes hung over her shoulders, the baby's shoulders, trailed behind them on the floor, even as he reached for something else. Lindy could tell he liked the color blue. It was her favorite color and had been June's, too.

The woman called out from behind the counter, "Come on, missy. I got something for the boy."

She had a bag of dried apples in her hand, passed one to the baby, and told him to chew it good.

"He'll choke on that," Lindy said.

The woman huffed out a laugh. "What they tell you girls these days, huh? That one's cutting teeth. Needs to toughen up the mouth."

"Oh, well. Sure."

Lindy looked at the baby as if he might answer for himself. He pulled the corner of something velour over his face and then peek-a-booed her with it. She felt like a dimwit, standing in the middle of this store, draped in somebody else's old clothes, taking advice. Did she look that needy?

"Anyway, how can you know?" she asked.

"How do the birds know it's going to rain? I raised twenty-one of my own."

"I'm a nurse," Lindy offered. "Used to be."

"Really." The woman eyed her uniform. "Aren't you the smart one. It don't seem to be helping you now."

Behind the dressing room curtain, the baby sat on the floor and held his ankles, watched her come free of her clothes. His voice was like a bouncing ball; he ran it in circles, high and then low, shrill and then soft. Her body ached. It was the travel, she thought, the hours on the train and the way she held her shoulders to hold the baby. She watched him launch forward on his hands and push himself up, bobble, then step. It looked like the first time, his first walking ever.

Lindy's brain went simple. Why wasn't June here?

The baby laughed and worked his hands at the air as if it was something to grab, and Lindy crouched to hold her arms out to him. She folded him into her lap. She whispered how good he was, thought how sweet he smelled, tried hard not to be sad. He was old enough now to be all different from when June died, doing all new things. There would come a day when Lindy would show him June's picture and tell him that she was his mother. She would explain about parents and grandparents, who she was and why he was with her, and how they'd come to be so far from home.

He pushed away from her, and Lindy watched him giggle and spit and fold his body back to stand up, and she wanted to leave her skin, it hurt so much.

She'd been selfish to take him. It was a hard thing to admit to herself, but true. Her mother doted on him, ran her days around his whims, and Lindy's decision that she needed him more made her a greedy woman. Fine, she thought. I am not all sweetness and light. Jimmy White wouldn't have him, and that was a worthwhile greed. Of that, she was sure. Wasn't she?

The baby would walk, would talk, and she would treat him as if he knew everything she did, and sooner or later he would.

She left her uniform in the dressing room on a hanger as though it belonged there. She paid for their things: a few loose sundresses for herself, a pile of bright cotton for the baby. The woman behind the counter was short with her, as if Lindy was a bad customer. Friendliness should not be so common, Lindy thought, that it was forever expected.

Outside, the sunset pinked at the sky. Lindy felt the heat of a Gulf town, the nearness of the water, and she thought of her grandmother's big house in Galveston. That was where her mother had gone after she left a boy at the altar in the springtime, years and years ago. Lindy heard about the whole thing when she and Cott became engaged, and not from her mother, but from her grandmother, Esther.

Esther was a sundowner. She had lived alone since Lindy's grandfather, Luther, died a dozen years ago, and she was fine as long as it was daylight, but after dark, her mind shorted out, and she forgot all kinds of rights and wrongs and pasts and presents. The problem was electrical. The lack of light opened the circuits in her brain and made her scattered, sometimes desperate, slippery, violent in her thinking. She knew it, too. With the shortening days of the winter before last, she bought time in a retirement center and put her big house on the market.

When Lindy's parents called the retirement home to announce Lindy's wedding, Esther had been offhand, dour; she said Lindy's path had been marked, she figured, a long time back. Her mother sighed heavily into the phone. It was ages ago, and she'd got married after all, hadn't she? It wasn't worth her time to talk about it.

Those were fighting words between the two of them, so Lindy just quietly hung up the extension and let them debate all the things her mother had done that weren't worth discussing. It was an old vein in an old conversation. Esther believed that she'd lived so long, everything was due to repeat itself before she died. Lindy, sitting in her mother's kitchen, her hand still on the phone, wondered why June's path hadn't been marked. But Esther's mind had been stronger when June and Jimmy White were married, in the summertime, at the courthouse. There was no altar to speak of. Lindy was the only one left to have a marked path.

Now, she hoped Esther's predictions were biology as much as fortunetelling. Why couldn't choice and mistake and just plain instinct pass in blood from one generation to the next, as cleanly as disease? She would never have imagined, that afternoon in her mother's kitchen, that anything could bring her to this street corner in Mobile, weeks before her wedding, with no Cott, June's son in her arms, with no June. Even now it was hard to say what had brought her here. It was as if she discovered that she would have a heart attack, but not for many years. She had to learn to live with what would kill her, with what had killed her sister, and she couldn't do it sitting still.

As children, she and June had spent so many barebacked summers in Galveston. Lindy could not remember ever having been in trouble there, not with her mother, not with her grandmother, not with her own self. The house was sitting empty; it wouldn't be the first place people would think to look for her. Not the last either, but maybe good enough for now.

She hailed a cab. She'd seen an ad in the paper at the lunch counter with the address of a man selling a car for cheap. They rode up Government by the big hotels and into the shade of white houses, live oaks. This was Highway 90, her way out of town, and once she was on it, she'd head west along the water, south when she got the chance. She'd make Galveston in a matter of days.

She rang the bell of a big Georgian house, and a man answered, a napkin in his hand. He was enormous, like a bull or a bear, the sort of thing you might not realize was enormous until you found yourself standing next to it.

"I'm here about the Cadillac car," she said, "and you're eating dinner," and she pointed to the napkin. She could smell food cooking, olive oil and garlic and peppers, and realized how hungry she was. How small she was. How alone.

"Please," he said, and stepped aside.

He led her through a tall white foyer, and Lindy could hear the coo of voices in other rooms, the sounds of glass on glass and foreign whispers. Through the open kitchen doors, she saw a woman, black haired and sloe-eyed, sipping wine and dividing oranges among the others at the table. Lindy was embarrassed to be staring, and she had to look away.

The man's name was Bruton Toliver. The baby, open-mouthed and drooling, watched him as they negotiated a careful path to the garage. Bruton said he was a softie for kids. He chucked the baby's cheek and stroked his head, his hand blanketing the small skull. He was telling how, the last time he tried to sell the Cadillac, a man came by and checked it out with his wife and three kids in full tow. All was well, and they shook hands.

He said, "The next morning at the bank, it's the wife and three kids hiking through the parking lot. I said, Where's the mister? and the wife said, He wanted to make sure we had a good car before he left us."

So Bruton gave them his Mercedes Benz.

"I have to sell *this* car," he told Lindy, "and you don't look like you're in for the pleasures of a vintage automobile."

He pulled the tarp off a car the color of old gold. The back seat stretched out like a sofa. He said it was his mother's, had always been his mother's, and she'd treated it with care, but it was old — from the looks of it, probably older than Lindy — and then his tone turned altogether and he stopped. He brushed his hand through the air as if he were waving goodbye.

"Go on," he said. "You've got bigger headaches, I'll bet, that you didn't have to pay for."

Lindy scuffed her toe on the cement floor. The baby squealed, and she hefted him on her hip. He drooled on the hood of the Cadillac.

"I need this car," she told him. "The price is good. Two hundred fifty is good."

Bruton sighed. "Sweetheart, the price is good because the car's a piece of shit."

So Lindy turned, took steps to the door, then stopped. She rocked back in her pockets, stood hipshot, and took a long look at her shoes. She didn't have to do as she was told.

"How about I take it for a test drive, see for myself?" she asked.

"Where are you from?" He really looked at her.

"Not here."

"And where are you headed?"

"Not here."

Bruton let out his breath and turned away. He made a production of polishing the door handle with his napkin. His voice was breezy. "If it were me," he said, "and I got on this highway right here, I'm guessing I might take it all the way till it ran out."

"Would you."

"Think of the pirates." He made a traveling motion with his hand. "All the way to Corpus Christi. Now, don't you want to know where I know that from?"

Lindy smiled. Propping the baby on the car's hood, she pulled out the bills she'd tucked away. She could see the keys in the ignition through the windshield, and she got real close to Bruton Toliver and slipped her hand inside his pants pocket. "In case I get stranded on my test drive, you'd be taken care of. Anything in there you'd like to keep?"

Bruton hung his head, and Lindy loaded into the car. She belted the baby, kicked up the engine, and it fairly purred. She smiled at Bruton as she slid the bench seat forward.

"Look," he said, "the engine has a slight exhaust leak, so don't keep it idling. The carburetor's been wired open and I don't know how long that'll last, the radiator's filled with oatmeal, she gets about eleven miles to the gallon, and the last time I drove her, the alternator caught fire and I had to stand on the fender and piss it out."

Lindy revved the engine. "I'll carry a bottle of water for that purpose."

"Well, it's been rebuilt since then."

"Thanks."

He stood, pressed a button on the wall, and the garage door raised up. He leaned on the window and the car leaned back against him.

"What about the title?"

"I'm just taking a drive." She smiled again, and her face ached. "We can work it out some other time."

She slung her arm over the seat and backed the car out of the garage. Bruton walked along beside, his hand on the window frame, telling her when the oil was last changed, when the fluids were last checked. He pulled a tire iron from the garage wall and passed it to Lindy, a first-aid kit, his business card, some spare spark plugs.

"Do you know how to change these?"

"No," she said.

"Well, somebody will. Look, is your baby going to ride like that?"

The baby had the shoulder strap from the seat belt in his mouth and was working to get the buckle end too, his cheeks shiny with drool.

"He's teething," she told Bruton. "He's just so struck by you."

Bruton fumbled through a storage closet and came back with a baby seat. It was all he had. It had been his little brother's and maybe wasn't regulation anymore. She could check that at the DMV.

"If you're inclined," he said.

"Yes," she said. "If I'm inclined."

Lindy pulled away into the coming night. Bruton stood at the edge of his house and waved goodbye as if they were old friends. She stuck her hand out the open window and waved too, waved when she made the turn from his driveway onto Highway 90, and as she looked back one more time, she could have sworn Bruton was following after her, some last thing he had to say hard on his conscience. Such a nice man, she thought; a truly nice person. And with that, she was glad to be away.

♒

It was spring evening on Highway 90 and Lindy rolled down the windows of her new Cadillac car, letting the breeze rush her ears, take up in her hair. After June died, she'd had a wreck. She hadn't driven much since then, so now she was deliberate, cautious. It was as if she had to get her legs back.

The accident had happened when she pulled out in front of a big four-wheel-drive truck. She wasn't wearing a seat belt, wasn't paying attention. Afterward, she remembered being alive and feeling the skin of her knees pull and swell from where they'd hit the dashboard. She kept saying she was fine, just fine, because she'd rather stick out some unexpected pain than spend the afternoon in the hospital. It could have been much worse. She slid out the passenger door, made certain the other driver was all right, and then cleaned out her car: the spilled-out purse, a case of exploded beer cans, the earrings flung out of her ears. She'd just been let go from the hospital; she wanted nothing to do with those people.

But she was bruised and stiff and sad. Cott took a long weekend from work, and they went to Carolina Beach to stay in a friend's house, with sandy floors and rooms full of double beds. When the swelling went down in Lindy's knees, they tried to make love, and when they were tired from that, she sat on the edge of the bed and brushed her hair, her head tipped over and the insides of her thighs fat with scent. After they got back to Charlotte, Cott ran her errands and she walked to work. Her car sat in the shop for weeks.

Off her left shoulder, the late sun made oxbow reflections where the highway ran with the Gulf, a growing pinkness, sadness. She thought of Cott and not being with him for the night, and then she passed through that moment and it came to be full daylight again, like a reprieve. It was warm enough in that sunset to take a swim. She told the baby he would learn to swim before he learned to run. He took his tiny, chewed-on hand out of his mouth and patted her as if she were a silly girl. He babbled something full of *p*'s, then sighed.

June had taught Lindy to love the water. Their parents' house overlooked the lake north of Charlotte, and in her mind, home was the backyard running to the water, running the fat, rolling lawn to the mud and knots of rock, the soft dockboards at last beneath her feet. She could feel the crack of her hands as she dove, the metallic, green scent, the cold deep beneath the sip of lake that got the sun. That was love, wasn't it? The place to which her mind was most attracted. When they were girls, she and June wore swimsuits to bed as soon as the weather was warm enough, goggles slung around their necks, so as to wake up and spend entire days in the water. The night before June went away to college, they slept out on a raft tethered to the dock, floating the night beneath the stars and the plunging bats, the lap of the lake at their hands when they wanted it and the moon glossy as new snow.

∞

Lindy drove the coast highway where the sand drifted onto the blacktop without dunes to stop its blowing, and the big car was like that tethered raft, wishing for the ocean. She and June had loved the ocean too, but that was different. That was with Esther, and in Galveston, and it didn't remind Lindy of home but of being away from home. The ocean was a colder thing to her, and she was glad to see it now for that very reason.

She steered with her knees and stroked the baby's long toes. She still felt wire-bound to the list of things in her head: she would feed the baby, find some rest, keep close to the water because it was good for her, and night would come soon. The highway took a curve coming out of Biloxi, and the fine old beach homes evaporated in neon light. Casinos glittered and spit over the Gulf. Lindy remembered when there'd been no casinos, only sand and shacks and little souvenir shops. Now, she couldn't tell what was over the water and what wasn't, and the whole stretch of road became migrant, as if on the constant edge of coming or going. It was the place to catch some rest that wouldn't be sleep, there in the night that wouldn't be dark, next to the ocean that couldn't be seen.

She pulled into the Sun Tan Motel in Gulfport. Across the highway was the Grand Casino, its lights washing over the night sky. An ambulance was parked at the motel office door, its beams lost on everything else. As she checked in, the desk clerk was signing some papers for an EMT who didn't seem to be in any rush.

Lindy asked if someone was hurt. The clerk screwed up her face in a kind of smirk. "Somebody up and died, that's how hurt they were."

"What happened?" Lindy said.

"Damned if I know." The clerk stopped her drawer-slamming. She folded her hands in front of her on the counter, her glasses perched on the end of her nose. "Did you know," she said, "odds are if you're staying in a hotel more than fifty years old, somebody died in your room?"

"Really," Lindy said. "Hotels or motels?"

"Either, I guess. Odds are, though." She laughed, and slid Lindy's key across the counter. "Ice at the end of the building."

Usually, Lindy liked motel rooms. They reminded her of Cott. Before they met, he'd spent most of his time on short jobs that took him here and there, and he always stayed in motel rooms. He lived like a circus man; he once told Lindy those were the days he ate glass, walked hot coals, the days when he slept on a bed of nails. She told him how she wished she'd known him then, but he said she was mistaken. She wouldn't have liked him much. It seemed impossible at the time, but people did change their ways. She'd bet Cott wouldn't like her much right now.

Tonight, it would have been nice to enjoy her motel room. She would have strolled down the covered walkway with a pair of high heels clicking, her back straight as a length of steel, a woman on her own by choice in the lee of so many choices. But her feet were bare, her toenails were not painted, and she felt not so much like a woman with choices but like some kind of woman traced on paper, not very tall, not very straight, and not very much to look at.

She shut the blinds and chained the door before she set the baby on the bed. The room was seamless black, with a dripping air conditioner and a heavy chandelier that Lindy left in blackness.

"We smell," she said. She and the baby hadn't seen a bath in days.

The bathroom had no tub, just a corner for a shower faucet and a curtain. Lindy's face in the mirror was a doll's face; her skin was flushed and tight. She looked as though she'd been painted on. She tipped her chin back, and her eyes weighted shut, as cleanly as if they'd been made that way.

She undressed herself and the baby, and turned the water to a warmish run. The baby's body was soft as suede and salty; he let her drift him into the spray and back out, finally tucking his face to her neck and easing in her arms. He seemed to melt into her, to love being held. She wondered whether she was enough like June to be a consolation to him. It could have been something physical, like smell, or something of habit, of manner. Maybe she and June showered the same way. She would never find out otherwise, but the baby was calm and peaceful in her arms, and that peace came into her own skin, cell by cell, as if by osmosis.

It was a term Cott used all the time: osmosis. People were slow as osmosis, dumb as osmosis. How did she figure on learning that, by osmosis? She wondered how much longer her thoughts would come dressed in his expressions. Her brain was reaching out for his. Maybe all her body parts missed him in their own discrete, practical ways.

The drain was clogged, and the water began to rise at her ankles. She wrapped the baby in a towel and set him on the bathroom floor so that she could use her hands to finish showering, but she talked to him the whole time to keep his attention, to keep him from crawling away. It was the most aware she'd been of another person in weeks, aware only because he challenged her to be so. She told him what she was doing, where they were and how they'd not be staying long. It was strange to speak and have no response, to have only his silent company. June had said that too, that after he was born, she had to remind herself to speak out loud to him, having spoken only in her head for nine long months.

"Hey," Lindy called out. "Tell me something."

The shower had run cold. He didn't make a sound.

"Hey," she said again, and yanked the curtain aside.

He sat in an inch of spill-off from the shower, chewing on a wrapped bar of soap. His face puckered and scowled, he took the soap out of his mouth, dipped it in the water, then chewed it again. He was so determined. Lindy knelt and sat back on her heels, held out her hands, and he crawled into her lap.

She dried and dressed herself, slipped the baby into one of his new T-shirts, and fed him a bottle of juice, a handful of crackers, some raisins from a box. They were quiet and clean, and she curled herself beside him, but couldn't make sleep come. Her head was thick with thoughts she could not keep hold of, her contacts gritty, her vision as if she were seeing through a screen. She felt the changing and lifting of things inside her, and she thought she should be still for that, should be sleeping, but the more she tried, the worse it got. Finally, the not-sleeping sat on her chest like a cat over a bassinet, as heavy as a superstition. She sat up to get away from the effort.

In Charlotte, she knew, Cott was asleep in his bed, his skin damp from his own night shower. He'd be working the concrete even in his dreams, raising some endless dream-building, one where he was made to walk high, high planks, another where he tied beams all night long. He'd wake tight and tired and lie in bed next to Lindy, let his day run minutes late for what he'd put himself through in the night. He'd sigh and stretch and say something like *Fuck all that.* And then he'd say, *I hold to just doing my job.* And he'd get out of bed, put on his steel-toed boots, and climb into his truck, and she'd not see him again until four or five o'clock, or whenever her shift ended at the hospital.

If she asked, he could calculate the figures of his dream-work, tell her how many cubic yards of concrete, how many tons of steel, enough to stretch or build or pave this much land the way normal people used it. It was like the dreams she had over EKGs and crash carts and how much blood a heart can beat through in a minute, an hour, a day. They were of the same mind, she and Cott. They saw what they saw in terms of what they did. He could not look at a building without seeing the concrete, the steel, how long it would have taken him to build it well. She could not look at you without seeing inside your chest, inside your skin, how much good your flesh will do when you are gone from it.

They shared their languages with each other. ·

She'd say, "A fenestration."

And he'd say, "The arrangement of windows on a building."

She'd say, "A surgery of perforation. Do another."

She knew he was beginning to understand that she was gone. He would have presents to return and people to call, all the plans to unmake. She'd not even left him a note; there'd be no fixing it with him. He wasn't the kind of man who'd come around to explanation, and there'd been no way to leave him with one. He could have talked her out of anything. Lindy drew her hands to her ribs, to her stomach. This is where you carry meanness, she thought, swallowed like a stone.

Beside her, the baby chewed on himself. She watched his silhouette. He looked like June in the cheeks, the perfectly round ears, even as he was fair where she was dark. Since June died, Lindy had studied everyone for how they looked like June: her mother, herself, Jimmy White. A gesture on the movie screen could be like June's, something her mother said, the arrangement of her own face. It was like being haunted publicly; the ghost was everywhere.

How long she watched the baby, she didn't know. Without talk between them, there was no way to mark the time. He gnawed his fingers, one by one, several at once, his palms, his wrists. When he stopped chewing, his cry was sudden and loud. She put her finger in his mouth; the ridge of a new tooth was pushing through, just as the woman in the store predicted.

Piling pillows on the floor, she nested him in so he wouldn't fall and went to fetch some ice.

Outside, the night air was nearly alive on her clean skin, like breath, or heat beneath a blanket. The highway hummed with cars; the casinos ran all night long.

She passed the room where the man had died. The door was broken off its hinges, because he'd locked himself inside. She reached around the tape to flip the light switch; green light came streaming, blinding. The mattress was bare, the room clean. She wondered how long he'd been dead, whether he died whole or in pieces, of himself or something else. It was hard to tell, just looking at the place it happened. She would've had to see the body.

She still remembered her first cut with the scalpel, like cutting through butter, and how underneath the flesh was rare and meaty and dinner-like, how it looked meant to be cut into, meant to be used. It was a feeling that never left her for as long as she collected tissues, and that had been nearly four years.

She took eyes, skin, veins, the mitral heart valves, the Achilles tendons, the patella tendons, anything in the lower extremities, the hips on down. She and two other tissue technicians would take a body from the morgue to OR where they set up, and these were just-dead bodies, some still-warm bodies. The blood would run from the table, because no one could use the blood anymore.

Eyes she removed herself, alone, in the morgue. She'd come to be most comfortable with that procedure because the calls came in the middle of the night, and the morgues had green lights and held all the hospital above them, and the slab rooms were cool and silent. It was a thing to be done alone. Sometimes the hospital that called was outside the city, and Lindy would find herself on a black road to Union County, the only car for hours, driving to take somebody's eyes, because that's the way they'd wanted it before they died.

The police had been through the motel room already. She went in. The phone was off the hook; on the dresser, a black suitcase spilled clothing, a pair of loafers, size eleven, a bathing suit. Why hadn't the police taken these things? Lindy found a photograph negative stuck to the bottom of the suitcase and held it to the light. The snapshot was of shoes, legs and feet, and a pair of man's shoes, possibly the loafers, as if the camera had snapped by mistake. That was all. She sat on the mattress, let her eyes sweep the room. What could she make of it, if she had to make something?

From June's house, the police had taken blood samples and dusted for fingerprints — her own, June's, Jimmy White's. They'd taken phone records and address books, bank statements, the rest of the money in Jimmy White's safe. It was a robbery, they said, and with robberies, there wasn't much to go on, but they'd taken boxes full of things away.

She filled the ice bucket and went back to her room. The baby was sleeping in his nest of pillows, a fingertip to his lips and white salt trails across his cheeks. For the first time, Lindy noticed the matches on the low table near him, the exposed wall outlet, the tangle of cords in the corner of the room. Why had she left him alone, on the floor? Why hadn't she taken him with her? She was out of practice at any kind of watchfulness. Her patients at the hospital were adults. She asked a question, and they answered if they could. If not, there was always someone else to ask.

She remembered June, days home from the hospital and rocking the baby to sleep, evening light coming in the bay windows, some gold skin caught in that light, and the look on June's face as if she were made for this moment, her body cast to hold a newborn child well. Lindy felt such awe that she'd had to leave the room.

The baby panted in his sleep. Lindy thought that if he were her baby, had grown in her body, fed at her breast, and if she'd tucked him into bed and got up with him in the night, if she'd done all those things, she'd have been as golden right as June in deciding what to do.

It was thoughts like these she had to stop having.

But the longer she watched him sleep, the harder it was, his sleep like a needle in her side. He was such a good boy, so peaceful and sweet and sleeping. Blood rushed to her face, traveled back to her heart and swelled it, slammed through; everything about her was twitching and thumping, and she was unable to sit still any longer.

She grabbed the baby's arms and pulled him fast to her shoulder. She was standing, striding, already crossing the highway, before he was fully awake. He let a thin, frustrated cry into her hair, and she felt better for it.

The nearly empty casino still flashed with light, with smoke, and the ting of slot machines. The baby's eyes were wet. Her feet were cold. Cut. Bleeding around the toes where she'd picked up glass in the parking lot.

She won sixty dollars, lost forty-five, and had two beers. The blackjack dealer was an Asian woman who could fold the chips in one hand as if they were attached, one to the other, like the leaves of a fan. There were people with pads and pens and odds written down. Finally, Lindy decided it was too boring to try to figure out what was only chance. It was Thursday, she realized. The handful of people around her knew it was Thursday. They knew what hour it was; they had to work tomorrow. They knew which clothes they'd pull from their closets. Lindy wondered what would happen to her closet, her clothes, her house, but she couldn't say she cared.

A security guard approached and asked about her shoes.

"I was just going," she said. "I'm gone."

❧

Back at the hotel, she stole pillows and towels and soap. It was early morning, and her headlights caught new-turned earth, beer bottles, trash cast across the medians. Moss dripped from the trees. She drove fast, and her empty stomach burned and bit, but when she'd think to pull over and eat, it would just get worse.

Mississippi went past in ribbons of small town dawns: Pass Christian, Bay of St. Louis; and into Louisiana, Pearl River and Flynn and the bayous, the swamps, the green lagoons. In New Orleans, she decided she must be hungry and, after crossing the bridge, stopped at a roadside café for red beans and rice, smoked sausage, white bread, and sweet tea. It was the first she'd eaten since Charlotte, and she ate all of it, in minutes. The baby palmed rice from her plate as if it was a game, and when the rice was gone he banged his fist for more.

Lindy had once loved to eat. She once loved to cook, and in her house back in Charlotte she had fine black pots on a hanging rack, pastry brushes and hardwood salad bowls, a mandoline, a sharp knife, a Roman pot, all gifts for her wedding. She'd unwrapped the boxes when they arrived on her doorstep, all the paper and packing and big white bows, and stacked them in her parlor. It didn't seem right to put the things in her kitchen until she was married — it would be like money spent before you earned it — so the gifts just piled up.

On her days off from the hospital, she used to start early in the morning with dog-eared recipe cards and yeast, fresh fruit, whole spices; the morning would spread to afternoon in loops of time spent peeling and kneading and walking softly through the kitchen. She would make brioches and crispy duck, tenderloins and timbales and sour cherry pies. Then, it was evening, and Cott would come home. They'd eat on her sofa, watching TV, her feet tucked beneath his thigh and plates in their hands. Now, she couldn't remember what that was like, making food for herself, being hungry for it. She had stopped cooking months ago.

Instead she stayed in bed mornings until after Cott was gone, stayed up until he went to bed at night, and she never put her feet in his lap anymore. Now, she ached to kiss him, do it well and right and wetly, with her whole mouth, and the ache became a spur in her chest sharp enough to make her gasp. She could see that it was better not to think of Cott at all.

She dusted beignet sugar from the baby's face and paid her check. From the parking lot, she had a postcard view of the railroad bridge crossing the river, green grass, and chestnut horses grazing under its trestles. The baby cooed and chirped, held out his hands to the animals. Lindy wanted to go back into the restaurant to ask for something the baby could feed the horses — an apple, a carrot, a cube of sugar. But she set him down on the hood when she realized what was happening, when she started to sweat and spit. Then she threw up her entire meal.

Afterward, there was that too brief moment of feeling better. She looked up at the soles of the baby's feet and thought how high a price she was paying for what she was doing, a personal, physical price, like suffering a pox. It was a kind of satisfaction. She'd expected this plan of hers to be difficult, complicated, and here it was, exactly that. She'd been right, but what could have been a horrible realization turned out to be different. Maybe she'd be right about everything.

She reached for the baby's toes and heard him gurgle and smack the hood of the car, the way you'd smack an animal's flank. She stood up slowly, spit again, and took him back into her arms.

I'm fine, she thought. And she wasn't long on the highway again before she started to feel much better.

৶৹

The sun was hot on her arm, cocked on the open window. The baby closed his eyes and opened his mouth, tasting the wind. He leaned forward in his seat to look at her; then closed his eyes, opened his mouth again. He kept himself occupied for most of Louisiana like that, gauging the limits of his actions.

Lindy kept to the back roads. She watched the fields tick past her window, sugar cane in Thibodaux, tides of rice in Lacassine, pastures full of cattle. It was all warm and springlike and new. She made stops to change the baby's diapers, to hold his hand and let him walk the parking lots of gas stations, and for several hours in the early afternoon there was nothing on her mind but the highway ahead.

Then, driving into Texas, she passed a man in his garden. It was a simple garden, littered with hubcaps, tin plates, and purple cabbages the size of watermelons. The man was old and bent around a shovel. He dug with his shoulders and back, with a solid determination, the way people dig to plant a tree or bury a body, regardless of heat or hardness of the soil. *The way people dig to bury a body* — and Lindy's brain snapped back to her like a dislocated joint, pulled in just the right direction, with just the right amount of pressure. She could almost hear it pop into place.

When she was in nursing school, some of the medical residents kept shovels in the trunks of their cars. They'd ask around about abandoned graves, because you weren't robbing what wasn't wanted anymore. They'd dig where they were told, treat the bones with quicklime, and keep them in their apartments. Before Cott, Lindy dated residents, fine-handed men with good voices, bad teeth, and skeletons in their closets. You had to come to the apartment, see the skeleton, hear the story, and maybe you made it to your morning shift in the same clothes you'd worn the night before. There were many things in her life Lindy had intended to be one way while someone else was thinking the other way around.

Her brain dealt these thoughts like a hand of cards, all of a suit, snapping down in front of her, one after another, everything she'd ever been ashamed of doing: she'd been cruel to other girls; she'd once let June's boyfriend kiss her; she'd cheated, lied, and stolen.

She'd called her mother from the clinic. She said she was coming by, would take the baby on some errands for the afternoon. She'd see her in a while.

Her mother was redecorating the house on the lake and told Lindy the paint fumes made her gloomy. She was wondering what amount of paint fumes it would take to suffocate a person. Her mother always thought in such big sweeping ways, made her dramatic and finer points. Lindy nodded into the phone, drew a ring of blue ink at her kneecap through her white nurse stockings, and said nothing.

"Ten gallons worth?" her mother asked. "One hundred gallons?"

"You're fine, Mother. Fine," Lindy said.

"I need a plan."

"I know."

"I can't handle this."

She meant June, the house, Jimmy White come by again to

see about his son. Who knew what all? And Lindy didn't ask. She nodded again and let a silence pass between them.

That was several afternoons ago.

Now the night billowed around Lindy like a woman's skirt, and she felt fear, her mother's fear, her own, the fear she must be causing. She passed a billboard proclaiming that this was a county in Texas where murderers walked free. What kind of place took pride in its murderers? She felt as if she'd entered a conversation in which no one knew what they were talking about. They were just talking, talking, talking, and she kept opening her mouth only to be talked right over.

She found herself close to tears. She'd driven a far distance and still had far to go. Texas was a huge treadmill of a place, and she'd just stepped onto the edge of it; already it was flying off with her. Her eyes started to lose focus, and she knew she had to pull over soon. She began seeing people beside the road, poised to run headlong into her path, and suddenly those people, disabled, dismembered, and disemboweled, were in need of her aid. Where her sickness that morning had seemed fair, this did not. She was down to seeing things that weren't there.

She took the next exit off the highway, pulled onto the shoulder of a two-lane road. She had to sleep, though it had been a long time since sleep had done her any good. It was as if she'd passed by the possibility of sleep a thousand miles back, and now there was no way to turn around for it and still get where she was going. The air started to close in, thick and high-throttled. She watched her rearview mirror. She breathed little breaths.

The baby began to wail, as suddenly as a hammer on iron. It was as if his good nature depended on their constant motion. Now that they were no longer moving, he chewed out cry after cry, tore off a breath, and began again. Lindy pushed her back against the doorframe and forced her jaw to release. She thought he might be teething, might be wet. She wasn't certain how long he'd been upset. He hadn't made a noise until now, but maybe she hadn't heard him. She brushed a tear from his cheek and tasted it, salty, like any tear. She felt as distant from him as if he were on stage.

She'd forgotten food.

Because she wasn't hungry, she'd forgotten about him. She dug in her purse and found a box of raisins, but he was too far gone to be placated, and soon he wore himself out. Lindy watched as he rocked himself to sleep, his head side to side and side again. She knew he'd rocked himself that way every night since June died; her mother had told her so. But this was the first she'd seen it, and it was so sad, she could not watch. She had watched a lot of horrible things, but a baby, this baby, so plainly alone, was beyond her.

In the bottom of her purse, she kept a stash of Toradol, Fioricet, Vicodin; samples from the clinic. She'd collected the pills slowly, and she hadn't kept them in the house because of Cott. She worried that he'd throw them out if he found them or, worse, that he wouldn't, and then they'd have been a constant temptation. That was what she thought. She didn't know. She never felt she had the right to ask what tempted him.

With the pills, it had been a mindless collecting; everyone at the clinic did it. Now Lindy had a purseful.

She worked up enough spit to swallow something down, and after that she sat in the darkness and the silence, with her eyes acting crazy and the sound of the baby's breath filling up the car. She sat until she could listen to her own breath as if it were coming from someone else's chest, ragged and running, right behind her. She locked the doors. She crawled over the back seat, unstrapped the baby, snugged him tight against her, and lay still. All she wanted was a few hours of some other place.

She pulled her purse into the back seat and fished out all the samples she could get her hands on, unlocked the door, and pitched them into the road. She closed the door and locked it again, and, someplace in there, started to dream while she was still awake, the most vivid dreams there ever were. She dreamed she was passing out, a slow spiral to the floor, and she was hearing through cotton, and she was in a library or a shopping mall, and a black man was there to help her to her feet. He was concerned. He asked her many times, was she okay? Was she okay? And she asked him the same thing right back.

She woke in a stickiness, with the morning coming through the windows of the big car and the baby's drool on her chest, but no baby. It was early still, warm already. Her head was thick from the Toradol, her stomach fragile as eggs, the car unnaturally quiet. She sat up and rubbed at her eyes with her fists.

The baby crouched in the floorboards with her open purse. He was chewing on something, but her contacts were cloudy from sleep and she couldn't see what it was. She pulled him to her. He held a silver packet, an empty packet, accordioned with teeth marks, his lips powdery with what had been inside. He'd found the last of her pills.

Lindy held him on her lap and wiped his mouth with a tissue. He was so quiet, as if he knew he should be scared, so Lindy whispered to him that it was okay, he'd be okay. But her voice failed her, and she made it worse. He whimpered, and she turned frantic. She swept her finger through his mouth to clear out what he hadn't swallowed, but she found nothing, not even a paste. A pill would have tasted bitter; maybe he'd spit it out. She checked the folds of his T-shirt, the floorboards. She dumped her purse out on the seat, and the baby started to cry.

She held his head to her shoulder. There would be a few hours to pass. He would be sick or not. She could get him to a hospital, but they'd take him away from her and wait those same hours. Without proof that he'd swallowed the pill, they'd wait for something to go wrong. She could feel the baby's heart beating in her hand at his back. A hospital would only be trouble. She had to get to Galveston.

She kept him on her lap as she got behind the wheel, kept a hand on him to feel if he was hot, if he convulsed. In that moment, she saw clearly that if something happened to him, there would be no reason to go back, no reason to go forward. He was everything solid she'd saved from her life, a tiny package of hope, and he seemed to need so little, she'd begun to think

"Yes, Alabama."

"Whereabouts?"

"All through it."

"But where is it you're from, in Alabama?"

"I'm not." She corrected herself. "Originally."

"This isn't going very well."

He asked for her license and registration. She went to the glove box and handed him Bruton's papers. She told him her wallet had been stolen.

"And I can see how upset it's got you."

Lindy sniffed. Officer Wilk stood tall and snapped his wrists from the cuffs of his shirt.

"So. This is . . . let me guess." He held the registration card to his forehead. "Your husband?"

All Lindy had to do was nod.

"Your address in Alabama?"

Lindy recited it back, and he told her she'd been doing seventy in a fifty-five.

"Speeding," she said.

"Oh, what do you think would be sufficient?"

"I'm sorry, Officer."

"Damn right you are."

He looked at her over the tops of his sunglasses. She had twenty-five hundred dollars in her wallet. She had her own driver's license, with her own name on it, but she was afraid to show it, because then there'd be proof she'd been in Texas. The rest would be easy to figure out when people at home started looking.

The baby puffed out a wet sound, and Wilk handed him a sucker from the breast pocket of his uniform.

"That boy's cutting teeth," Wilk said. "Makes 'em sore at everybody. I suppose it tries a woman's patience too, don't it."

"Yes," Lindy said. "It does."

The baby threw the sucker to the floor.

Wilk walked back to his patrol car and Lindy watched in the rearview mirror as he picked up his radio. She could run, maybe. Now. She'd have to cross traffic in either direction, but she thought police probably didn't fire at women with babies. Sweat ran down the underside of her arms, the front of her ribs, and she felt sick again.

She took a deep breath. She'd promised herself she would move slowly, think about what she was going to do before she did it, consider the safety of the baby. He had apparently survived the pills. Something would save her from this ticket. She watched Wilk write for a long time, and her head came forward to butt against the steering wheel.

He was standing at her window again.

"I'm going to have to ask you to step out of the car."

"Pardon?" Lindy said.

He opened the car door for her. "If you'd just step out of the vehicle, please."

"But I have the baby here."

"To state the obvious, bring the baby with you, little lady, and step away from your automobile."

Lindy and the baby stood near Wilk in the breakdown lane. Her brain was racing with the traffic; the concrete rising up ahead to accommodate more cars, the sound rising. Officer Wilk riffled his ticket book. The baby coughed, startling Lindy. Wilk laughed.

"What?" Lindy yelled.

He leaned toward her, put his mouth near her ear. He smelled like candy. "I know what you're doing." He let his eyes drop over her.

"What?" she said. She could feel her face flushing.

Wilk laughed again. "I'm just trying to decide if you need calling on it."

"I'm sorry," Lindy said, "I don't know what you mean."

"Well, I noticed you're in a hurry."

Lindy sniffed.

"And you've got quite a handful with the baby there." Wilk snorted. "If I had to, I'd say you're related. But you ain't this boy's mama."

"His mother is dead."

Wilk slapped the ticket book against his thigh. He looked at a spot on the asphalt beside Lindy's left foot. Traffic whipped past them. He looked at her face and spoke again. "Yeah. Anyway, I was trying to decide if I need to take you in, sweat all this out at the station."

She jostled the baby on her hip for something to do and wiped at her nose with the back of her hand.

"I believe I have some tissues on the front seat back there," he said. "You go on and see if you can find them. Lean right in the window."

"Like the witch in the oven," Lindy said.

He laughed. "Go on."

She was going to have to run for it.

She walked backward, away from him, toward the patrol car, alongside the flying traffic. And then, up ahead on the beltway, there was the sound of brakes, of metal on metal and glass shattering. Lindy saw it first, a hundred yards in front of her. A car broke through a guardrail on the overpass and plummeted to the highway below.

It landed in the breakdown lane, on all four tires, bounced a few times, and was still. The driver's face was sour, like turned milk, her hands tight at the wheel. Lindy watched her lay her head back on the seat, blood coming from her nose and lips. She spit teeth from her mouth she'd just have to find later.

Wilk ran to the woman, opening her door and kneeling down. He spoke into a hand-held radio. Lindy couldn't make out what he was saying, but she could hear sirens coming up the highway and then passing by, exiting for the overpass, an accident up there that the woman had swerved to miss.

Wilk had dropped his ticket book. Lindy tore off the top sheets of paper, the tickets in Mrs. Toliver's name; there were several copies. She took the ones that looked to be her own for the fairness of it, the honesty. She slipped into the driver's seat of the Cadillac, strapped the baby in tight, tucked the tickets beneath the sun visor. The engine started up with a purr, and she eased into traffic, ever so quietly, ever so slowly, and then she was gone up the beltway, another car among the hundreds.

At the very least, Wilk knew she was lying. He probably figured that people were looking for her, and he could have her description on a wire that very moment. All she needed was to go another fifty miles, but she didn't know how chancy that might be. Her head was full, she couldn't think, and suddenly she realized it was Saturday. Had everything been different, she and June would have been shopping. Had she been home, she and Cott would have been using his day off. They'd spent the last dozen Saturdays going over the details of their wedding. All of that was gone now. The pressure in her head gave way. She was beginning to feel the ease of total failure.

✑

Galveston came up ahead late that day in bright light and mirrored surfaces. She crossed the bay to the island, and there was the pyramid from some museum, glinting in the noonday light, like a birdpan in the garden. She felt blinded. She reached for the baby and grabbed his foot.

"We're here," she said. "Here we are."

She remembered child things about Galveston, running and hiding, being wet and sunburned, fed well and watched over. She would fill her days with the baby, all the old things and remembered things she could find to entertain him. It was a mother's house: Lindy's mother's, her grandmother's, and her great-grandmother's before that. She was going there with a baby not her own, but a baby most dear, and she hoped the best would come out of the building itself.

In Esther's house, there were three taps in every bathroom: hot, cold, and rainwater for your hair. There were Florida palms painted in the corners of the dining room, a garden, and a grotto with walls of beach glass and bright metal. The grotto was a place in wait for something, with water and darkness, a single shaft of sunlight you could tell time by. It was there that Esther held her foot-washing ceremonies on Sundays, after dusk. She'd say, *Whatsoever you do to the least of us, you do unto me,* and she'd pull a wide Turkish towel from a steamer trunk, pat your feet dry with as much care as she'd give crystal, and sometimes she'd even kiss your toes.

She wanted Esther first of all; she'd go to her in the retirement home and tell her she was hiding out, ask her to keep her secret, and bounce the baby on her knees. Esther loved children, and always said she'd wanted more than Lindy's mother, but some things just aren't possible. She had the next finest thing: the house she'd been born in, a place in which to raise flowers and peacocks and, someday, to die. Lindy always understood that, the compromises we make, the next best things. She would take that now, if she could get it, over the bridge and down the causeway, as fast as her old gold car would carry her.

◈

Those first days in Galveston, April came, and Lindy lingered in bed, restless like a sleep of naps strung together, only there was no sleep, never sleep, just some kind of shut-eyed distance from the present hours. Esther's beds were half-tester beds, meant to be slept in sitting up. Esther said it aided dreams and digestion, but really the beds had been her mother's and she loved them too much to throw them away.

Lindy kept the Cadillac parked down the street. She did not leave the house during daylight. She kept the doors unlocked, the blinds pulled, the windows shut, just the way she'd found things. In the backyard, there was a hatch to the crawl space and the belly of the house, but she didn't lock that either. Nothing had been locked when she got there. She heard the odd creaks and moans in the foundation, the house's settling breaths, and her brain stumbled with the kind of fear she put on herself. Someone would be coming for her; it was only a matter of time.

In the newspaper, there was no mention of her, but missing women and children were everywhere. A little girl, taken by her father; a boy missing; a baby switched at the hospital. A woman disappeared from a husband, a house, and two kids in Houston.

60

Just down the street, someone broke into a house to watch a woman sleep. Later, another story told of a woman held down by a man in a black mask who painted her toenails. She was pregnant. He was very gentle, the woman said, but still, she hadn't wanted him in her house.

Who cares if anyone's here with me, Lindy thought. I'm not really here myself. But she knew who would care, who would notice. There was a real estate agent, and also the man who took care of the garden, who'd known her since she was small. He had a son near Lindy's age, and she and June had played with him whenever they came to visit Esther. Lindy remembered the boy, Orrin, a tease. She hadn't seen him since she was in high school and he was even younger. She wondered whether he was still living here, wondered whether she'd find him if she went looking. He used to draw flowers on her feet with a calligraphy pen Esther gave him, and they lasted on her skin for days afterward.

The baby found Esther's stash of calligraphy pens while Lindy lingered in bed. He marked all over himself and the closest wall, chewed the nibs to rickrack before Lindy realized what he was doing. She cleaned what she could with nail polish remover, and left the rest to wear off. When the baby smiled, his mouth was black with ink. He looked as if he carried fever.

She was learning to orbit him. He became her clock, in need of her every few hours, and she was grateful for that. She fed him, changed his clothes, wiped his mouth and his behind, and when she finished that, maybe he'd sleep a while, and then she'd do it all again. She spent her mornings watching him pull himself up on the furniture and bump back down. The heat was hard upon them for only springtime, and her skin was always moist and smelled like cloves, and the baby's like sweet hay. She'd fill a tub with cool water and watch her sweat drift away from her body like milk.

Nights, she lit the back rooms, kept the shutters closed upstairs, and from Ball Street it looked as if no one was home.

She became still, where she'd been in motion. She was tucked away, where she'd been exposed. She walked the house to keep from thinking what she'd done to get there, and for those first days, it worked. In the parlor, the walls were lined with cabinets filled with Esther's trinkets: tiny glass, china dolls, things made of teeth and bone. Lindy found secret panels, false bookcases, locked doors, interior windows that opened to other rooms. Every clock was set to a different time zone, leaflet Bibles were tacked open at every doorway. An iron ring in the kitchen was heavy with keys, none of which opened the doors that were locked. There were nine pianos, one in every common room, uprights and grands, baby grands, boudoir and cabinet and cottage pianos, even a Wurlitzer, in the downstairs bathroom, that could be played from the throne. Esther had been a performer, a pianist. She traveled the world until she had Lindy's mother. After that, home became important, and making her house a riddle became everything.

Lindy sat on the crest of the stairs with a hot needle, a pair of tweezers, and the baby's knees across her lap. He'd picked up splinters crawling across the floorboards, and she needed the light from the chandelier to see by. Sleepy, he was circling his fingers on his scalp behind his ear, but if she was slow about it, he'd lie still and let her pick. She talked; it kept him quiet.

"These are old floors," she told him. "An old house. Who knows where this wood came from, or where it was before?"

The baby let his serene eyes settle on her face. He didn't know to be frightened of the needle, of her, so he wasn't. He yawned, rubbed his head, and Lindy flinched at his slightest movement.

"You were June's," she said. "Before that, I guess you were God's own, and before that, well, you tell me."

The baby rolled from her then the way a plane rolls, in all dimensions, and started backing down the stairs. Lindy watched him, concentrated, as if that plane was disappearing on the horizon, growing smaller and smaller and smaller. Soon, she thought, she'd have to squint to see him at all.

"Wait," she called, scrambling. "Wait for me."

In the kitchen, whatever he could reach was food. A pot handle, a dust bunny, a rock. He was faster than Lindy, and by the time she got to him, he was chewing on a wooden spoon. She tied him into a ladder-back chair with a dish towel and set about finding him some dinner.

She was still not keen on the business of eating, and had decided that breakfast could be a long shower, lunch a can of peanuts, dinner a pot of coffee. She liked the idea that something so small was satisfying. She felt full when she fed the baby; watching him eat was her food. She knew she leaned heavily on him, pulled on him like a magnet drawing filings, and he was too small to put up fight. Some nights she went and tickled his long toes to wake him, to watch him come awake as if it was effortless to pass between the two. She didn't like to be alone the way she thought she would. She'd pick him up, knowing it was pure craziness to wake him, but he was just a baby.

Jimmy White had hung on his son like that, come without being called and for his own reasons, come, like Lindy, when the baby slept soundly. She hated to align herself with Jimmy White. They were no longer confederates, and there were more reasons for that than she could tell.

After June died, Lindy was the only person who would see Jimmy White. At first, it was her chore to check on him, to make sure he had food and had eaten it, to see that he had clean shirts, a made bed. She'd report to her mother sometimes just the condition of the house when she stopped by, and that had seemed enough. Her parents had taken the baby home with them from the funeral. The trouble came when Jimmy White asked for him back.

It wasn't that he was a bad father, but he was a shady man, a dangerous man even, and Lindy's parents believed this danger had killed their daughter. They would not be so careless with their grandson. It came to words; Lindy's daddy threw Jimmy White out of the house and said forever, never, and ever again.

But Lindy still looked in on him. She'd find him at the Sardine, have a couple of drinks when Cott was working late. She'd stop by the house every once in a while to fold his clothes. She was careful to tell no one. He'd call her at work. "Meet me here," he'd say, and she would.

They'd throw darts, shoot pool. They spoke to each other only when necessary, and were perfunctory, monosyllabic. Then there was the afternoon just weeks ago when they'd both had too much bourbon. He turned honest and sad. "I think the corny things," he said. "If only this; if I'd once that."

Lindy studied his face in the darkness of the bar, the shadow of his jaw across his neck, the set of his mouth. His cheeks were wet. He turned his eyes on her, and she wanted to cover herself. "I see her face everywhere I look," he said.

Lindy let her glass down on the bar, pushed back her stool, swiveled her hips, and set her feet on the floor. She left a twenty for their drinks and never said a word in parting. She could offer her company as long as it was only that. She couldn't bear to hear about his grief. Her own was already too much.

When she got home from the bar, Cott met her in the driveway. He took her arm as she stepped from the car. "Where you been?" he said. "Driving like that."

She didn't want a scene. She let him lead her inside, but then she locked herself in the bedroom, stretching out, not on the bed, but on the floor, and pulling a blanket over herself. She listened to Cott's boots outside the door. Sometime after midnight, the engine in his truck turned over, and he left for his house. The next day she lost her job at the hospital.

To explain her actions to Cott from the beginning was too daunting, so she didn't try explaining at all. When she saw him again, it was as she looked up from a spread of wedding plans on her kitchen table. She asked if he wanted to wear an orchid in his lapel, or whether a rosebud would do just fine.

He bent and put his lips to the top of her head. Whatever, he said. He'd be there. His eyes were red, bloodshot, tired. She did not study what she found.

"An orchid would be nice," she said, and wrote that in her book.

✣

The baby fell asleep with a cracker in his hand, his head against the ladder-back chair. She wiped his face with a warm cloth, gathered him in her arms, and carried him upstairs for bed. His eyes came open on her shoulder, but he didn't stir, seemed to understand the inevitability of sleep, until his head hit the pillow. Then it was thin, whimpering cries as he began rocking himself, his eyes squeezed shut as if he were in pain, like someone who'd been bitten. Lindy knew what she was supposed to do: go away, shut the door behind her, and let him cry. But none of this was the way it was supposed to be.

She crawled into bed beside him and put her hand to his shoulder, gently at first, and then to hold him still, to stop his lonesome rocking. She stroked, and whispered, and then she moved her hand away and only breathed, with a meditative patience, powerfully waiting, as if putting a trance over them. If only she herself could sleep, she thought, he would have an example to follow.

Hours later, she pushed herself slowly from the bed and went back into the hallway. Stapled to the high transom of Esther's bedroom door was a verse from the Song of Solomon: *Comfort me with apples, for I am sick of love.* Tired of love, or sick from too much love? Lindy could understand it either way. Esther's house was full of things like that.

June had come down when Esther first put the house on the market. That was before she got pregnant, but she wanted children, thought all the time about children, and called Lindy from the payphone down the block to tell her about their mother's closet, full of toys, her walking dolls, her toe shoes, her hoop skirts. Esther had saved everything, every space filled and safeguarded. *So many keys without locks,* June said, *and doors without keys.*

When June came back to Charlotte, she found out that she

was expecting. But now, inside her body was piping and cotton and chemicals, Lindy's own diamond ring. Lindy couldn't say for certain why she'd done that, other than that she'd wanted to do something, and the things she'd known how to do there was no time for.

She hadn't seen June laid out at the funeral home; she'd wanted June burned in the backyard, wanted her sunk in the lake and floated to the ocean, no casket, no dirt, no weight, but her parents had her buried. Her daddy told her later that her mother had seemed fine, but then she'd not liked the way June's blouse was opened, not liked her necklace, wanted her to wear this old, old ring. She'd crawled in the casket with her daughter and come apart. The mortician assured her daddy that it happened all the time and helped her mother to the car, into the back seat with Lindy. Her daddy drove them around the beltway until he could remember the way home.

Her parents were separated these days, but they weren't calling it that. Her father worked late. He had calls to make in Atlanta or Raleigh, Washington, D.C., and maybe he'd be home on the weekend, or around midnight. But her parents had not slept in the same bed since the winter, and neither seemed to care.

The day Lindy went to get the baby, her mother was alone. "I have no idea where your father is," she said. "No idea at all."

She was leaning close to the mirror in the master bathroom with a tube of mascara, her head wrapped in a towel and her robe opened to her waist, a straight slip of tan skin. Her hands shook. She reached for a tissue, wiped away what she had done, and tried again.

"What you doing?" Lindy perched on the edge of the tub, ran her fingers in the still warm water.

"Looking for boys who look like trouble."

But her mother wasn't looking anyplace but back at herself and up into her own head. The house ached of paint and new perfume. Lindy put her damp fingertips to one temple and then the other. "You called me at work," she said, but in truth it had been the other way around.

"What did I want?" Her mother turned from the mirror, reached down, and took a tube of something from the baby. He was in his seat on the vanity, kicking his legs.

"He ought not to be up there, you know," Lindy said.

"Oh, pooh. In my house, you never say no to babies or dogs."

Her mother leaned down and nuzzled the baby's stomach. It was a mother's business, she said, to be accommodating, a woman's prerogative to change her mind. It was she who had decided that Jimmy White would not have his baby any longer. She said, *He was June's, so now he's mine.* Jimmy White had yet to bring the courts into it, though it was a possibility they all saw in the near distance. He had the money, and sooner or later he'd be able to use it.

"Drink?" her mother asked, scooping up the baby.

"What you got?"

"Champagne, water, or formula. Apple juice. Take your pick."

They took their champagne outside in big glasses full of ice, glasses like bowls they held with both hands. They set the baby on a blanket and stretched out in the sun on their elbows.

Lindy was still in her whites from work. She should have been at work, but her mother didn't seem to notice. Nobody worked anymore or needed to be anyplace other than where they were. Nobody but husbands.

Her mother said, "If your grandfather were alive, he'd have shot your daddy by now."

"Not before now?" Lindy asked.

Her mother lifted her shoulders and set them down again, not a shrug, more a pretty breath.

Lindy swung her legs in the air and peeled off her stockings, worked the skirt of her uniform up around her hips. Her skin was still winter-white and laced with veins, her blood so close to the skin. By the second glass of champagne, she'd tugged the zipper on her uniform down about her waist.

"You're as fine as china," her mother said and tripped her fingers along Lindy's collarbone.

"I haven't been outdoors lately."

"You'll relax after the wedding. You'll feel as if you have all the time in the world," she said.

The water on the lake rippled. Her mother sat up and poured the rest of the champagne into their glasses. The wind was high, the sky strange. The predicted storm was yet to come, and in moments the sun was hot, then dark, then bright again. Lindy and her mother and the baby closed their eyes.

Everyone had tried to keep June married. Lindy talked to Jimmy White; June talked to her mother. The first time divorce was brought up, they'd been married only a year. The second time, Jimmy White had shot the man on their patio. It was hard for everyone to reconcile that, but they did, and there was a lot of talk thereafter about standing by your man. Then the baby was on the way, and everyone figured it would all settle down like rain.

Jimmy White hit June once, only once, and it was while she was pregnant. June said it was an accident, that they were arguing and she was riding him hard, calling him cheap-hearted and criminal. He'd gone to slam his fist on the table but caught her hand instead. He broke four tiny bones and cracked a joint in her index finger, and the hand had doubled its size by the time she let Lindy look at it the next morning. Somehow, the bruising had leaked up her arm, almost to the elbow. Cott wanted to go over and break Jimmy White's hand right back, but June wouldn't hear of it.

Lindy called their mother about June moving back home for a few days. She'd had enough of the circles being run; something drastic was in order.

Her mother said, "Why?"

"Mother, he broke her hand. Broke it badly, in several places."

"June says it was an accident."

"And you believe her?"

"Lindy-loo." She sighed. "There are times you have to take a pregnant woman at her word. Don't make the situation bigger than it is."

"Fine."

"You make it bigger than it is, and there'll be no going back. See? Lord, if you knew half the accidents your father and I had, starting, of course, with June herself . . ."

June had made it clear that there were things she wanted in her life, one of which was a man like Jimmy White, a man she could steal a horse with. She held the philosophy that from time to time, and among other things, a woman should be decorative. She loved old movies and making herself cry, loved Lindy and her parents and her little baby boy. When you got down to it, Lindy knew Jimmy White hadn't killed June. But he hadn't kept her safe either.

Maybe no husband ever loved his wife well enough, long enough, often enough. There was a time in Lindy's memory when her family was driving south and got pulled over in a sleepy town. Her daddy couldn't take the ticket on his license and still keep it, so her mother took his place in the driver's seat, all limbs and gearshifts. And then she was smiling at the cop and speaking in Spanish, *No comprende, con permiso.* That was the last clear memory Lindy had of her parents together, really together, and laughing and kissing each other on both cheeks. She must have been eight or nine.

The day she told her parents she and Cott were getting married, her daddy took everyone downtown to a big hotel and they had bottle after bottle of champagne, most on the house. Lindy's mother was excited, and June was kissing her cheeks, and when Cott left the table for the men's room, her daddy leaned over and whispered the truest thing in Lindy's ear.

He said, "I can see how much you love him, and I am jealous."

When Lindy thought about that love now, she was jealous, too.

✢

It was dawn, and Lindy had been sick again. She wanted an egg cream soda, and she'd spent the last few hours of night looking for a pair of socks. She hadn't paid attention to her body in months in any clinical way, but she wasn't stupid. She was pregnant. She drew a glass of water from the bathroom tap to rinse her mouth, and it tasted like blood. It was April. By her guess, she was three months along.

She knew that at three months, a baby has decided on its sex, and her baby was a boy, like June's. She knew he somersaulted and drank the fluids he floated in. His heart beat twice as fast as hers. He would have a little heart, little fingers, fingerprints like nobody else's which he'd carry until he died. He'd make little motions, but he was only three inches long and could make himself felt only in waves, like seasickness or fatigue. It was he who wanted the egg cream soda, whose feet were cold; he who wanted Cott, his father, closer at hand.

She leaned into the doorframe, and braced a foot on the sink to pin herself upright. She and Cott could have started over somewhere together. They could have lived here in Galveston, in this very house, and been happy. The sun would be here, and the ocean. The storms would be seasonal and dramatic, like the blizzards up north. But this was a new thought; she'd already gone ahead and acted differently.

She let herself onto the cool tile floor. She told herself this is past, and that is past, and what is past will lie down for always. She'd left Cott in Charlotte. That fact would never change. She could come back to it another time and worry, or never again think about leaving him; it would make no difference. What's done is done. That way of thinking was what Cott loved in her. She never asked for explanation or orchestration, not flowers or gifts or high discussions.

"I'm sorry," he'd say, and she'd shrug.

"No. I am. I mean it."

"I'm sure you do." Then she'd sit on the edge of her high-heaped bed and slip a shoulder out the neck of whatever she was wearing.

"You," he'd say. "What do you want?"

And that was what he meant: what do you want, what can I give you, do for you, me and you, skin to skin. He'd trail his fingers as far as they'd reach, and her breath would come through her mouth, catch, break, catch again. She'd want to lie down, want to tell him something but could never think what it was. It didn't matter, did it, if she couldn't say it out loud.

June once told her the opposite of love is fear.

"Doctors like to tell you that it's death," Lindy said.

"No. Fear. The opposite of life is death."

Lindy thought this was true, in the way that all things lie close to their opposites. She and Cott had come to be like old-fashioned medicine, like blood-letting and poultices and sweating out a fever. They'd found a way of getting at each other that worked by accident more than design, touching that took so much from Lindy. When it was through, she couldn't remember where she'd started.

They'd touched each other less and less after the winter, and then hardly ever. When Cott grabbed her arm after her night with Jimmy White, it had been rough, unpracticed, the way you'd grab a child stepping in front of a train.

Cott had a wife before Lindy was to be his wife. He'd been married for six months, six years ago. There had been no children, and Nadine had left him. She called Lindy from Nevada to say a friend had sent her the engagement announcement from the newspaper and she thought it only fair and right to tell what she'd learned, having been married to Cott for that brief time.

Lindy started to hang up. She took the phone away from her ear and halfway to the cradle, but then she thought, I'm a big girl. I can hear what this woman has to say.

"Oh, honey," Nadine said. "The stuff you ought to know.

The things that I could tell you." But then she didn't tell her anything.

So when she and Cott had dinner in her kitchen that evening, she didn't say she'd spoken with Nadine, and he didn't see it on her face. She thought maybe he'd ask what was wrong and then she'd tell him. But the longer he was there, the less she wanted to talk about it, and then she just wanted him inside her. That would mean something definite, yes or no, up or down.

He had gone to bed afterward and she'd stretched out on the sofa with a glass of wine and Miss LaVelle White on the stereo, but she let the wine get warm in her hands, and when the CD played out, she didn't start it over.

Around midnight, she got up from the sofa and slipped down the hallway to where Cott was sleeping in her bed of flannel and down, his clothes piled on the floor, his hair damp from a late, lone shower. She reached her hand to his long broad back and let it hover there to feel what he gave off. She lay down in his heat, closed her eyes, and tried to feel warm herself, in her pores, like sunbathing. In the morning, she listened to him dress and drink his coffee, listened to the screen door slam when he left.

Now she had something to say to him, now that she knew she was pregnant, a whole thought made from her nights without him. It sounded like the truth when she said it in her head. If she could have that morning back, she'd run after him in her nightclothes, catch his sleeve the way that building had caught his sleeve and sent him to her in the hospital, and she'd say to him, *We are ways and things with each other we could never be with anyone else.*

She would tell him how being in love has nothing to do with being healthy, how we do not always act on what's good for us. Then she would make him come inside and hold her until the morning passed, hold her down, as if to herself, and what would happen then, who could say.

But she'd stayed in bed that morning and listened to his

engine start up and turn over, listened to the sound of his wheels in the driveway. When she opened her eyes, her thought was to break her heart for good. What made her love a man and not want to be with him? She didn't want to be with herself, so she'd thrown Cott over with the rest of it, her life elemental and prime to her, as indivisible as glass. A tiny, growing part of him had tagged along.

Driving to dump the car before she left Charlotte, she'd detoured past the house where Cott and Nadine had lived together. It was a small house; there were children's toys cast across the treeless lawn, an empty driveway, an overturned garbage pail by the curb. Lindy stopped and got out of the car, but there was nothing the house could tell her. She had an aerosol feeling in her mouth, a taste inhaled by accident. She could not convince herself that she was upset about Nadine and Cott; the two of them were long since gone.

There'd been another stop. She had one last conversation with Jimmy White.

She stood in his dining room and told him she was leaving, that she was taking the baby with her and didn't know when she'd be back. June's wedding dishes were stacked on the sideboard, bone china with a gold filigree rim. Lindy counted eleven dinner plates. What happened to the twelfth one? Jimmy White offered her a drink, but she didn't take it. The baby rested his head on her shoulder.

"What kind of man," he said, "would let you take his son from him?"

"A man with no other choice."

She said her parents would try him for June's death. They needed to hold someone responsible, and he was the one available. It shouldn't matter to him that she was taking the baby now; it was now or later, her or her parents. She whispered when she spoke so as not to disturb the baby, and she believed what she was saying, believed she was facilitating time, the cards were laid, the shape cast. As she spoke, she came even more to believe herself, so she grew louder, more earnest.

"I didn't have to come here," she said. "I wasn't planning to. It would have been easier just to go. I guess, now, you don't have to let me go."

His eyes were flat as dimes.

"But you will," she said. And she believed that too.

He stood up quickly and grabbed her elbow, pushed her as much as he could push her, with a baby in her arms, through the kitchen, into the laundry room. There on the floor was a basket, full of June's things. She saw a sweater of her own, borrowed and never returned, a snapsuit of the baby's, too small by months now.

"These," Jimmy White said, and he kicked the basket. "These are June's. There are two skirts, a sweater, a nightgown, some underwear, and a towel. Some stuff of his, and some stuff of yours. If you get real close down there, it all still smells like her."

Lindy watched his face break, watched his thoughts come apart before they left his mouth. He was pathetic, and she felt her convictions bowing under his weight.

"Get down," Jimmy White said. "On your knees. Like this."

He dropped to the floor, his mouth working for evenness, his voice working. She could hear the gristle in his joints. And then he laughed. She hated him for laughing at her. She turned her face to the baby's body and whispered, *Shhh*.

"You're a hard woman, Lindy," he said. "But are you hard as this?"

"I'm going," she whispered at the baby, but she didn't.

Jimmy White pitched himself onto his back, his head cracking on the floor. He made his hands into fists, stacked them at the crest of his skull, and stared at the ceiling.

"Look at you," he said, but he wasn't looking at her. He was looking at the fluorescent light humming overhead. He cleared his throat. "Look at you," he said again. "You're skipping town. You're taking, you're *stealing* her child. Nobody's going to say that you killed her, but I'm the first place they fucking look."

She left him there on the floor, like a dropped handkerchief, a fingerprint, a clue to her whereabouts. She shook, with lack of sleep and panic, but got into her car and drove, broke her window, caught a cab, bought tickets, and was gone, all in the space of an hour. Least of all, she feared his following her, because he did not have the strength.

ॐ

In Galveston, weeks and miles away, there was no list of things to be accomplished, no travel to plan, not even the baby to tend, only herself on the bathroom floor. She had heard how horses could be made pregnant by the wind. She wished for that now, a baby that was hers alone, not part of any other living thing, not stolen away, not carried in secret. From where she lay, she could see the blink of streetlights through the shutters down the hall, could hear their electric snap, and, far off, hear the ocean.

She was coming to understand that there were whole swaths of her life, important, heavy parts, she would share with no one else. Here in Galveston, what she thought, what she felt, what she worried over and cried over, the way she walked the floors at night, all of these were hers to have. If she went a run of days and hated June for dying, hated Cott or her parents, no one else would know about it. It wouldn't show on her face or in the tone of her voice; Cott wouldn't feel it in her touch because there would be no touch. If she went back, she would never have to explain her feelings, only her actions. If I go back, she thought, and it made her feel like a swinging chain.

LITTLE MEN
AND
LITTLE WOMEN

SOMEONE WAS CHECKING ON HER; she heard it from Esther.

She had taken the baby to the retirement home in the middle of the night. The reception area was nearly a living room: wingback chairs and gas logs blazing in the fireplace, coffee tables, framed snapshots. The baby squirmed to get down from her arms, but she sensed it would be rude to let him run around. She picked up a photograph. It was of a spaniel paddling in a plastic kiddie pool. Whose dog, whose pool, she had no idea.

She asked for Esther at the front desk. The attendant was a resident, a woman of eighty or so, dressed as sleekly and well as if she owned the place. An ivory-handled cane rested in the crook of her arm.

"I am not my sister's keeper," she said. "Sign in here, please."

Lindy wrote something illegible in the guest book. She shifted the baby from one hip to the other. The carpet was so thick, she felt it on her feet over the edges of her sandals.

"Should I open every door?" she asked.

"After hours, you rather take what you can get, don't you? I should say you're lucky I'm here at all. I don't imagine I'll be a bother to this earth much longer. My hips are gone. My heart is twice the size it ought to be."

"Just a room number might be helpful," Lindy said gently.

The woman sighed. "No one who has any choice about it is in their rooms at this hour. We've slipped all the controlled substances we can spare to the night aides. In exchange, we are free to do as we please after seven o'clock."

Lindy stood quietly as the woman told her that sitting at this desk was not what she herself would choose to do, but the girl who was paid for such work had called in sick, and they all had to pull together, didn't they, if their little scheme was to continue. All for one and one for all, and all that jazz. As Lindy wandered away, the woman punched furiously at the keypad on the telephone for the number, any number, of someone who might come and take her place. She seemed to have forgotten Lindy altogether, and maybe that was for the best. The phone she dialed was not plugged into any wall.

Lindy found Esther in the basement, in the bowling alley, a room low and damp and rich with wood. The lanes had buckled with the sea air, and the buckling had been waxed over and over until it shone like heat on pavement. Old people bowled as if they were swatting flies. An attendant boy in a sharp red uniform reset the pins and jogged the ball back down the lane, pin-monkey style, the only kind of bowling Esther could feature as a sport. She believed that in golf, one should have caddies; in tennis, there should be ball boys; and hunting ought to be carried out on horseback. Very little was ever worth doing without an audience.

And so Lindy found her holding court in a high leather banquette before a half-dozen old men she had to shoo away so that Lindy could take a seat. There was a scramble of canes and bowling shoes across the parquet, and then Esther and Lindy were alone.

Esther was not surprised to see her. She was so not surprised, it was as if Lindy had gone out for milk. She held her hands out for the baby, smacked them together, and held them out again. Lindy gave him over, and Esther, as always, cut to the quick of things.

"Really, other people's little details are no longer important to me," she said. "How is my garden?"

Esther had aged as well as a man. She'd looked the same for as long as Lindy could remember, slender and silvery where she caught the light, only a little more than the last time they'd been together. Lindy reached across the table to kiss her cheek, as soft and strange as the skin of a fish.

"Your garden is green," she said.

"You laugh. But I am a magnificent gardener, even in my absence."

In truth, Lindy had not set foot past the garden gate since she'd been at Esther's house. Dread held her inside the house, maybe for her own good, and she was loath to press against such strong feelings. She had seen, through the slats in the shutters, the winged tops of palms. She could say they were as green and great as ever.

"Listen here," Esther said. "When your mother was a little girl, I chased your grandfather into the koi pond we had out there. He'd been caught with great expectations for some skirted thing or another, and I was angry, the way you get angry at a dog for barking. When he fell in that pond, I had him trapped. I leveled a gun at his head, and he ducked under the water. Leveled the gun, and he ducked. This was before filtration or chlorine or anything, and there was vegetation in there I should have been more careful about importing; growth with bones to it. So Luther came up for a breath, and I leveled the gun again, on and on like that for longer than was funny. Finally he called out, 'My God, woman. Go on and shoot. You won't let me in the house since I've been in this shit anyway.'"

Esther jounced the baby on her lap, and he laughed with her, a spitting laugh.

"He could be so funny," she said, "at his own expense. I love that in a man."

"You shouldn't point guns at husbands," Lindy said.

"Oh, I don't care for your tone," Esther said. "It's such a good story."

"Would you've shot him, if you could have?"

"If I'd wanted, I certainly was able. You know, Lindy, Mr. Clyde Barrow named his favorite guns after me."

Esther was convinced that all of history had happened to her and in Galveston, so Clyde Barrow had been here, Jeb Stewart, James Dean. The margarita was invented here by the Mafia for Peggy Lee, and Esther had the phone numbers of seven men who would break legs for her; she kept them alphabetized in her jewelry box for easy reference. All the handsomest outlaws, all throughout time, had been in love with her.

Esther lived in the fine-texture detail. Who was to say what was too far past for her to know? She could tell you more about it than somebody who had been there, and not one living soul knew her true age for a place to start the unraveling. Lindy grew up taking Esther at face value, at the risk of either being fooled or learning something, which one, she'd probably never know and ceased to care about. It was from Esther that she had learned to measure out the truth, and the million different things to call it when she was done: a good story, your own protection, how she remembered it at the time. The possibilities, she'd learned, were limited only by the material at hand.

Behind Lindy, bowling balls cracked in the lanes like thunderclaps. She watched the baby flinch, laugh, and flinch again.

"Don't you people sleep?" she asked.

"Some." Esther shrugged. "But it's a waste of time, isn't it?"

"I thought there'd be regulations. In a place like this." Lindy waved her hand vaguely at the room.

"Oh. Of course. But I suppose there's not much difference between the old and the two-year-old when it comes to rules. You don't seem much for rules yourself."

Esther held up her palsied fingers for one of the sharp uniformed boys, and sent him for ladylike drinks, a snack for the baby. The boy disappeared through a set of swinging doors. Esther sailed a hand across the tabletop to draw Lindy's attention back to her.

"I've decided I'll not worry about what you're doing, Lindy-loo," she said.

And Lindy said thank you.

"There seem to be plenty of others to do that," and it was as if she had lifted her hand to strike Lindy in the face.

"A man called here Thursday," she went on. "He wanted to know whether I'd seen you lately. Asked whether you'd been around or dropped by. He didn't ask whether you were living in my house."

Lindy tried to keep her eyes on an old man across the room, squatting over the path of his released ball, even and focused and willing it to roll one way more than the other. Her heart burst in her chest like a ripened fruit.

"Who was it?" she said.

"I didn't get his name. How many are you expecting?"

Lindy didn't answer, but Esther wasn't waiting for a reply.

"Good Lord, before you go losing all your starch. Where do you suppose your mother came running when she left a man on the church step? Here, right here, back home. If you were so concerned about not being found, perhaps you should have thought with somebody else's head."

"Somebody else's head?"

"Yes. How's that saying go? To catch a thief, you have to think like a . . . what?"

"Like a thief."

"Yes, but there's a niftier way to say it."

Esther told her how it had gone thirty years before, how Lindy's mother left college suddenly, midsemester, hitchhiked home, and climbed into her bedroom window off the balcony. Three days passed before Esther knew she was there.

"So, at the outset, I was completely honest with those people from the university, the boy. I had no idea where she was. Then one morning I got up, and she was drinking milk at the kitchen table. I fell in with her immediately, of course. I mean, really, she looked so possessed of herself. A glass of milk, stockings, a pressed dress. The papers were full of women who wouldn't wear bras, and there she was at my table, graciously, completely dressed."

"Do I look like that," Lindy asked. "Like I know what I'm doing?"

"I have practice, Lindy. I threw him off well."

"What did you say?"

"I said, 'Lindy? Lindy who?' And he said, 'Your granddaughter.' And I said, 'My granddaughter is dead.' And he said, 'Your other granddaughter,' and it went on like that."

"Do you think he believed you?"

"Yes." She raised her chin. "Yes, I would say he did. He believed that I had no idea what I was talking about. Which, ironically, would be the first anyone beyond these walls believed a word I've said in months."

The light in the room was suddenly the color of mustard. It made Lindy dizzy, made her sick to think of mustard, and the clap of the balls against wood beat a pulse in her head. She cupped her hands over her ears and propped her elbows on the table.

"How did you know —" She licked her lips and began again. "How did you know not to tell him anything?"

Esther was breezy. "I think it's this place, living here amongst these ancient people. What's ever to be said that would make any difference? As I told you, Lindy, I've had practice galore."

The boy arrived with their drinks. Lindy took hers from his tray, tipped it back, thick with juice and rum. Her stomach flipped. She set the drink down and moved away from it.

The baby ate cake. Esther's hand trembled the fork from the plate to his mouth, losing half as much as she got there, as bad as any drunk. Lindy watched another boy in uniform appear to take the fork and plate and feed the baby for her.

Esther sat back and told Lindy not to worry.

"Silence visits on us all, dearie," she said. "One way or another."

But Lindy didn't know what sense to make of that. The man on the phone might have been her daddy, Jimmy White, the police, might have been Cott, and none of those men was the sort to be silent or the sort to be visited by anything uninvited. Some men were made hard and difficult by emotions that crossed them, and those seemed to be the only kind Lindy knew.

Yet sitting in that bowling alley, Lindy found a slender part of herself wishing it was Cott who'd called. She wished for him not to turn hard, the way she'd expected, but to go against himself, go looking for her. She'd felt that same clutch in her own chest so many times on his account. It was a chain of thoughts that made her more nervous about herself, not less. When had she grown such an appetite for pain?

She stood up from the booth, caught herself on the edge of the table, and stood again. She couldn't find her bearings, her foothold, and panic lofted inside her head, febrile and fat. She was like a bird under the gun; all she could do was rise.

She had to go, she told Esther. She had to move fast, and she scooped the baby from his cake and hurried out into the midnight streets, to the house, the safe, silent hiding.

A return to Charlotte would be impossible, a return in the physical alone. Every tie she had was torn, and she would not go back, not under her own power, and not by some man's force, even Cott's. When she realized she was pregnant, that what she carried was half his, she'd felt the pull of fairness, of rights. She'd thought the words *If I go back*. But fairness had no part in what she was doing. She'd stolen her sister's baby; she'd let her family think the worst; she was stowed away in her grandmother's house like a criminal; and this was the way she'd planned it from the start.

Keeping her pregnancy to herself followed course. She had June's baby, and now she would have Cott's baby. She was her parents' only child, and so had taken pieces of them into herself and would have those too. She would find a way to live

It was the females that got you, June always said; the females that bit. Lindy smacked at herself, caught blood on her calf, fanned at the air before her face. She felt the baby do the same from his perch on her shoulders. He knows me, she thought. He knows he's with me and, left on his own, he'd follow after me. She was grateful for that companionship, small as it was.

Sunday would be Easter, the baby's first birthday after that. Lindy tried to think what one-year-olds were capable of, what he would learn in the coming year: to open doorknobs, to walk up and down stairs, to feed himself, to talk. He made sounds now, but she imagined that his voice in words would be different, more like hers, or June's. Lindy would watch him for the rest of her life as if he were June's magic trick, a little way for her to cheat death. For her part, Lindy would always tell him, no matter how hard it was to say, *That there, boy, that's just the way your mother would have done it.*

At the corner, Lindy caught a flash of blue lights down the cross street. Two dressed-up girls had their hands spread on the hood of the cruiser. They were Hispanic girls, their skirts white and crinolined, their braids long on their backs. A little white dog circled their feet, and, behind them, cops filtered from a shotgun house, one after the other after the other, like clowns.

Lindy had left her traffic tickets in the Cadillac, underneath the sun visor.

Sweat slipped along the notches of her spine. She watched a cop bring the barrel of a shotgun up beneath one of those white skirts, lifting the fabric to the breeze. There was a time when she would have run the five or six blocks back to the seawall, but she had a baby on her shoulders, slumping against her, growing tired and heavy to carry. She was tired herself, and she thought about leaving the tickets in the car. She couldn't remember what she had told Wilk that gave a clue to her whereabouts. She couldn't remember any of the details of that conversation, and she waffled in the street like an animal in the path of a tire. The girl in the lifted skirt furled out a long, hot run of Spanish. Lindy couldn't take the chance; she turned back.

She'd always relied on her memory, but now her mind seemed organized by strangers, a card catalogue, a librarian. Once she'd done it, thought it, someone else filed it away. She would search her brain for something, and it was as if she had to wait in line to check it out. She held the baby inside her responsible. Pregnant women could never remember a thing.

She cut over a block to find shade, to be farther away from the cops and their shotguns. Those girls, Lindy guessed, were sisters.

The baby threw his weight backward to look at the sky, to look behind them, and Lindy was like a horse under reins. She took him off her shoulders to walk beside her, but their slowness became excruciating. Her legs moved as if she was in one of those chasing dreams where you can't run, but you can't be caught either. It was just endless. She swiped at the sweat on her lip with her free hand.

Back at the seawall, the cars were parked solid along her left and to her right; the Gulf was so close, she caught the spray off waves against the concrete. The baby dragged her to see the souvenir shacks, with their seashells and keychains and floppy hats, the hot dogs and the Sno-Cones. The birds keeled. The hulks of tilt-a-whirl and roller coaster on the public beach sallied at the clouds. Everything was glaring and quick except Lindy. Her body moved behind her want for it, as if she was leaving a trail of herself as she moved.

She didn't recognize the big car when she passed it, so she kept going until the seawall was a sidewalk for the Gulf. She turned in the other direction, knowing she'd missed the car, not knowing where or how. Panic began to beat within her like a hammer. She studied license plates, looked for the cars she'd parked near, told herself it would be the very next block, the one right after that — and she kept walking until she was down in the new part of the island, and nothing at all was where she remembered it.

She'd been out all day, when she'd planned only a single, fast errand, and now she was lost, really lost, lost even to herself. She had a quick, mean flash to her parents, Cott, to how panic must have beat in them every day since she'd been gone. Was it like this, this immediate, this loose in the gut? Yes, Lindy figured. It was not knowing what had happened and when it might end; it was enough to make you consider giving up.

When the old gold Cadillac with the Alabama plates revealed itself, she couldn't remember what she'd been looking for otherwise.

She reached into the car and took the tickets from beneath the visor, unlocked the trunk, and got the tire iron Bruton had given her when she pulled out of his driveway. She pried the plates off the car and dropped them into her bag, although she wasn't certain what good they'd do. She had the urge to take the whole car apart with that tire iron, like you'd drop something into a shredder, but she just slammed the trunk shut and was gone.

She phoned Bruton Toliver from the corner Big Save Store. A woman answered, her voice thick with sleep. Lindy said her name, why she was calling. She could hear the phone passing across sheets, the cradle slipping off the nightstand, and some soft cursing in a Romance language.

"You've broken down," Bruton said.

His voice was distant, throaty. Lindy was embarrassed.

"No. Actually, the car ran like a dream. I didn't even have to change those plugs you gave me —"

"You've wrecked it."

"No. Bruton, I got stopped in Houston. A few weeks ago. I don't have a driver's license with me, and I . . . well, the officer assumed I was your wife. Before I knew you had a wife."

"I don't."

"Yes. Well."

"Just a minute."

She heard the closing of a door. He'd made himself alone. She told him she knew it was her fault, her problem, but she was sorry, she shouldn't be driving the car. If he wanted to come and get it, she'd understand.

90

"Good thing you called, I guess. I saw your picture down here, yours and that baby's." He dropped to a whisper. "Apparently not your baby?"

There was water running, the tap of a razor on porcelain, the muffle of a towel across his voice when he spoke again. "Where did you say you were?"

Lindy hung up. Slowly, carefully, she took the baby's hand and walked away, as if the phone were a wild animal, as if it might pull itself out of the ground and follow her. The license plates from the Cadillac scissored in her purse.

But those plates were precious little to hold against Bruton's tracing his car to Galveston. And once he found his car, he'd find her. Maybe there was a reward attached to those posters. Maybe Bruton would get rich just by pointing her out in a crowd, the baby snatcher, the car thief, the missing one.

Of course, if he'd had a mind to find her, he would have done so already. She hadn't made it very hard. She had to trust it was something more than laziness that had kept him from turning her in. The same went for Officer Wilk. He'd known she was in some kind of trouble, and debated her fate on the side of the freeway. In the end, he'd let her go. But how far could she trust the good faith of men she didn't know? She left herself no choice.

It was a very slender thread to hold, but she gripped it tightly. That was what she lacked in this new life: a benefactor, a slayer of dragons. She had to trust that such a man was still around.

❧

As Lindy and the baby came up Ball Street, she saw a man in Esther's yard, crouched in the tawny light, his back curled to them over some machine. She felt her joints tighten to bolt, felt the run in them now that had been missing all day. The pavement rose beneath her feet, and her thoughts leapt like fire jumping highways, as fast as fast could be. I cannot hold my ground right now, she thought. But I'm not going back.

She steeled herself to keep her pace, to walk past, and then to run, until she saw his face.

It was Orrin.

*

Esther used to say summers were for children, because it got too hot in Texas to act like an adult. When Lindy first met Orrin, she was five, he was the age of June's baby now, and it was summertime. His mother was dead, so he was always attended by one willowy baby sitter or another, who'd drop him by Esther's house near dusk so that his father could take him home after work. They lived on a farm off the island, but the baby sitters were always a kind of pretty from the big houses along Broadway, pretty and blond, and lean, and loose with money. They were always more interested in Orrin's daddy than in the baby boy himself.

June, however, loved Orrin the way a girl loves a dog. She'd bundle him away from the baby sitter on her hip, and the three of them would disappear into the late-light garden, endless and wild and never the same as it'd been the day before. The baby sitter would have a kiss for Orrin's daddy and be gone.

In the garden, Orrin's long legs dangled halfway down June's own, and she'd lean him over to touch leaf and flower, telling him how everything was in its place. She knew the names of all the plants, had written them down and committed them to memory: red wing, crepe myrtle, heliotrope, Texas sage. It was like that every summer.

"June," Lindy said, "let's do something else."

They were at rest on the banks of Esther's koi pond, spread among the toad flax and Solomon's seal, Orrin's hard head on Lindy's shins. She was ten, Orrin was five. June was sixteen, and for what seemed like hours, Orrin lay on Lindy's shins while June fished. Lindy would carefully nudge her legs out from under him, but as soon as his head hit the ground, he'd reach for her again, and they were right back where they'd started. He was watching June.

June had a bamboo pole and was catching the same fish over and over, not even bothering to take the hook from its mouth before she threw it back. You could get away with that in front of Orrin, but Lindy saw exactly what was going on. Each time June made the fish break the surface, Orrin pushed up from Lindy's shins, squatted by the pond, and stuck a finger in the water.

"Look at that," he said. "Another one. There must be millions in there."

Then he'd return and lay his head across Lindy's shins once more, coming down hard enough to make a sound and then apologizing, patting her bones the way you'd fluff a pillow. It seemed to Lindy that they'd go on this way forever, if she didn't speak up. June would be going out for the evening. Lindy wanted to do something fun before she left, but it looked as if they'd be stuck entertaining Orrin.

"I love fish," he said. "Hey, June. Tell me how come I'm not a fish."

June knew the answers to questions like that, questions too long and complicated to ask, questions that everyone else answered with *because*. June kept a notebook, which she carried in the back pocket of her jeans; it was full of long words, labeled sketches, lists of names and dates. Lindy had stolen the notebook once. She couldn't make heads or tails of it, and the truth was, if she'd only asked, June would've been happy to explain everything in it, line for line. Lindy felt stupid for stealing it, the way you'd feel about stealing a book from a library.

To tell Orrin why he wasn't a fish, June explained how the chance for that had passed him up millions of years ago. She told him she figured everything on earth in the beginning was the same. Everything looked the same, acted the same, ate the same, thought the same way. Slowly, the things that would become birds began wishing to fly. They wished hard enough, and grew themselves some wings. The things that would become fish began wishing for the water, and so they popped out gills and fins and pretty skin. It went on and on like that, she said, bears wanting bear things, horses wanting horse things. At the beginning, she thought, it was as pure and simple as getting what you asked for. But now, Orrin was a boy because, millions of years ago, his very most distant boy relative had wanted it that way.

"Too bad," Orrin said.

It was what he always said when June told him something from her notebook. Lindy imagined he meant it was too bad that he couldn't understand what she was telling him, but usually it was the fitting thing to say. She swept her legs out from under his head and went for June's fishing pole. She flipped the koi onto the grass, held its body down with one hand, and slipped the hook from its mouth. The fish hit the surface of the pond with a broadside splash.

"Let's do something else," she said.

June shrugged. She said, *Sure. Something else,* and then she took Orrin's outstretched hand and dipped back into the greenness of the garden on the path that led toward Esther's house.

Esther was having a bridge party in the parlor. Her bridge parties were famous for never involving a hand of cards. Orrin's daddy had worked all the week before in the garden, edging the paths, pruning and preening. In the evening, when the cards were left on their tables, Esther's guests would filter out into the garden and go on and on about the hollyhocks, the four o'clocks, the blue delphiniums. *And in the salt air!* they would say to Esther, but amongst themselves they'd whisper about Orrin's daddy and which devil he had to sweet talk to get his four o'clocks to grow.

Now, the catering truck arrived, the florist, the serving girls with their black skirts and silver trays. Everything was beautiful, and Lindy and Orrin were told to stay outside or upstairs unless they wanted to clean up and look pretty. June had a date and could do as she pleased, but Orrin was spending the night and was therefore in Esther's charge.

Orrin's daddy had gone to shoot the rampant snow monkeys

west of Dallas. The snow monkeys had escaped from a research project and were eating the crops or stealing the dogs or something like that, and people had decided they ought to be shot. That morning, Esther suggested that Orrin stay with her for the night, rather than go off hunting. Lindy overheard how it all got planned; that summer, she overheard everything.   ˎ

"The girls enjoy him," Esther said.

"I won't bother you with it. He's about old enough to hold a gun anyhow."

"Save that for another year. Please, the girls enjoy him."

"I won't bother you."

"I insist."

It went like that for whole minutes on the back porch steps, the girls and then the bother, neither Esther nor Orrin's daddy moving an inch. Esther fanned herself with an open hand, leaned out from the porch to cast an eye up at the flawless sky. Finally, Orrin's daddy just thumped the brim of his hat with a forefinger and walked away.

Now when Lindy reached the edge of the garden, it was Luther on the back porch, alone with a tall drink and a worked-up forehead. He rocked on his heels at the edge of the steps, drained his drink to the ice, and stared out at the tangle of the garden. Lindy could have sworn his eyes were on her, but he had the expression of a man who thought he was alone. This summer, she was learning how people held themselves when they thought they were alone, what you could see about them that you wouldn't have been allowed to see otherwise. She could tell Luther was itching for a fight; it was in his forehead, the set of his jaw. Later, if it happened, she wouldn't be surprised.

Suddenly, June's arm snaked around her neck. June was never afraid to touch, would never stand behind a true myrtle and watch someone who thought they were alone. She was never afraid of aloneness, not ever, and she never hesitated. Lindy leaned into her shoulder and indicated Luther with her chin.

"He was up late last night," June said. "I heard them fighting."

"About what?"

June didn't say anything, and when Lindy turned to look at her, she gave another shrug. From inside the parlor drifted the ladies' laughter. Luther drew a heavy breath, spat on the floor of the porch, and walked around the side of the house.

"Hold the baby," June said and passed Orrin's hand to Lindy.

June's legs were long, and when she moved into the open, she was like an unpenned horse, loose hair flying, all heels flying out behind her. For a moment, Lindy thought she'd keep going and going away, and she wanted to call out, call her back. She wanted to tell her to wait until Luther was around the side of the house, but stopped herself for being stupid. He was their grandfather, and just because he was mad at Esther didn't mean they had to avoid him. But Lindy's sympathies always fell with Esther, and she had the kind of mind that ganged up, that was always for or against. June, on the other hand, would run through the middle of a battlefield.

Lindy looked down at Orrin, his small hand in her own. He watched June too, and Lindy could tell he hadn't learned how much his face showed about him. He was a boy. Maybe boys weren't as aware of it as she was.

"Hey, Lindy," he said, tugging on her index finger. "Pick me up."

And she did, even though he was five and lanky and she was small for ten. She squatted down and caught his legs behind his knees so that he could ride piggyback. He pushed her ponytail around the side of her shoulder and tucked his face into her neck. His body was very warm and not so heavy. She didn't mind carrying him.

"What's this?" he asked.

"What?"

"This part of you." He tapped a chubby finger at the base of her skull.

"The nape of the neck."

"It's nice."

"Thank you."

"You should always have one of those, I think."

"I will."

Then June was back with a pecan pie she'd stolen from the bridge party, leading Lindy and Orrin down the winding path to the grotto. Lindy thought she didn't naturally like Orrin as much as June did, didn't have as much patience with him. She'd have to try, but he seemed to understand that about her and was patient too. He said nice things when he got a chance. When they reached the grotto and she let him down, he didn't run over to June; he sort of made his way to her side, and Lindy appreciated that, too.

June passed Lindy a handful of pie. It was sweet and full of nuts and made Lindy eat fast so as not to wear it on her shirt. June flipped her notebook to a blank page and wiped her fingers on the paper. Lindy wondered whether she would keep that page or tear it out and throw it away. You could never tell what June might decide was important. Orrin took a bite from June's pie and wiped his mouth on her book. He put his face on the edge of her crossed knee to chew, swallow, and then return for another bite.

Soon, June's date would come for her. While they ate, she told Lindy and Orrin that he was older, a college boy whose parents ran the Galvez Hotel on the seawall. He lived there in the summertime, when he wasn't at college, in whatever room he wanted. He was going to pick her up and they'd leave in his car, maybe stay out all night long. She wanted to sleep on the beach in front of the Galvez in a pair of deck chairs, wrapped in blankets, because she imagined the only way you could do that was if your parents ran the hotel and you lived there in the summers as if it was your house.

Lindy felt the vague plummet of concern in her belly for June with the words *older, car, hotel, night*. She didn't know much about the trouble you might get into at sixteen, so she had no clear idea to go with her uneasiness. It was this blank, bad feeling. It could have been the pie.

"What kind of car does he have?" Orrin asked.

June didn't know. She couldn't remember.

"My favorite car is a Lincoln," Orrin said. "If that college boy drives a Lincoln, I think you'll have a nice time."

June touched his head with the clean heel of her palm.

"Orrin," she said. "Old ladies drive Lincolns."

"I like the black ones especially."

"Old ladies or Lincolns?" June asked.

"The ones with the suicide doors."

June said, "You are such a little man, Orrin. You know that?"

But Lindy knew what he was trying to say. He was worried for June too, and had decided a sign in his own direction would be something to look for. It was a good idea. For Lindy, she never met anyone without learning their favorite color. It could tell a lot about them. Orrin's favorite color was orange.

By way of thanking him for speaking up, she offered to trim his eyelashes.

"That'd be great," Orrin said. And then, "Why?"

"They're long," Lindy said. "I think you'd see better without them. Run go get some scissors from Esther. It won't take a second."

When Orrin was gone, June told her she shouldn't take advantage of him like that. "He's just a kid. He'll do anything we want," she said.

"Anything?"

"It's the way kids are."

"You're a kid, too," Lindy said. "We're all a kid to somebody, if all you've got to be is older."

June gave out a laugh that wasn't laughter. "Don't be so contrary."

And then she was quiet. Lindy again felt the distance between them, long and pretty much unknown territory. She had no idea how it would ever come to pass that she'd go on a date, sleep on the beach, use a word like *contrary*. But, then, she wanted June's arm around her and it was there, without her even asking. Maybe the rest would be easy, once she was old enough for it to happen. It looked easy for June.

"Okay," Lindy said, "I won't."

Orrin returned without scissors. He hadn't even been up to the house; he got turned around in the brake and thicket beyond the grotto and could only find his way back, not forward. He held a small thing in his outstretched palm, a small moving thing, breaking free of its shell. June and Lindy shoved close to see it better, but Orrin held them off with a finger to his lips. "Be quiet," he said. "It's frightened."

"Is that a bird?" Lindy said.

"A baby," he said. "It fell out of the sky and I caught it like a baseball."

The three of them constellated in the growing darkness of the grotto. It was impossibly quiet, impossibly still. Lindy felt herself grow heavy in her shoes, as if to move would soon be impossible, but she didn't care. It was funny how she could be so restless one minute, then turn like this. Even inside herself, she was cool and quiet and still.

June whispered when she spoke. "As Esther would say, a bird in hand —"

They'd all heard Esther say it a million times.

The bird shivered into the midst of them, and Lindy held her breath to see it moving, so tiny and wet and breaking open. She wanted to be like that bird, pecking at her shell, stretching her limbs into some new open air for the very first time. She wanted June looking down at her with wide eyes. She even wanted Orrin there, when she thought about it, but she wouldn't want him catching her out of the sky.

Then came the sound of the college boy's tires on the pavement, and June was gone. Orrin forgot to see what kind of car the boy drove; Lindy forgot to see what color he wore; and June moved away on her long colt's legs with a blown kiss over her shoulder, as easily as ever before.

Lindy and Orrin studied the bird as it worked its way free. Lindy scratched in the dirt beneath a tree with a trowel and found some grubs to feed it, but it wouldn't eat. She thought maybe she needed to chop the grubs up, but then Orrin noticed that something else was the matter.

"Look here," he said. "It's only got the one leg."

The bird wobbled, tufted and peeping in Orrin's palm. It was as though a leg had been plucked away. Lindy shivered. Orrin turned the bird over from one hand to the other, trying to see where another leg might have been misplaced. He poked through the shards of eggshell, where it might have been left behind. He looked at Lindy as though he had made a horrible mistake. He wanted her to do something.

"It's okay," she told him. "Sometimes it's like that. You didn't catch that bird like a baseball, Orrin. That bird's mother threw it out."

Orrin was confused. Lindy explained how a one-legged bird would be killed by a cat, or whatever else killed slow, crippled birds. Its mother had the instinct to push it out of the nest and spare it that kind of death, give it another one. A nicer death, she said, and he accepted that.

"Its mama meant for it to die," Orrin said.

"Yes," Lindy said.

"I guess I shouldn't have caught it, then."

"Maybe not."

They watched the bird, blindly reeling in Orrin's hand on its one leg. Orrin hadn't put it down since he caught it. Where before Lindy had been sorry for the bird, now she wanted Orrin to put it down.

"I don't think we ought to just leave it out here," Orrin said.

"No?"

"Its mama didn't want a cat to get it."

"No," Lindy said. "You're right."

She took the bird from him and quick, snapped its neck. The small body went soft in her hands, as if it had never had any bones to speak of. She laid it in the dirt she'd scratched out for the grubs, wiped her palms on the pockets of her shorts. She wished she had a page from June's notebook to save whatever was on her hands, whatever she'd taken from the bird. She'd have saved it and looked at it later and figured out something; she didn't know what. But she knew she wasn't frightened by what she'd done. Not once, and that was something she would remember always.

Orrin bent down and arranged the bits of eggshell around the bird, first in a circle, then a halo, then scattered over the top of it like petals on a church aisle. His hands were trembling, so Lindy helped him. They patted the powdery dirt over the bird with their fingertips, then the toes of their sneakers. Lindy found a rock, and the grave was made. They went back into the garden.

Late that night, Orrin appeared at the door to Lindy and June's room, their mother's old room, with a glass of water in his hand. He stood at the threshold and called Lindy's name until she woke.

"I thought you might be thirsty," he said.

Lindy slid over and flipped back the sheets for him to get in with her. They did not mention the bird or the fact that June was not home yet, but they traded their thoughts one to the other like a queen of spades. He wore a pair of pajamas with feet on them, covered in trucks. They were pajamas Esther must have bought for him; Lindy could see the folds where they'd come out of the package.

They were an hour in the darkness until June slid open the balcony window and climbed inside. She was cold, shaking. She slipped into bed behind Lindy and tucked into her back, close and tight the way Lindy used to tuck into June when she'd scared herself with a nightmare. June's cheek was damp on Lindy's shoulder. She tried to turn, to see her face, but June held her tight, and she couldn't move.

Lindy could see Orrin's eyes in the dark, gray as pelt, and they didn't look frightened at all. It was as if he wasn't the same boy who'd stood on the threshold an hour ago with a glass of water and a quiver in his voice. He seemed smarter, as smart as Lindy herself.

June whispered then, about the dreams you have where you fall through the air and wake yourself when you hit the ground. The dreams where you fly. She told them how much she loved to swim, how long she could hold her breath under water. She said she still had all those bird parts and fish parts and horse parts inside her, and she was going to start wishing very hard, right then. She was going to wish to be something other than June, and she recommended that Lindy and Orrin do the same.

Orrin slipped out from under the sheets and walked around the bed to June's side. Lindy couldn't see what he did, but June began crying, the kind of crying you need to do, and Lindy thought how brave Orrin was to go to her. Whatever he was doing was a brave thing. She felt June's chest shudder, then sough, then go to smooth sleeping breaths, her face still damp on Lindy's shoulder. Lindy lay awake the rest of the night, feeling June against her back, breathing with her, in and out. She knew, even though they didn't say so, on the other side of the bed Orrin was doing the same thing.

The last time Lindy saw Orrin, he was nine years old and she was fourteen and June was away at college. She knew by then that a fledgling bird still in its shell had probably been stolen by a predator, not pushed out of the nest, and she imagined Orrin had learned that, too. It didn't really matter. She had acted on what she'd found, and she was certain, in the end, that she'd been right.

The last time they saw each other, it was across the crowd at the public beach arcade. Their eyes barely met; they recognized each other and moved on. He had never been the kind of boy who would tell on her, who'd make her feel bad for something she'd done. She had never been the sort of girl who'd give him that chance.

✥

Lindy hadn't seen Orrin since they were children. Now he was lanky and golden, taking her hand and smiling at her, acting like any man she might have known from home, and she shook her head for how the panic let her go. What had she been running from, moments before? He's twenty, she thought. Maybe twenty-one.

"It's so strange," she said. "You're a person now."

He looked to her for what to make of this, and she could imagine the blankness in her face, her mind having already moved ahead to what she'd say next. His fingers in hers were dark, oiled, slipping from her grasp and leaving their touch on her skin. He laughed, and she went like a fast animal to the how and where to lie.

"Jesus, Lindy. I guess," he said.

"No. I just meant —"

She waved her hand across her face and began again. "Would you like a cool drink?" she said. "To come inside? Or we could sit out back in the garden. I'm just so tired and didn't expect to find you here."

Orrin reached into the bed of his truck and took a couple of beers from a cooler; the bottle he handed over was cold and wet and stinging in her palm. Lindy took a long pull so as not to talk, and then put the beer to her side. She swept the baby from her hip and squatted by the rear wheel to be low to the ground in case she needed it. Her stomach was strung like a bow. She knew she ought to say something, anything, to head off a question she wouldn't want to answer, but she couldn't think. Every turn blew up in her face.

He asked after her family, after June, and it got worse inside her head. He hadn't heard the news. There came the need to spit something from her mouth, not words, but a taste. Not a taste, but a whole extra layer of herself, sloughed off and spit out on the driveway, from the inside out.

Orrin sat on his heels in front of her, the sleeves of his T-shirt pushed high on his shoulders.

"This is June's son," she said.

"Honest?"

He reached out and smoothed his hand over the baby's head. His face gave way, becoming soft and open, and Lindy thought how easily some people loved babies.

"Does he take after her much?" he asked.

"Yes," Lindy said. And then, "Orrin, something happened."

She went to say her sister's name and couldn't, so instead she told him about herself, how she was to get married in the coming months, but now she wouldn't. She told him she was lying low for a time, and, actually, no one knew she was here. She told him about the train and buying the old gold car, about getting lost on the seawall earlier, and finally she told him she had heartburn so strong she thought her ribcage was dissolving. She was crying, and she thought it was too dark for him to notice.

"I got Rolaids in the truck, baby. I'll be right back."

Lindy let her head kick back against the wheel well. Orrin had said *baby* long and slow, like it had to do with things other than women and children. She let it come to her lips a few times while he was gone. It was only Orrin, she told herself, the way it ought to be here, at Esther's house, the way it had been when she was a child. He only wanted to know whatever she wanted to tell him.

He was standing over her with a bottle of Rolaids.

She said, "I've heard we have a second, tiny brain in our stomachs. It's where we get butterflies, and sinking feelings, ulcers, gut reactions. It's not a fact." She looked up at him. "What do you think?"

"I think that sounds like something June fed you."

"It's not."

"Well, then. Now that you're all grown up yourself, what puts such ideas in your head?"

She told him she'd been a nurse.

"I'll be damned. Well, that's great. I've got some bad itching.

It's not poison ivy or anything I got into, because it won't scab over like that. It just itches. Here. See?"

He hiked the leg of his cut-offs and turned his thigh so that she could see the flat inside. She bent close.

"Is there a rash or a peeling?"

She reached out to run her fingers over the skin, and he jerked back.

"You touch it, and next thing I know, I'm going at my leg with a bottle opener."

Lindy raised her eyebrows.

"You think I'm kidding," he said. "I swear it spreads like a gas fire."

He'd taken over his daddy's yards the spring before, he said, and was forever plagued by rashes and reactions of one kind or another. She asked him about detergents and chemicals he might have come in contact with, anything recent and unusual. She was grateful to talk on and on about his itching, the common causes of itching in general, talked until she could think of nothing else to say on the matter, and that was a good long while.

He didn't ask her anything else about her situation, made no judgments. She was banked again and again in relief, and the burning in her stomach lessened, then quit altogether. She remembered that whenever she'd been with Orrin, June was always just around the corner, coming or going. They'd been a threesome. It was a strange turn in her head, but it stopped her feeling pressed to explain where June was now. She half-expected her to be right along herself.

Yes, he loved babies, Orrin told her. When he had one of his own, he was going to call it Peanut or Cookie.

"Kids should have tasty names." He pulled on the baby's long toes. "What's he go by?"

"He needs a nickname," Lindy said. "I don't know what would suit him."

"God forbid what's on his birth certificate. I heard of a baby the other day called Hermione Jane. Can you imagine going though life like that? You are what you eat; you know what I mean?"

Orrin reached over and took the baby from Lindy's arms and squared the small feet on his knees. He and the baby considered each other, made canted sounds in their throats.

"He's a man, isn't he. A whip-smart little man."

"Little Man," Lindy said, and it was done.

They moved to the porch and sat in the rockers, where they could watch the street and the sky. Orrin fetched his cooler from the back of his truck, and Lindy found a fan in the parlor to keep the mosquitoes away. Her thoughts were kind to her, easy things, like how, when they were little, Orrin wanted to be an astronaut. He wanted to live in Houston, to have pretty wives and be weightless for weeks on end. He wondered what the weather would be like in space. There had been a handful of times in her recent life when she'd looked at the sky and heard that question of his in her mind, seen him standing on Esther's porch in a summer evening lit purple with the sunset, turning to her with his question and a handful of pie or lemonade or salt peanuts. It occurred to her that maybe Orrin was one of the things she'd come all this way to find again.

Suddenly, she wanted him to hold her hand, to reach for it as naturally as he'd reached for hers or June's when they all played together in Esther's garden, way back then. She wanted touch, the way touch had been when they were kids.

"What's that look?" he said.

"I was remembering how you wanted to be an astronaut."

"Yeah." He leaned his chair back. "Still do."

He laughed, but it was a possibility for him, to still be choosing, deciding. In the dozen years since she'd seen him, she'd been to college, become a nurse, met a man, and promised to marry. Then she'd lost her sister and walked away from the rest. Orrin had become tall, and what else she didn't know, couldn't tell. She hoped his life was still elastic, still clean, that he'd yet to take an irrevocable step.

"What else do you want to do?" she asked.

"Man, I'm glad I ran into you. Nobody asks me questions like that."

She couldn't tell if he was being flip, and he didn't answer her. Instead, he asked whether June still kept her notebooks.

There had been hundreds — under her bed, in her closets, in her purse and glove box. One day after the funeral, when Lindy was over to leave food in Jimmy White's fridge, she gathered all the notebooks into shopping bags and took them home with her. She spread them throughout her house, just the way they'd been in June's. For weeks, she'd open a cabinet and a notebook would fall out, fall open, and there would be a thought of June's that Lindy couldn't quite understand without her.

"Hundreds," she told Orrin.

He brushed Little Man's toes with the back of his hand.

"I bet this guy sent her to the moon," he said. "I bet she's got a world of theories over him."

"I bet she does."

The lie was easy and temporary. At some point, Lindy figured, he'd ask when June was coming for her son. He would sound expectant, and she remembered the time she'd carried him piggyback to the grotto, and, once she put him down, he was so casual, even at five, moving in June's direction. He had loved her company then, probably always would, however that love would work now. Orrin had never had a mother of his own.

"I was wondering," Lindy said. "What do you remember of your mother?"

"She died before I was Little Man's age here."

"But I was wondering whether you remember anything. I don't know if memories go back that far, but maybe, if there's no other choice, they do."

"Like how people with no arms can use their toes for fingers?"

"I'm serious."

"I am, too. That's the wildest thing. You see some woman in the grocery store, picking up a cantaloupe with her foot."

"A cantaloupe?"

Orrin lifted his boot and circled his foot around in the air. Lindy had no right to pry, and she was bad at it, had no practice. At the hospital, people had handed over details of their lives because she was a nurse, a confessor for the body; perhaps they thought she could do something with them. In all the years she'd known Orrin, years when it would have been more appropriate to ask, she had never mentioned his mother.

"It's hard to tell," he said.

He looked off at the far streetlights, let his brows knot up, and picked at the label on his beer bottle. She thought that was all he was going to tell her, either about the cantaloupe or the workings of his mind, and she felt stupid for asking questions when she herself didn't want to answer any.

Then he said, "There are some things I like that I can't explain."

"Like?"

"Smells. Lilac, and lilacs don't grow here. I think it's a lady-like smell, and I can count on one hand the ladies I was around as a youngster. I love the smell of molasses bread, and I've come across her recipe card for it. I have handwriting like hers."

"What was her name?" Lindy said.

"Caroline. I understand it was a family name."

"It's a pretty name."

Orrin tipped his head at that. He leaned forward in his chair and rested his elbows on his knees. He was never still.

"I guess her family never got over her leaving Virginia with the likes of my daddy. I sure as hell don't know any of them."

Lindy smoothed her hand along Little Man's round calf, let her hand keep on to her own leg, to the weathered cane of the seat, and then back up again. She spoke out into the night with old confidence, the way she used to speak to Orrin years and years ago. "I think part of getting older is coming to realize somebody in the world is going to hate you for something you've done. I think it's the first thing you lose, that idea that you're a nice person. Nice is temporary."

"Well, who wants to be nice?"

"You know what I mean. The kind of nice you seem to others."

He drew his eyebrows down. "How long have you been down here all by yourself?"

She shrugged. "What day is it?"

"Tomorrow's Easter Sunday. Now I bet, in spite of yourself, you're going to be a nice girl and go spend Easter Sunday with your grandmama in the home."

"I don't think Esther celebrates Easter anymore."

"Esther celebrates holidays they don't have religions for yet. She celebrates Easter with fried chicken and deviled eggs, like anybody else, I bet you."

"They don't let old people have eggs."

"No eggs on Easter?"

"Cholesterol."

"Well, now, that's a crime. That's a damn crime. As many folks as must hate those old people," he said, "seems to me they ought to have eggs."

She kicked at his chair. "Are you picking on me?"

He grinned at her, as wide and white as a child.

"Then you can pick me up right here. After dark. We shall see Esther for ourselves."

She wanted an indication of when she'd see him again, so she simply declared that it would be tomorrow, the way she'd ordered him around when he was five. It seemed fine with him, and for her it was familiar, comfortable. This was the first time since June died that something felt the way it always had, and she couldn't help herself. She clung to it.

They kept to the front porch and their talk until late in the night, with the mosquitoes, the mossy oaks, and the closeness of the neighbors. Little Man dozed on Lindy's shoulder, and then lay, belly up, across her lap. From time to time, Orrin reached out to touch his head or his hand or his toes, and Lindy saw his expression again, big-eyed with want, the way high school girls got when they were around babies. She'd guessed some men loved children like that, but she'd not seen it so clearly until now, with Orrin, and it made her want to kiss his cheek. How sweet, she thought; how glad she was to see it.

"There's a couple in a slow waltz," he said, and pointed the neck of his bottle at the shadows of a man and a woman beneath a streetlight, caught close together.

"They're kissing?" Lindy said.

"Yeah."

"I see them."

"But they've gone around the corner."

Orrin leaned over against her shoulder to see what she was seeing.

"From where you sit, those are two trees," he said.

"Eternally kissing."

"Yeah." He took a long pull on his bottle. "Until fall."

"My eyes aren't so good."

"You stick with me, Lindy baby," he said. "We'll just see about what you're good for."

Then he set his bottle on the porch boards and said he ought to go. He tucked something small and cool into the pocket of her sundress with a halfway sleight-of-hand and looked away afterward, as if he hadn't done anything at all.

Then he did go, climbed into his truck, and pulled out of the driveway, with a long arm slung out the window. She watched his taillights all the way up Ball before she went inside.

That night, when she pulled her dress over her head, she found his milagro fallen to the floor, a winking eye. It was the first of many small things he would give her to carry, slipping and tucking and not talking about them then or later. She never knew how much they meant to him, those small gifts, but she kept a list of them in her head as if they would add up to something, some other time, when she might need it most.

*

Esther, wrapped shoulder to toe in terry cloth, answered their knock at the door of the retirement home's sauna, holding her spray bottle. She was a fan of heal-alls of any kind, and this was hydrogen peroxide mixed with spring water, good for sinus infections and other demons. She liked to say she'd picked up the cure in her Oriental travels.

Now she had a go at Lindy and Orrin and Little Man. She misted inside their ears and down the necks of their shirts, their heads and hands and feet. They stood still, because that was what you did for Esther. You let her talk you into anything, even when she wasn't saying a word.

When she was satisfied, she settled back into her bench and gathered a towel around her shoulders as if it were a length of finest velvet. "Come and say your hellos," she said. "Hugs and kisses all around."

Lindy swept up Little Man, stepped inside the sauna, and Orrin closed the door behind them. The air was thick at the draw, the cedar walls padded with heat. The ceiling seemed too low to let you stand. Little Man pushed at Lindy's chest to be let down, but gave up and flopped beside her on the bench. It was strange to see a baby sweat.

"Idleness," Esther announced, "is what does us in. Bones break because they're idle. Stiff joints worsen faster than those that still work. Am I right, Lindy? Those are the things they tell us about here."

"Idleness is one thing," Lindy said. "You attacked us at the door."

"I do what I can for you children. I don't expect to live much past Thursday."

"Oh, now," Lindy said. "That's not necessary."

"Hush. I didn't say which Thursday."

Girls wearing thick white towels and turbans hovered with pitchers of water and armfuls of terry cloth. Orrin studied them like a menu, loosening and retucking themselves, combing the napes of their necks with free hands. He wiped his brow, his lip, looked away, and was drawn back. He'd been made serious by the heat and the female company, whereas Little Man panted like a dog.

"I have never understood the inclination to sauna, myself," Esther said. "But so many cultures carry on the practice, it's like rice in China. How can one billion million be wrong? The Scandinavians, the sweat lodges, the little children burying themselves in sand. I understand when we finish roasting, we are to beat ourselves lightly with birch boughs."

Orrin fanned the neck of his T-shirt. "Well, I sure appreciate your having us over."

"You'll get the sense that we're enduring something here," Esther said. "I've chosen to ignore it myself."

She told them of her dreams the way she might have reported the weather. The dreams, this week, were graphic. They were the sort she'd had in her younger days when she was trying to compose; full of history and time and the occasional inappropriately naked person. What was creativity without distraction? In her younger days, Esther had her travels to distract her. She had touched every continent but heaven, and now she dreamed of that.

"Last night, I saw Luther," she told them. "And he's been dead for ten years. I asked him. I said, *So how is it?* He said, *Well, this is a big place.* And then we stared at each other a while, me in my skin and he in whatever he had to wear, and I said, *So, did you see God yet?* He said, *No, sugar, this is a really big place.* I was so pleased to hear he'd kept his sense of humor. I hated to think it had died with him."

She smiled thickly, rubbed her hands together, and turned to Orrin.

"So," she said. "How is my garden?"

☙

Waiting for Orrin that afternoon, Lindy had been uneasy. She started at every car going by, every door being slammed. It was as difficult to know the person coming for her as it was not to know, and she worried the skin of her collarbones between her fingers. Finally, she cuddled Little Man into her lap and closed her eyes, waited for someone to put their hands on her, whoever got there first.

Orrin's touch came on her foot. He'd climbed in the window from the balcony.

"You asleep?" he said.

"No. Just waiting." She was breathless. "It can look like sleep."

He squinted out at the westerly sun. "We have a couple of hours until dark. Can I take you for a ride?"

Lindy beat him to the truck.

As they drove through the late church traffic on Broadway, Orrin pointed out the other yards he kept, the big Victorian house museums, the homes of the Sealys and the Moodys and the Kempners, the oldest money on the island. They caught glimpses of the bay, then the Gulf. It was a good bright evening, a holy Sunday, and Lindy could not remember what had had her by the throat at Esther's house. She felt as spotless and crisp as an apple.

They lazed along, cutting the streets toward the retirement home, and then away, parking on 81st Street across the railroad tracks to eat pistachio nuts and watch the highway come onto the island. Orrin was content to do the talking. He told her about his work. It meant knowing the land, the difference between mud flats and salt meadows. He pointed out cord grass, sedge, rushes, and sea oats. If she squinted hard across the water at his fingertip, she could see Tiki Island, Texas City, the big ships in the distance.

He said, "You can eat green cattails like corn on the cob."

"Do they taste like corn on the cob?"

"Not at all. But you can eat them like that, typewriter-style. They're not bad if you're in a pinch."

"What kind of pinch might that be?"

Orrin shrugged. "They grow all around my daddy's property."

Then he was quiet, and Lindy realized she'd never seen this

property. Years and years ago, Orrin's daddy had been in prison in Pennsylvania; Lindy heard he'd not been released but got himself out, so he was a frightening man to her when she was a child. She never spoke to him unless he spoke first, and she'd never thought to follow Orrin home to his house. She guessed it hadn't been a happy place, and she felt a twinge of shame for that, an impossible responsibility.

"Some people weren't meant to be parents," she said, as if they were talking about another boy, long ago, whose father left him to eat what he could find.

"I know how it would be if I had a kiddo," Orrin said. "I'd tell him the reeds in the bayou were for people living beneath the water. I'd say they have towns and televisions and pizza parlors down there, but you've got to breathe through reeds, like they were snorkels. Kids love that kind of thing."

"Is that what you think?"

"It's what I'd say. But I don't have a kid. You don't either, for all your laughing at me."

"You're right." She shifted Little Man in her arms.

"I guess," Orrin said, "a nephew is a sort of kid who's yours."

Lindy let the breeze carry her hair across their faces. She could have told him then that she was pregnant. She'd have to tell him before it became obvious, or it would hurt his feelings, but she held back. It was the sense that everything between them would be changed once she said those words. Orrin brought so much old goodness with him, hints of June, of herself when she was so much better than now, and she liked his company. She wasn't sure how she could go back to being alone, if it came to that. She couldn't find the thing inside her that would weather it, that would be okay if Orrin walked away from her, right there on the edge of that bayou, and she never saw him again. She'd learned to be prepared for some people to do that; it was a lesson she had taught herself.

"Why did you bring me here?" she asked.

"Women like to see the water."

"Did Esther tell you that?"

"No, that's my own thinking. Esther says, and I think it goes like this, that she's always found extravagant recall of trivia most attractive. That's what brought to mind the cattails."

"You've used all your tricks on me already."

"Don't you worry." He smiled. "I know a couple more."

The sun set lavender behind them. They passed the shipbuilding and processing plants, a shed roof peeled back by a storm. Lindy watched the darkness come down outside the truck, the pavement holding the very last of the light. She could hear electricity buzzing in the high lines overhead. At the tracks they waited for a Sante Fe with a red caboose to pass, but the train stopped for them, backed up in the other direction, and cleared the way. Orrin could not figure how that worked.

"I think we're charmed," he said. "All the way through."

⁂

Now Orrin was leaning close to Esther, telling her about her garden, the jasmine on the back pergola, the calla lilies, the banana shrubs in bloom. She asked about the hybrids, the palmate tulip trees, the glass myrtle, the yellow thing in the bucket.

"Yellow in a bucket?" Lindy said.

"Scientifically still unnamed," Orrin said. "It's part of the plan for sending it all with her."

Esther plucked delicately at the top of her towel. "I've let it be known there's poisonous vines back in our little plot of green. May have intimated a carnivorous mistake or two more deathless than kudzu; I can't say for certain just how the fear of God got given out. The agent's as dumb as a stump. She apparently trusts us."

"Trusts you in what?" Lindy said.

"She has shown the house but once, to a family of highly superstitious Arabic people. Orrin happened to be there. He showed the wife a few botanical experiments that, well, frightened her, I suppose."

"Plants that bite?"

Orrin shrugged. "Stuff that looks like human heads. Muslims seem to have a problem with that."

"I'm sure anyone would have a problem with that."

"Anyhow," Esther said, "the agent came shortly afterward to say she thought the house showed best by photograph. What with the troubles in the garden, she said. She would be in touch if anything developed. I don't worry much about it. Orrin keeps me abreast of the situation."

Esther laid a hand on Orrin's as if they were long-time confidants, and he smiled shyly to himself, as if he didn't smile to himself very often. Esther had always insisted that Orrin spend his time at her house, with her grandchildren, in her kitchen, in her garden, at her table. An omniscient Esther was no stretch for Lindy's imagination. She trusted Esther to have made Orrin's life easier at every possible opportunity.

She'd bet he knew it, too, and that was why he seemed to polish like brass under her attention now.

Lindy got to feeling like a girl with a crush, only worse; like a girl with a crush on a horse. There was a line with Orrin she couldn't cross, for all her sudden, surging affection for him, a line as hard as biology. That would be okay if she could keep him for herself, own something in him, feed something, see him when she wanted to. But Orrin wasn't as easy as a horse, or as the child he was when she'd last seen him, and what she felt was a childish thing. She was sorry for herself and her pulled, dumb, aching heart, as bad as a spoiled little girl. Orrin's attention was like candy.

She smoothed her hem over her knees and took a glass of ice water from a passing girl, took another and handed it to Little Man. He turned it over in his lap, patting the melting cubes into his shorts, and looking up at her as if he'd discovered the reason for ice. He reached into Lindy's glass for more until she held it above her head. In sips, the water traveled down her throat and spread through her chest as if she'd breathed instead of swallowed. Orrin held out his hand, and she passed the glass to him.

"I feel like a spoiled child," she said.

Orrin drew a look along her outstretched arm, across her shoulder bones.

"You're not," he said, and dumped the glass into his lap.

"Don't be foolish," Esther said. "Men have no timetables. They will never be governed by a calendar. But there are seven stations to a woman's life in which she may behave like a spoiled child."

She made to check her watch.

"You're up to number six," she said. "If you're counting."

Orrin crossed his wrists behind his head and skinned off his T-shirt. There was his long back again, and even Esther seemed taken with it.

"How long has it been since you and Orrin were playmates?" she asked.

"I hadn't seen Orrin since I was fourteen, until yesterday."

"How on earth you missed each other, all those dozen years." Esther addressed Orrin. "Did you manage to see June the last time she was here?"

Lindy felt the room skip, as if someone had cut the lights and flipped them back on. Everything was different, altered, and she was suddenly cold. It was here, she thought, she would regret not having told Orrin about June's murder. She caught Esther's eye, but there was nothing she could do to draw short the course of things. The telling would begin here.

"Let's see," Orrin said. "The last time I saw June . . ."

He was hard at work pretending to put on Little Man's shirt, his face filling the body, his hands flopping out the neck.

"Orrin, you'll tear those seams." Esther misted in his direction. "I am talking to you."

"I'm sorry." Orrin folded the shirt neatly on his lap.

"You were such beautiful children," Esther said. "Fair and dark, aesthetically symphonic. People used to stop me on the street."

"People always stopped you on the street," he said.

"Yes. But with the bunch of you, they had a true reason."

"I told you, Miss Esther. I don't have time for this today. It's Easter."

"I see that."

"You haven't seen clear since God was a boy."

"I see fine," Esther said. "I just do not give a damn to study what can easily be ascertained. It is Easter, and you are busy, but you want to take time to humor your favorite me."

"I swear, you are stubbornness incarnate." Arnaud began fiddling with the control panel on his chair, forward and back, forward and back. "You are so stubborn, you aren't ever going to die and leave poor Arnaud in peace. They'll just stand you up, come Judgment Day, and shoot you like a lame horse."

Esther smiled and presented Arnaud with his bowl. He took it gingerly.

"And that baby is going to get your drum," he said.

Little Man had pulled himself up on the edge of the tray and was hammering the side of the teapot with the clapper from the gong. Esther's hands fluttered over the coming disaster. Arnaud, sensing his advantage in the disturbance, handed his tea bowl to Lindy.

"I don't know how you can possibly say you enjoy this, no sugar, weak as bathwater," he said. "I really do have to be going. My people have to get on back to Mobile tonight."

Lindy dropped the bowl, and it broke cleanly into three pieces, splashing tea up her bare legs, across the parquet. Everyone stared at her as if she'd fallen down herself, and there came a scatter of girls in white towels from the sauna to wipe the mess away.

Arnaud began backing himself toward the hall.

"Thank you for joining us," Esther said tightly. "I sometimes find it difficult to demonstrate harmony, respect, purity, and tranquillity without a worthy adversary."

"You haven't got a thing to worry about, Miss Esther," he said, and his look was devilish. "You're as sharp as a . . . What might you be sharp as? Viper? Witch's tit."

"Sharp as a tack." Esther let her hands clatter on her tray, raised her voice. "I am sharp as a tack, Arnaud, and I'll have you know I plan to grow sharper as the days wear on. Soon, you're not going to have anything of me to grab hold of."

Arnaud whistled. "I'll still be able to get your hair up, don't you worry."

"Oh, that's where you're in trouble, dearie," she said. "I am going bald all over."

They could hear Arnaud laughing his way down the hall. Esther took a moment to compose herself.

"You serve the honored guest first," she said. "Then you worry about the rest."

She brought out her spray bottle and misted everything she could reach.

"Arnaud's people ran two of the finest bordellos on Postoffice during the dark days; Luther's favorites, really. His stepmother gave Luther the most beautiful ivory-handled walking stick before she died, her favorite client's when she had been of service in Paris. It was a walking stick that had been carried in a handful of minor revolutions. I had it myself for years, but I apparently lost it in a cheating hand of bridge."

"I saw that cane last week," Lindy said. "The receptionist had it."

Esther shrugged. "I would not be surprised if the thing made its way back across the ocean. I believe our belongings find their own places to rest."

She let a small silence pass in observance of something only she understood. The teapot dangled from her hand; then, just as quickly, she came back to herself.

"Did you know," she said, "during the war, there were more whores per citizen here in Galveston than in Paris, France?"

"More than Paris?" Orrin said, accepting his tea bowl.

"More than Paris, Shanghai, and Chicago put together. Arnaud's stepmother remarked on that constantly."

Esther told them about the many boys there were in this town back then, sailors and soldiers on leave, gamblers, bootleggers, medical students, still boys, clean-shaven and starched.

They needed knowledge under their belts, and fast, so they drank and gambled and sailed boats and shot each other.

"They did all those things," Esther said, "but you could see the boy on their faces when they passed you on the street. It stirred your heart."

She raised a hand to her chest and Lindy looked at Orrin, could see the boy on his face, lit as by a flashbulb, shiny and clean and sweet. He shifted, and it showed again.

"It made sense to me at the time," Esther was saying. "And there wasn't anything nasty about it. All those boys needed all those women."

Orrin stood. He drew up his chest, bowed carefully at the waist, and produced a small flash of something for Esther out of no place Lindy could see he had to hide it. It was an Easter gift, a small gold filigree egg, as perfect as a new penny in his outstretched hand.

Esther blushed, and palmed the egg away. For moments, she was lost for words. The room grew quiet and immeasurably heavy, as though they were still inside the sauna, and there was no talk to stir the air. Lindy felt all the trouble she was in flicker across her shoulders and move away, as light on its feet as Arnaud, as perfectly shaped as Orrin's Easter egg, as quickly gone as it had come.

"Yes, sir," Esther said finally. "I've always had a bent for boys, myself."

Lindy and Orrin drove the alphabet streets in the late Easter evening, the darkness beginning to bloom, Little Man beginning to sputter with want of toy or sleep or food. Lindy rested an animal cracker on his knee, and he took it, so she did the same again. To her, it was as if they were speaking to each other, a conversation tuned to how closely she paid attention to him. It took long moments for Orrin's voice to reach her, because she had stopped listening for voices altogether.

She asked where they were going, but he wouldn't tell her,

other than that he needed to pick up his posthole digger. They didn't cross Broadway toward Esther's house but cut west, into bayou brush and houses with tin roofs and wide front porches. Lindy once more felt under his power, whatever was releasing her into the tiny events of the present. Little Man stuck his hand out the open window into the current of air and had it slapped back to him, so he had to do it again, and yet again, making a high, keening squeal for happiness. She admired that in him, his ability to make himself happy in such small, immediate ways. She hoped it was a trait of babies, something passing back into her own bloodstream from the baby she carried. She let her hand skim along her belly. It would take time, she thought. Her baby was barely the size of her fist.

She watched Little Man's eyes go heavy until his head lolled against her shoulder. In minutes, he was sleeping, but just as quickly, he could be awake.

Orrin's truck slipped through the dusk and into the night, headed out near the airport, where the island widened, through the loudness of the crickets and mud bugs and night birds. He pulled to a stop in front of a Spanish-style bungalow. The sound of its yard rose up to meet their ears, the wetness of the tires in the grass. The yard was sown with cement sculpture.

"Your house?" she asked, but he shook his head. He lived in town. This was one of the yards he kept from time to time.

"And you left your posthole digger here?" Lindy asked, but Orrin's mind had moved on.

"This is the curandera's house," he said. "She's from the southwest of Mexico, where all the great witches are made. She can make you invisible to whatever's after you."

Lindy saw how honest he was, how he wasn't making fun. She could feel a change in the cab of the truck, the way breath leaks from a punctured lung, and it made her bite her lips and whisper. "Orrin," she said, "when did you ever need to be invisible?"

But as soon as she spoke, she knew what string she had pulled. He would tell her something intimate and sad, and she would do the same — and rushing to the top of her throat was June. She could nearly taste the words in her mouth. She understood that the knowledge of June's death would kill something in Orrin, and tonight she would have to pass that knowledge on. It would all be lying at their feet in a matter of moments.

Orrin looked as sweet and unprepared as a child handing over a blanket. Lindy watched him in the blue light and saw the boyishness draw back into his face, his eyes going heavy-lidded with its ebb.

He told her he used to smuggle out of Laredo with the landscape business as a cover, back and forth across the border for fertilizer, plant material, some very nice marijuana. It was something that Wolfie, his daddy's partner's wife, had set up. Wolfie was from down there, the kind of woman who knew the people to talk to, the places to go, and the ones to avoid. For a while it was neat money.

"How much neat money?" she asked.

"I moved into town. I made myself comfortable. I've got a good bit stashed away."

"I wouldn't have guessed."

"You're disappointed," he said.

That wasn't it, but she looked away, and he was quiet.

In the night-lit yard, the curandera's house was long and low to the ground; the sound of wind chimes came from its porches and porticos. It was a woman's house, well-kept and planted, its statuary shining white. The rocking chair by the front door was just like Lindy's chair back in Charlotte.

"So this is a witch's house," she said, but Orrin didn't answer.

And inside, she thought, is a witch, someone who could find cures in whatever form was available, sometimes in simply the sheerest of hopes. Lindy did believe that hope could take you far, the way clean clothes could, and good food, a solid night's sleep, what she had done for patients at the hospital. But she knew that what was wrong with her was past that possibility.

"So this is a witch's house," she said again.

"Well, then," Orrin said, "you'll be fine."

He heeled open his door and slammed it shut behind him.

She watched him stalk past the fenders. She had nipped something, saying what she expected from him. Outside, he snapped his wrists, chipped his shoulders, his nerve coming off him and into the night like steam off a horse. She put Little Man on the seat and closed her eyes. She could hear Orrin kicking at the dirt. She would have to apologize. She would have to explain.

But she didn't want to go into this house to do it.

Then, at her ear, Orrin made a sound with his tongue and the back of his throat. When she opened her eyes, his elbows were resting on the open window near her.

"You hiding from me?" he said.

"I don't need witches, Orrin. I have enough that haunts me."

He laughed, as if she was kidding.

"Maybe you have the ghost sickness," he said. "I don't know what all kind of foul she'll make you eat for that."

"This isn't a joke, Orrin."

"I'm not joking. Come on, baby. Get out of the truck."

"Why?" Lindy's voice turned brittle. "I don't want to."

"I want you to." Orrin sighed. "You're in some kind of trouble, maybe trouble with the law, I'm thinking. You left too much back in Charlotte for this to be some parking tickets. You don't want to leave Esther's house unless it's night. It's bad when somebody's that plain about it."

"Plain?" Lindy was yelling.

"Yeah. Obvious. I thought about calling your sister, but it's really not my business. So I brought you here. This is where I'd bring myself."

He opened the door and held out his hand to help her from the truck.

He caught her sandal as she made to slip across the seat and away from him. She was fast, but he was strong, and he hauled her limb by limb out of the truck and to his chest, held her beneath her knees and around her shoulders, tight. She already had his keys in her hand.

"What in the hell are you doing?" Orrin said, quietly. "I'm depending on those keys to get us out of here."

She untangled herself from his arms and stepped away. The keys fell to the grass.

"Well, now," he said. "Would you have come back for me, or would I have had to hitch it back to town?"

"I don't know." Her voice barely topped her throat.

"You woke the kiddo for your trouble. You'd've tanned my hide if I'd done that."

Inside the truck, Little Man perched on the seat, with his hands folded on the rise of his stomach, like an old man on a park bench, a pot-bellied god. He watched Lindy with a cool face, rimmed with curls, cool as the light of the moon.

"I have to sit down," Lindy said. "I have to sit down now."

She leaned against the pedestal of a high-breasted goddess and slouched back to see the stars, to let the cool air wash her skin. She was dizzy with anticipation, the way she would have been if she had something good to say.

Orrin wet his hands in a bird bath, touched the water to her cheeks.

"What's got ahold of you?" he said. "You're burning up."

Somewhere in his face was Lindy's mother; she was like a child with a fever, a scrape, a bad dream. She closed her eyes and felt his careful hands on her and thought of all the times her mother had touched her face, her hand, her shoulders, as if the touch would make it better, and sometimes it did. So it was in this feeling that she put her hand over Orrin's on her cheek and said what she had to say.

"Orrin," she said. And she told him about June.

She watched his face over her, watched him sway and break, his fingers slipping away from hers. She said it again.

She told him how June had been murdered in her dining room, in winter, and by a thief, probably somebody who knew there was money in the house and had picked a bad time to look for it. She told him about her hands on June's body at the morgue, about how she'd given her engagement ring to June, and now, in a way, had given her the whole engagement. When she finished, she looked back to the stars, to the night sky, and let that cool air dry the bird bath water from her cheeks.

In the far off, there were cars, crickets, a rustle in the grass. Little Man whimpered in the truck, once, twice, then quieted himself. A light flicked on in the witch's house, casting its yellow glow over the lawn, but they were far outside its reach.

Orrin stood beside her. She held out her hand to rest on his arm, but didn't let it touch him, just let it hover above his skin, and turned her face to his. She watched the heavy things she owned come over his shoulders, his poor, sweet boy's face. She decided she would never tell another person these things, not as long as she lived.

"Who did it?" he said.

"I think they'll arrest her husband."

"It was him?"

"I think the husband always gets arrested."

"Goddamnit, Lindy," he said. "I asked who. Who?"

"What difference does it make?"

That made him angrier, but she had nothing more to tell him. She'd never had to explain June's death before, and there were no details that made it real or recountable, a murder in this house, on this day, by this person, for this reason. As she told it, it was a story meant to make you angry, and that was the way it would be forever.

But when she asked what difference it would make if he knew the details, Orrin snapped. He went to the bed of his truck and pulled out a steel-handled, flat-bladed tool and began swinging it.

Statuary fractured in a wide arc, chunks of head and ear, whiskered nose, taking to the air with each nicking contact of the blade. He went at that yard like a boy with a bat and a broken heart, and as she watched, time itself turned strange, more in Lindy's stomach than in her head. It seemed to hang and tear on that pinging sound of steel against cement, the way a thorn will snag a stocking. In that moment before Orrin swung, she had time to roll away, time to think he had no idea how badly he would hurt when he ran out of things to break.

When he was spent, he planted the tool in the earth at Lindy's side and slid his body down the handle to her feet. He pitched his head into her lap, was rough about it, but Lindy let him be. Even with all the work he'd spent in his anger, she couldn't tell whether he was breathing. The ground around them was littered with concrete and plaster, stark white in the moonlight, and Lindy found herself wondering whether the shards could knit themselves again, like bone. It was quite a mess to leave in someone else's yard.

She brought a light hand to Orrin's head, the way you might put a hand to a wild animal. His hair was thick beneath her fingers, she thought, and then he rolled away.

"June's been dead all this time," he said. "Since January. How could she be dead that long and I didn't know?"

"I should have told you sooner," she said.

Orrin stared as if what she'd said had no bearing on what he was thinking, and yet she was trying to take some of the blame for what he felt. At the hospital, she had spent time honing a way to make an announcement of death to a stranger, the right words, the right moment to lay a hand to a shoulder. But for this, with June, with Orrin, she had no manners. She tried again.

"There was a fortuneteller," she said, "at my bridal shower, Christmastime. The woman talked about wheels in my future and wanted to know whether I was a salesman, or something. When I asked her if I was going to be happily married, she said she didn't answer that kind of question."

Lindy glared at Orrin and tried to smile.

"She told June's fortune, too," she said. "Can you imagine?"

"I'm sorry," Orrin said quietly.

"For what?"

"That I brought you here."

"Oh." Lindy gave a little laugh and waved her hand across her face. "I'm sorry I came."

She covered her mouth, and her hand smelled of Orrin's hair.

"I don't know how long they'll let me be," she said. "I've heard the posters are out there already."

Orrin let out a long breath. "I imagine you're more clever than a piece of paper, Lindy Jain. I imagine you've always been that."

And with those words, a latch inside her snapped tight. He did not speak warmly or strongly, but something in his tone told her he'd be around. She'd been wrong to doubt him; he would prove her wrong. He would help her; he would protect her; he would bear up under the most awful news there could be.

She said, "I may be pregnant. I may have been for some time, I don't know."

That was a lie, about not knowing, but it got at the truth, so Lindy let Orrin take it up with the rest of her he'd taken up that evening. It was all out, all said, all in Orrin's hands, and she was a little better for it, a little more accountable. He was someone now who knew her. She had lashed herself to him, along with all her particulars, as if he were the raft she meant to float away on.

The next thing he did would tell her what she needed to know. She hoped he understood that, but he was quiet, and she couldn't see his face in the dark.

"Orrin?" she said.

"I heard you," he said.

"And?"

And he didn't leave her. He took her hand and led her back to the truck, drove back across the island to Esther's house. He walked her and Little Man to the porch steps without a word. Lindy watched his taillights fade up Ball Street, and she thought, These are the times we do the things that mark us forever, forward and back. Sometimes they're gentle things, like fading taillights, and sometimes they only seem that way.

And though Orrin didn't come around for some time after that, the stretch of nights that followed brought the chatter of blackbirds in the garden, hundreds of them roosting in the trees from darkness until dawn. The din through the shutters was as insistent as a knock at the door. In the morning, the trees were empty, the birds vanished. But they were back the next night, even stronger than before.

∽∾

The night before Little Man's first birthday, Lindy woke to screaming. Dizzy with sleep, she thought first of the black-birds in the garden. But this was a different sound, clear and bursting, a single word, coming from right beside her. Little Man. Her mind swirled like a drink in a glass. Little Man was screaming.

He was screaming for juice.

She ran the steps to the kitchen and fumbled in the darkness for a sippy cup. She could hear Little Man upstairs like a fire engine, a shrill siren. Was he asking for juice, or was that what she herself had decided? Now his words were muffled by the ceiling and the floor to a long, lonesome sound. Then she was running back up the stairs with his juice, and his voice was getting louder, not clearer, but at least she was doing some-thing. She pressed the cup into his hand. He sipped; he was quiet. And then he was asleep.

Lindy was flattened. She stood over him, catching her breath, her eyes adjusting to the darkness. She was amazed by the swiftness with which a need could begin and end.

Tucked into her place in bed was a paper sack. Inside it, she found three heads of garlic stuck with pins, a vial of rosy fluid, two horseshoes wrapped in red ribbons, two black wax dolls, a deck of Mexican tarot cards, and a slip of paper from Orrin, saying that the gifts were from the curandera. He had come and gone without her knowing it, and left the sack with Little Man. His note said, *For what it's worth.*

She went to the window, but saw no sign of Orrin on the

balcony or the street. She had no idea how he'd got in and out while she was downstairs. He must have been watching her. He must have been watching her for hours. She looked for a clock of Esther's that told the time in Texas. There was Japan, the Pacific Rim, and maybe Paris, but central time was broken or lost. Beyond the shutters was thick blackness. She hadn't seen Orrin since the night at the curandera's, and she was glad to know he had been thinking of her.

Little Man sighed in his sleep, contented and full. His appetite had grown in the past weeks; he ate constantly and everything: fruit, grain, meat, plaster, rock. Lindy had seen him put pieces of paper in his mouth and chew them, and she'd actually thought, *It's only paper.* He sucked on her fingers. He chewed the hem of her skirt. When she left a room, he followed after, eyes cast down to find a fallen raisin, a knot of string. He was bottomless and happy with whatever he came across.

Lindy took the empty juice cup from his hands. Her wants were not so easily fetched from the kitchen; they were vague and wistful, a fog of wanting. She watched the sun come up.

Then Little Man was one year old.

She spent the day baking, Little Man barricaded in the kitchen with her, drinking air from a soup pot, water from a dish cloth. She fed him batter and frosting and milk, and, always moving, always reaching into and under things, he ate some wisp he found beneath the refrigerator. It's his birthday, Lindy thought. He should do as he pleases. But when he started chewing on the lids to the pickle jars, she called it quits. The popping metal made her nervous.

Her back ached. Her head was heavy. Her face was on posters in Mobile, but that was Mobile. When she checked the Galveston and Houston papers, she found nothing. If her family knew she'd gone as far as Mobile, wouldn't they assume that Esther's house was the next place to look? She doubted, no matter how much practice Esther had with such phone calls, they'd trust her word against logic. Lindy was certain somebody was on the way.

She put her back against that fact. She could count on it, so there was no need to worry over when and where and who. The time was coming when she would have to face someone from home, and what she did in the meantime was done in the shadow of that.

She packed a birthday party for Little Man. When evening came, they took a picnic basket to the retirement home. She and Little Man wandered the halls, checking the bowling alley and the sauna. They found pool tables and massage parlors, a poker game without its players, but no Esther, anywhere.

The attendant in the reception area was young, Lindy's age, a nurse in white.

"What happened to the woman who was here before?" Lindy asked.

The nurse smiled at her patiently. "I'm sorry," she said. "Can I help you?"

Lindy imagined she addressed everyone that way, as if they were doddering old folks, as if they hadn't heard her. She spoke louder. "There was a woman here, the last time I came. She had a beautiful cane —"

The nurse smiled again, even more brightly. "May I help you?"

She asked for Esther. The nurse gave her a room number, pointed down a long, antiseptic hallway, not unlike the hallway of a hospital. Lindy hadn't noticed before how sterile these halls were, the blank-faced walls, the rows of doors, some open on the residents in their beds, curled on their sides. She had never grown used to the frailty of old people sleeping. So many here were sleeping. It was just past nine o'clock.

She pushed on the door to Esther's room and found it locked. Not locked, but weighted shut, and she knocked softly.

"It's Lindy," she said. "It's me."

"Just a moment, dear," Esther called. "They're ministering my fortifications."

"What do I care?" she said. "I'm a nurse."

"Oh, my goodness," Esther prattled. "You should care enormously. Throughout history, narcotics have performed important tactical roles. Did you not know that Santa Ana was addicted to opium?"

An orderly, big as any house, cracked the door. Lindy put a hand to his chest and he pulled away, like an elephant before the mice. Lindy smiled. She knew orderlies; they liked to do the touching themselves.

"It's true," Esther went on. "And he was the president of Mexico something like twenty-seven times."

Lindy stepped into the room to see an RN break the needle on a syringe and whisk past in a stiff white breeze, as Esther smoothed her skirt over her hip. She had that shivered look Lindy recognized as the endpoint of pain, icy and blue around her mouth. She settled into her chair, pulled a blanket over her knees, and held out her hands for Little Man.

"It was the opium," she said, "that ended it for him. The afternoon of the attack on San Jacinto, we captured Santa Ana in his tent, smoking his smoke and trifling with a half-breed girl. That girl was forever known as the Yellow Rose of Texas."

"What is it you're taking, Esther?" Lindy said.

She tried to follow the RN, but the orderly blocked her way, not so much on purpose, but because he was large and unaware of himself. He leaned in from the doorway like a leaf to sunlight.

"God's truth." Esther held up her palm to the orderly. She'd found her better audience. "And that's not the all of it."

She took a deep breath, sat up tall and pretty in her wingback chair.

"I was the Yellow Rose of Texas."

"Esther." Lindy sighed. "You're as white as mayonnaise."

Esther ignored her.

"I always planned to do something in my life worthy of a song," she said.

"But you didn't do that."

"I did better." She pointed a finger at Lindy's heart. "I wrote my own songs."

The orderly was gone. The room grew heavy, and hot, and ghostly empty. Esther took her spray bottle from beside her chair and misted her face and neck. There was the thrum of air-conditioning, the chirp of monitors from other rooms. Lindy was embarrassed. She had no business calling other people down from where they'd traveled to, especially Esther. She started to apologize, but Esther beat her to the words. "I'm sorry, dear," she said, "but there's been another call for you."

Lindy looked down at her hands.

"What did they say?"

"That you'd run off. That they didn't know whether you wanted to be found or not, but that you had June's baby, and that was another matter."

"Did they mention a course of action?"

"It's not war, dear. You've snatched a baby."

"But he's my nephew." It sounded thin, even to her.

"At any rate, the plan seems to be to hunt you down. I said again that I hadn't seen you, but . . ." She sighed. "We do like to make our lives complicated, don't we? I think we even need to."

They passed several minutes in the close, hot room with only the sound of Little Man's baby mouth. He chewed the fringes of Esther's blanket, his new teeth snapping on the threads like the ticking of a clock. Lindy didn't feel complicated. Streams of questions rushed her head, but Esther would know or she wouldn't, and whoever was calling would stop or call again or show up. Her thinking was linear, clear-eyed, of emergency caliber. She would follow what she had already planned, the way she would have handled the reappearance of a disease.

She could sense the hardness in her face, the weight of her gaze spreading into the room. She was glad. Sometimes hardness could be used like strength. But when she felt Esther's hand cover hers, she knew that trick worked only with strangers.

Esther rose to the occasion. "Well," she said. "Did I hear you say cake? My kingdom for a slice of cake."

"It's Little Man's birthday." Lindy tried to match Esther's tone. "It's his birthday cake."

Esther clapped her hands. "Wonderful. Let's get down to it."

So Lindy pulled Esther's china from the basket she'd brought, sliced a wide hunk of Red Velvet cake for each of them, poured glasses of lemonade from a screw-top thermos. She'd forgotten forks. Esther didn't seem to notice. Her words came in rushes between mouthfuls and gulps.

"You bake like your mother. Pure confection. I have no idea where she learned to bake."

"Not from you?" Lindy asked.

"Surely, surely not from me. One of her many un-inheritances."

Esther licked the icing from her fingers, her face chemically bright, her eyes glassy. Her tongue was red as roses from the cake.

"You know," she said, "the Chinese eat almost everything digestible, except for milk and milk products. Makes you wonder. It's also the country in the world with the most pigs."

"You are high as a kite, Esther," Lindy said.

"I know. It sharpens my edges. I've eaten sea urchin in Japan, chapulines in Mexico . . . Do you know what chapulines are?"

Lindy shook her head.

"Grasshoppers. Tiny red grasshoppers. They are an excellent source of protein. Of course, too much protein makes us tall and stupid."

"I think you've told me that."

Esther batted at Lindy's knee with a shuddering hand.

"John the Baptist had a strict diet of locusts and wild honey, and that was probably what made him holy. Myself, I was never called in that direction, but diet is so important."

"I've been trying to eat better," Lindy said. "For the baby."

"That's it." Esther clapped her hands and crumbs scattered. "Let's tell some birthday stories."

Little Man settled himself into Esther's lap and drew her

arms around him like a shawl. Lindy felt washed out, left behind.

"Your mother, Lindy," Esther began, "started to be born on the day of the greatest fire in Texas."

Esther talked about April 1947, about waking to rattling glass in her windows, her bedframe skittering across the floor. Luther was on the roof. There'd been a storm days earlier, and he was repairing loose shingles at nine in the morning. Sleep being what it was for a pregnant woman, Esther yelled at him as if he'd woken her on purpose. Luther came running. He'd seen a fireball and fifteen feet of water crossing the harbor. He'd seen big hunks of metal flying through the air; they needed to hide out.

Esther was old to be so pregnant, she said, and she'd lied to the doctors about just how old that was. She knew in her heart, when her pains began, that she had to get to the hospital. She told Luther her baby had not heard of hide out, and they had to go right then. There was orange smoke in the street. There was burning cotton in the air, and that hum that comes across a place when something horrible is happening. But Esther put her hands over her head and let Luther lock the doors behind them.

What she did not know was, in Texas City, right across the bay, dockworkers had tried to treat a fire on a French cargo ship with more fire, and the explosion had blown up their town from the docks on back. They'd blown up their fire station and all their firemen. They'd broken every window within two miles of Galveston Bay, and they were the ones who started her labor, four weeks too soon.

Lindy understood Esther's fear, her call to action in the face of something gone wrong. She thought of the accidents attendant on her own life, all the way back to her mother's birth, all the way forward to her sister's death, her job at the hospital, her trip to Galveston, and the freeway full of wrecked cars. It was as if she gathered accidents around her. She seemed to be good at them.

In the aftermath of the Texas City fire, the emergency room of the John Sealy Hospital was crowded with bodies and parts of bodies, people without fingers and hands and arms. Esther did not remember the smell of burning. She did not remember seeing burning skin, but she felt its company, she said, as heavy as Sunday night. There were people everywhere. She waited in that emergency room for five hours before a doctor could take a look at her.

"I knew," she said, tapping a fist to her chest, "I knew it was the wrong time. I held my breath and twiddled my thumbs, and when I couldn't sit still any longer, I walked those halls amongst all those burned-up people."

"You were frightened," Lindy said. "It only makes things faster."

"But I was counting on your mother. Especially then, in ways I only half believe myself. All those burned-up people on stretchers, stacked up like traffic. I passed a woman who was holding a package from the butcher. Her nylons were melted into her legs, but she had her fingers laced through that butcher's twine as if you were going to have to fight her for her lamb chops. Isn't it strange, how you can set your life on something so small?"

"Yes," Lindy said. She tried to feel her own baby ripple inside her, her own small anchor.

"I knew your mother was to be a girl," Esther said. "She was a second chance at what I had thrown away, with all my travels, my men in every port. Perhaps, in my heart, I knew that where I'd gone wrong there was no righting. Your mother was the last piece of me I thought I might keep good with God."

Lindy thought of her mother back in Charlotte, in her house of new paint. She had always been a mother, had never worked at anything else, and now that her daughters were gone, she probably believed herself as far from God as possible. Lindy felt a twist of shame. She had changed the course of her mother's life, the same as her mother had done with Esther, but her mother would never tell the story of the day June died or the

137

day Lindy had taken Little Man. She could not meet Esther's eyes.

"So you see," Esther said, "how disappointed I am in the man upstairs. Your mother seems to be serving all our shares of penance these days."

"You hold God responsible?" Lindy said. "Why not me?"

Esther nodded. "Oh. It's women who plan it. But it's God who carries it out."

"You don't have to make excuses for me," Lindy said. "I could use a lesson."

Esther laughed. "I suppose it's not so simple as a lesson, is it? You're too old for that."

"Yes." Lindy sighed. "I guess I am."

"I will tell you this," Esther said. "I have concern for the child you carry. The keeping of secrets is a dangerous thing."

"I trust you."

Esther tossed her hand. "No one trusts me. I imagine that holds for God, as well, but he can't keep a secret either. Anything he ever did, he told someone about it first. But women, we die with secrets all the time."

"June and I often tried to imagine what you'll take to your grave."

"Mind, there isn't much I haven't told to someone, somewhere. I used to have a friend in Sweden who was an excellent pen pal. Her grasp of English was not so perfect, but nonetheless. To keep secrets is to ask for trouble."

"I told Orrin I was pregnant."

"It's important, Lindy, that there is one person in the world who knows you at all times. You lose that person, and I believe you become lost too. If a tree falls in the empty forest —"

"Does it make a sound."

They were quiet, watching Little Man. He was rocking himself to sleep in Esther's arms, his head tolling back and forth, back and forth. Fine trickles of sweat traveled along Lindy's ribs, but she didn't move to open a window or the door. She wanted to keep the three of them clustered together, a peaceful configuration, an isotope. She tried to keep her breath from disturbing the room.

Esther put a flat hand to her stomach and let out a small, delicate belch.

"I have a bellyache," she said.

"What's the matter?"

"I'm full to the top of my chest with today," she said. "Really, that's it. I've eaten too much of today."

"That can happen," Lindy said. "Our eyes are bigger than our stomachs."

"In Thailand," Esther said. "Or perhaps it is Malaya? Bhutan. In Bhutan, they cook orchid flowers in a bit of onion and butter and serve them to you in a grass bowl. It is marvelous food there, what of it is vegetarian. You must go. We all must go."

She was quiet.

"Let's go," she said, and then she slept.

Lindy spent the night in the chair across from Esther. It was the nurse in her, come back. She thought Esther should have someone watching over her, and it seemed natural to be required in this professional way, to sleep in a chair, wake at another's stirring, to keep her comfortable and clean. At some point, Little Man slipped down from Esther's lap, and Lindy tucked him into Esther's bed rather than leave. She felt safe there, the three of them together. When it was light again, she kissed Esther's sleeping cheek and took Little Man home.

⁂

On Ball Street, there was a Big Wheel tethered to the front doorknob with a birthday wish from Orrin. Little Man knew instantly it was his, wanted down from Lindy's arms, and was happy to sit on the thing tied to the doorknob.

Lindy braced herself on the handlebars and pushed him up and down the slats of the porch, making noise like a freeway, laughing, and making more noise. It was morning, still cool and blue-skied, and the neighbors were coming to their front steps for their newspapers, with their mugs of coffee and their little dogs underfoot. If they'd seen Lindy's picture on a poster, read her name in the paper, it wasn't foremost in their minds. It was far gone from Lindy's, too. She cared about the boy between her arms, his laughter in her ears, the boards beneath her feet, and that was all.

✼

Lindy decided that if Orrin could find her so easily as to slip into her house while she was sleeping, she could find him. She'd have to go looking.

May days were humid, and to go outside was to pass through a steam whistle. She and Little Man left the house early, while Lindy could feel the breeze off the ocean, the sunshine on her back clumsy and harmless. When Little Man got tired of walking, she carried him, and she spoke to people only when she had to, which was not often. She began to forget how to have a conversation. It was as if she were from another country; and instead of being lonesome, she was contained; instead of struggling against it, she acquiesced.

She began to feel the weight of the baby inside her, in her days, in her thoughts; another presence to account for, extra time for the accounting. She was solicitous of her own restlessness, her high tears, eggshell stomach. She saw the habit of balance at work; as much as her leaving Cott was forever between them, so this baby would be, an absence steadied by a presence, a real thing, not a promise made in church. When she was in a wishing mood, she wished for a baby who looked exactly like Cott, so that she could look at her son and see his father. That was the way it should be. She would tell her son of all the ways he was like his father, the way she would tell Little Man about June.

She went to town. Orrin had told her he lived in town, and the Strand was the center, the strip of restaurants and T-shirt shops and bars spilling tourists onto the raised sidewalks. She would wait, and he would come. She had nothing else to do.

She bought divinity candy and ate it until she was sick. At the candy counter, Little Man wanted taffy, and they sat on the steps outside the store, Lindy unwrapping and Little Man making shapes. Each piece of taffy she handed him he mashed into a ball in his lap, taffy along with gravel and bits of lint, his spit and hair. Every once in a while, he'd start to put the mess into his mouth, and Lindy would hand him another piece to keep him busy.

She though he might become an architect, a boy who so favored the prospect of material over the satisfaction of finished product. Cott always called the architects suckers for their own game, and he'd as soon shoot one as look at him. She was thinking those words — *as soon shoot one as look at him* — when Orrin crossed her line of sight.

He was a familiar motion on the street. It wasn't Orrin she recognized as much as his gait, the tuck of his hands in his pockets. When he turned the corner toward the wharf, she stood and took Little Man's taffied body in her arms and followed after him.

She intended to catch up, say hello. She'd thank him for the present he'd left Little Man, but, in truth, she needed to talk to him. He had, since the night at the curandera's, become central to the way she thought about her days in Galveston, and she wanted to tell him so. But her body moved more slowly than she expected, and then Orrin shunted into an alleyway, pulled down a fire escape, and climbed up the side of a building. She watched him shoulder open a window and leg himself inside an upper floor.

Lindy counted stories, buildings and worked around to the front of the street, to the entrance of the one he'd climbed into. She found a name on a mailbox — O. CORDRAY — and thought it must be his, suddenly aware that she had never known his last name, had never asked.

She could hear voices above her in the hallway, Orrin's and a woman's. They were whispering, disagreeing. Lindy was practiced at eavesdropping to determine relationships; it had been a useful skill in the hospital. She stood still, made quiet motions over Little Man and listened to Orrin and his woman, but she caught just riffs and fragments. He said *only* and *sorry* and *sad,* and she sounded sometimes sincere, sometimes not. They were lovers, now or at one time. Lindy was certain of it.

She was about to go when Little Man squealed. His taffy lay at her feet. Lindy's first thought was quick — hand it back to him — but the sound was already out into the air. So she made fast for the door and the street and Esther's house, where she would not be embarrassed found lurking in the stairs. But before she could go, she heard Orrin call her name.

He leaned over the banister. He could tell which way she was going, so she stopped. "I wanted to thank you," she said, putting a hand to her forehead as if to shield her eyes from light. "For the tricycle. How did you guess it was his birthday?"

Orrin shrugged and toed a spindle of the banister, sending scatters of grit down her way. He looked tired of explaining himself. His face was strange from her angle. "I could tell he was due. Come up. I'd like you to meet someone."

She was a woman about a decade older than Lindy, slender and sky-eyed and pretty. She wore a man's undershirt tied off at her ribcage, and her belly was an even tan. When Orrin introduced her, Lindy shook her hand. Joy Ballinger.

"Orrin tells me you're a nurse," she said.

"I was."

Lindy said it easily, the words slipping from her mouth before she had time to consider them. She was disconnected, floaty. Joy began walking backward, leaning into the conversation but moving away from it, heading for the stairs. Maybe she didn't feel like answering questions, either.

"Orrin tells me you're expecting a baby," she said.

"Yes," she said. "I am."

"You have a pregnant face," she said.

Lindy shrugged. "Who's to say I haven't always?"

Joy gave off an edgy laugh and descended the stairs without

saying goodbye. Orrin watched her from his doorway, his arms folded at his chest, his body leaning into his shoulder. When he spoke, it was over the sound of the outside door hinging closed.

"She used to be a real nice girl. She would've found out how long you were going to be in town, and if you'd want to have tea sometime. She was always real big on tea and on bridge. These days, it's a good bit of jogging and Bible study."

"I'm sorry I interrupted. I know you weren't expecting me."

Orrin's eyes were still trained on the staircase. "Before I met her, she was in girlie magazines. Then there was me, and now it's Bible study."

"Orrin. It's really not my business."

He looked at her. "Well, then. What is your business? What can I do for you, Miss Lindy?"

Lindy's face was hot. "Really, I just came by to thank you."

"Come inside, then," he said. "Let's not be shy."

Lindy was sorry to seem so needy. She let Little Man to the ground, and he bobbled like a top, handed his way across the distance from her knees to Orrin's, everything about him sticky and determined. Orrin scooped him up and disappeared inside.

She could hear the rattle of cages, Little Man's squealing, and she followed them into the apartment.

Orrin held Little Man on his knee in a wide chair, in a butter-colored room, streamed with light. Cooking drifted from the kitchen: cumin seed and sesame and corn, toasted, tan scents. Lindy let her back find a wall, let her shoulders loosen. Orrin was telling something, his voice a low run of Spanish. The air was swollen with birds.

There were song birds and tropical birds, talking birds, electric-colored birds like the spectrum. He kept them in wrought-iron cages, floor to ceiling, but now the cage doors were open, and the birds tunneled and dove in the air, their feathers sifting to the tops of tables, lampshades, books, to the floor at Lindy's feet. It reminded her of weather: a featherstorm, drifts and banks and floods of feathers.

"You collect birds," she said.

"They have some pretty loose definitions of poultry down in Mexico. I sort of figured I was rescuing them from tacos."

"You brought all of these from Mexico?"

"They come from the Yucatán, from South America, but I picked them up at the market in the DF. I was into breeding for a while; I was going to open up a shop in town. Exotics."

Lindy could not help wondering when his collecting had started. There was always a moment that seeded an idea like this. She thought of the day he'd caught the baby bird out of the sky in Esther's garden. She'd begun something that day, too, something far more practical than Orrin's enterprise. She'd begun the ushering of life into death. Maybe each had borne witness to the other in some small way. Maybe he'd remembered her, off and on, since then, as well.

Orrin rounded the birds into their cages; he whistled, and they came, some growling and barking like dogs in a fight. These were birds he'd raised at his daddy's farm, Orrin explained, in the same shed as a litter of pups. Parrots were highly impressionable.

Little Man let out a long low growl, imitating the parrots. He liked his sounds more than he liked his words lately. Orrin went on with his talk about parrots and Little Man went on with his growling and Lindy had the feeling she was there alone, that it was Little Man and Orrin and the parrots in the aviary cages, the cages somewhere in her mind, and her body taking its space elsewhere. She spoke, simply to reassure herself by hearing Orrin reply.

"The other night," she said, "Little Man woke up screaming. He was screaming for juice. I ran downstairs and got him some, and he went right back to sleep."

"So he's a talking man now."

"Not really. I mean, only in his sleep."

"Well," Orrin said, "that seems ideal to me."

He reached over to one of the perches and took a baby parrot on his finger. He touched his finger to Little Man's shoulder and the parrot high-stepped onto the child's skin and growled into his ear. Little Man nearly lost his balance, leaning back to see the bird.

"My man, Little Man," Orrin said, and swept him up high on outstretched arms, the bird fluttering away, Little Man's feet fluttering behind. Orrin laughed and the parrots growled and Lindy felt even less present than she had before. There was something Orrin wanted in Little Man. It was clear to her, watching them, how important that thing was.

"Did you always wish for brothers?" she asked him.

"Yeah. Sisters. Anybody." He slung Little Man over his shoulder like a sack of grain. "It was pretty lonesome in the wintertime. You and June were back home with your folks, and there wasn't as much work for my daddy, not as much to bring him into town."

"You had schoolmates."

"Yeah. But it wasn't the same. I mean, you had schoolmates, too, but not like June."

"No. Nothing like June."

Little Man squirmed, and Orrin set him down and offered his hand to Lindy. "I have some caldillo on the stove," he said. "You'll stay for lunch?"

Orrin's kitchen was long and narrow, barely enough room for two between the cabinets. Lindy helped herself. She found big white bowls and silver spoons, found glasses and filled them with sweet tea from a pitcher in the fridge.

Being in Orrin's apartment was strange. Lindy hadn't yet completely believed he was old enough to take care of himself, but here he was, with comfortable chairs and hardwood floors, straw mat rugs and throw pillows and a peg rail near the doorway for coats. It was a nice apartment, as nice as Lindy could have afforded back in Charlotte if she'd still been working at the hospital.

Suddenly, Orrin seemed to remember himself. He took her hand again and drew her to a spindle chair in the corner, poured her a glass of milk, left the room, and returned with a pillow for her to sit on. He stood over her, chewing his lip, trying to think. She knew what he was going to ask.

"When's your baby coming?"

She leaned back and brought her fingers to her lips, smiled, then laughed. She had not been asked that ever before, and though she'd anticipated it, she had had no idea how happy the question would make her. She wished Cott were here. He should have heard the answer from her lips, no matter whom she was about to tell it to.

"I'm not sure," she said. "Fall. October, I think."

"Fall is good."

"Is it?"

Orrin blushed. "Anytime is good."

Lindy and Orrin ate from the bowls held close to their mouths. Little Man pulled dish towels from the handle of the refrigerator, dragged them over his head, and crawled around, bumping into the walls, the cupboards, Lindy's feet. When he hit something hard, he'd fall back on his behind, adjust his dish towel, and set off in another direction.

The television was on in the other room. A child was missing in west Texas. They were searching for someone who, until two months ago, didn't have a little girl. They were looking in doctors' offices and grocery stores, places the child might have been taken by whoever had stolen her away.

Lindy set her bowl on the counter and wandered into the other room to hear the news better. She hoped she was being casual, hoped she was still partly invisible to Orrin in the wake of some small drama of Little Man's, some new affection. The newscaster gave a number to call with information about the missing girl.

Then Orrin was standing behind her, whispering, "You didn't tell them you'd be taking Little Man, did you?"

Lindy sighed but didn't turn to look at him.

"I told his father," she said. "But I didn't wait to find out what he thought."

She could feel Orrin's eyes on her as if she were laid open

before him; he could see where parts of her turned wrong, where she was white, gray, black. She could not meet his face. She stood suspended, her back to him, until he put a hand on her shoulder, squeezed, and let his touch drift down her spine.

"At the hospital," she said, "I had patients with growths. Decay, cancer; things like that. They'd be facing the loss of some body part and they'd tell me how they loved their leg. That pain was mostly what they thought about."

Orrin was still behind her. "I've never seen anything like that, Lindy."

"Oh, I know. But I was thinking, someday, maybe I will come to love this fear of being found. It is so much a part of me now, it's nearly a comfort. I think it's a matter of waiting for it to turn to love."

"Does it really work like that?"

"All the time, I think." She turned to go back to the kitchen, and let her eyes catch his. "All the time."

On the kitchen floor, Little Man cried with no sound, dish towels scattered and silent around him. He held his breath and his face went red, then purple. Lindy checked him for burns, scrapes, but he'd just been alone too long. She picked him up and whispered in his ear. She rocked him in her lap and tried to make him stop. He would calm down or pass out, one or the other, she told herself, but it was like holding a ticking bomb.

"Orrin," she said, "do something."

So Orrin started pulling everything out of his kitchen cupboards — pots and pans and lids and bowls — and soon Little Man wanted off Lindy's lap, wanted to follow Orrin around the kitchen and look in all his containers. Lindy let her head down on the counter's edge.

"Thank you," she said.

"You can owe me," he said, and Lindy laughed.

"As if the end of the rope could be handed off."

"Oh, now. I find it hard to believe Little Man here is more of a handful than, say, an emergency room."

"It's not that. It's not him. It's that so often I can't tell what's wrong. In an emergency room, somebody isn't breathing and there's a reason for it. You can put your finger on something."

"If you know what to look for."

"Yes. If you know what to look for, I suppose you could find anything."

Orrin asked what she had done at the hospital.

"For a while, I collected people's organs," she said.

"Like hearts?"

"Smaller than hearts. Hipbones, and saphenous veins, and femurs to make bone grafts. People promised themselves to us before they died, and we'd take what we could use, the way you'd strip a car for parts. We used to talk that way about it. It was like any other job."

But she realized how much she missed that job, the puzzle of it, cutting blind all the way around a bone in a smooth stroke, and knowing there was but a handful of people in the world who would do such work. She did it well. She had once been able to point to being a nurse and say, *Here; this is where I am right.*

"So why did you stop?" he asked.

Lindy shook her head. She had stopped because she'd stopped everything. She could see where Orrin wanted her to be a girl for him, a girl with clear reasons and clean feelings about what she'd done in life. It made her ache down in places she'd forgotten she had.

"I had a patient who died," she said. "Her husband had her cremated. He took her ashes home and ground them into dust, baked it in the oven for a whole day, poured it into capsules, and swallowed her every morning for a year."

"He loved her," Orrin said.

They were quiet with that thought. Little Man banged his pots on the floor, watching Lindy's face for a reason to quit, but she let him go on, would have let him go on until the neighbors complained.

"You know what always breaks your heart?" she said.

"What?"

"One person doing what two used to do together. It doesn't have to be people, even; dogs, birds, whatever. It's the separation that's so sad."

"What did you and June used to do together?"

"Think. We thought. And I miss her constantly."

Little Man crawled into Orrin's lap and laid his head on his shoulder, tucked his arms underneath himself as if he were ready to be carried off. It was as though Little Man could sense their past connections, how they'd all been playmates, and he was put at ease. It made Lindy glad. It made her want to be wrapped up and carried off too.

"I was wondering," she said, "you being a gardener. Why do you think people keep houseplants? Is it to be closer to nature, to bring nature indoors?"

"I don't know. Maybe the same reason people keep dogs."

"You've given me all these little trinkets," she said. "I want something of yours that would be like keeping a houseplant."

He looked up into the sky of his apartment, the lilting, heavy flight of birds with weakened wings, birds who flew only indoors, in cages, birds in all the colors Lindy could think of.

"I have no problem with birds," she said.

"Well, then, it's lucky you're here."

When she left, he gave her an old brass skeleton key tied with a blue ribbon. He didn't tell her what the key was for, but she assumed it was the thing she'd want to keep. It would have been rude to ask him, and, in a way, not knowing made it better.

*

When she and Little Man reached the house on Ball Street, she carried him up the porch stairs, his mouth a-drool on her shoulder. She did not check the driveway for cars; she walked right into the foyer and was halfway to the bedroom when she heard the footsteps overhead.

The real estate agent was showing the bathroom. Lindy heard her shrill tones, could picture her high starched hair and the bow on the neck of her blouse. She backed slowly down the

"That's okay. We can go inside."

Lindy set Little Man on the ground and they all went inside the house, like neighbor women. Esther took her spray bottle from her purse and misted their faces. There was lemonade in the refrigerator, birthday cake in the pantry, the parlor was cool from the sea breezes and the sunset. How would this have seemed to the agent? Esther didn't act concerned.

She settled on the piano bench, licked cake from her fingers, and surveyed the room. "I wanted to talk to you. Your mother called this time."

Lindy was silent. Little Man sat on his Big Wheel and hummed.

"Yes, it was harder to lie to her." Esther smiled bitterly. "Although I've had lots of practice."

Lindy could hear Esther telling her mother she didn't know anything about her and Little Man, the two women with sugar in their voices, the sweetness and care of a mother talking to her daughter. Lindy would have given anything just to say hello. Only hello, and to stop there, but that would have been impossible. She flung her body back in her chair, let her chin pinch down on her chest, her arms hang limp beside her. She bit her bottom lip, and it bled.

"I want you to understand," Esther said, "that you are being cruel."

"I don't mean to be."

"Intentions are for children."

"Don't be hard on me, Esther. Please."

"Well, then, get on with it." Esther's voice was heating. "Do what it is here that you set out to do. If it is Orrin you think will heal you, then have him. I've already said more than I planned."

Lindy tasted her blood. She wanted to save herself, wanted to say she'd do whatever Esther asked. But she hadn't asked anything; had just stated the obvious.

"You are on your own now, dear. I have reached my limit. I've become passive in this endeavor, a conscientious objector.

From now on, I will not hold myself responsible for your well-being."

"Am I being evicted?"

"More like excommunicated."

They became silent, divorced. Lindy stared at the floor, Esther at the ceiling. Time passed by the clock set in Paris. They watched Little Man; he hummed and scooted on his Big Wheel. Lindy got the idea that she was being abandoned, yet Esther was there, across from her, when she looked up.

"Maybe I should be the one to go," she said.

Esther made a patronizing face. "I don't believe that was what I was talking about. I said *get on with it,* not *go.*"

"I mean now," Lindy said. "If you want to stay here, you shouldn't have to deal with me."

Esther didn't answer. Her eyes examined the ceiling, panned the room, and when she spoke, it was as if they'd just walked through the parlor doors and sat down for tea.

"You know why they'll never sell this house?" she said. "It doesn't want to be sold. Now that the agent's gone, the faucets will stop dripping, the doors unlock. The plaster will smooth and straighten. Underneath your feet, the floors are leveling. Before your eyes, the paint is whitening. The foundation is saving itself."

Lindy looked away, but Esther's hand shot up to catch her jaw and draw her back. "This house watches after you, doesn't it?" she said. "You feel safe here, don't you?"

"Yes," Lindy whispered. "I feel invisible."

"Well, pay attention then. Let me tell you why."

She let go of Lindy's face and absently, gently stroked the piano; the keys drawing her fingers along them like a cat arching its back. Her voice was level and controlled. Upstairs, she said, and out of sight, her great-grandmother reclined upon her favorite tester bed for a nap. Luther, in his big leather chair, wished for cigarettes, and somewhere June was tending Lindy and the boy. The whole house was watched over, haunted; it wanted to be safe and sound and theirs forever. It had been that way since Esther was a child.

"Listen," Esther said, "to what I'm saying. There is no place in this entire world that is truly empty."

Now her fingers drummed the keys, and Lindy knew that Esther did not want to be playing, hadn't wanted to play in years but couldn't help herself. It was true, she thought, the pull our talents exert when we're at a loss for anything else. It was true, not all talents were ones you'd be happy to have.

HARD SUGAR

THE HOUSE BECAME LINDY'S. It was her exile, her small conceded country. In exchange, Lindy understood she was not to visit Esther at the retirement home, and soon Esther could start pretending Lindy had never visited her there at all. Allegiance was a simple matter for them; it moved through blood, and the nearer the blood, the tighter the sway. Despite what Esther claimed, Lindy knew her mother was difficult to lie to; she had had practice in that, and wished it on no one.

And so she was cut loose. There would be no more news of phone calls from home, and if she avoided the papers and the television, there would be no more news at all. It was she and Little Man, and he was almost a new child from the one who'd been on the train from Charlotte. He walked, he made words, he ran circles around her when she lay on the floor. He could occupy himself for hours. If she kept herself right there, right in that space and time, she was happy to let him.

Also, there was Orrin. For a span of nights, he came to her when she was sleeping. He did not wake her, but always left behind a mark of his having been there, a pressed flower, a feather, a charm. Lindy thought of the woman she'd read about in the paper whose sleep had been watched in secret. At the time, she thought it was eerie, but now she looked forward to

Orrin's private visits as if they were a living, recurring dream. At last, she felt her sleep was true and, best of all, watched over, not so much in secret as in a secrecy of occupation, the way angels and saints watch over you because it is their job to do so.

Gradually, Orrin came earlier and earlier in the night. Soon, she was awake to see him, as if her angel or her saint was making himself known to her, and once again she knew the safety of being in his presence. She didn't think about anyone tracking her down; the possibility seemed vanished. She thought about the next time she would see Orrin, and she told him so. "It would be nice to see you in the daylight."

"I have work," he said, "and all those birds to take care of."

"It was just a thought."

So he began to come before sunset. He brought dinner for the three of them, flautas from the Mexican restaurant on 14th Street, oysters from Gaido's, fresh shrimp from a man whose yard he kept on the bay. Little Man waited by the door for his truck in the driveway, patiently, the way you'd wait in line to see a show, and Orrin would push him up and down the hall on his birthday Big Wheel until it sounded like a dragway. Lindy stayed in the kitchen and picked over the food Orrin had brought, going about her evening as if it was what she did by habit, so Orrin's presence became a part of every evening. There was sleep, then Little Man, then Orrin, and then it began all over again.

After Little Man went to bed, she and Orrin played cards at the kitchen table — double solitaire, Russian bank, gin rummy. Their concentration on the game was like a conversation, taking the place of conversation. Orrin said that's what you did with pregnant women, played cards, and then he'd deal another hand.

It was while waiting for Orrin with the deck of cards that Lindy felt her baby move for the first time. She was hot and tired and stretched out on the kitchen floor, the linoleum cool against her shoulderblades. Summer was hard upon the island early — it was only May — and Lindy would have given anything to be away from the narrow air of the house, but where did she have to go? The floor was stiff beneath her, a therapeutic pain, and her back arched like a rubber band pulled tight. She put her hands over her head, and that's when her baby butterflied inside her belly, as soft as if she had imagined it.

She held perfectly still, wanting it to happen again.

The linoleum was cool, the air heavy, the night darkening. Upstairs, she heard Orrin promise to take Little Man to the dirt-track races, heard Little Man laugh and make motor sounds, and, above that, the night birds cawing, the sea breeze stirring in the garden, and, all the way out, the Gulf breaking itself on the sand. She felt time passing in her blood. She knew her baby was growing, moving, his brain making folds to make knowledge and memory and action, but knowing that and feeling it were different things. Somehow, she was nearly embarrassed. It was as though a stranger had presented her with a piece of old family jewelry. It's too much, she thought. You are too kind.

Orrin came into the kitchen and drew himself a glass of water from the tap, made space for himself at the table, shuffled the cards for Russian bank. He dealt his hand and waited. Finally he spoke. "Are we playing, or are we lying on the floor?"

Even if she sat at the table and played cards, she would think only about the baby, and she didn't know how to talk about that to Orrin. There were the movies in her head now, TV commercials where the kid puts his ear to his mother's stomach to feel the baby kick. It made her queasy with sentiment.

"Let's do something else," she said.

"Like what?"

She rolled to her side and propped her head on the break of her wrist. "I guess I wish we could go out. To a movie or to eat. I feel like strolling in a museum."

"A museum."

"Yes. I like museums. And movie theaters. They're always unexpectedly cool."

Orrin plucked a ring of keys from the table and rolled it in his hands. She watched his fingers, tapered and tanned, fanning the keys into his palm the way you'd fan a hand of cards.

"You aren't a museum person, are you?"

He smiled. "You still got that key I gave you?"

She pulled it from the pocket of her skirt, dangled it over his palm from its blue ribbon.

"Come on," he said.

"Where?"

"Just down the street. Just for a minute." And she left Little Man inside the house, asleep, in bed.

She followed him to the front porch and into the street, a few steps off his pace, so he'd turn, look at her, and wait, drawing her ahead. The streets were dark and empty, and Lindy could taste the air, the moonlight full blue and foglike over the street, enough to make her think she'd passed through a mirror into a dream world, out the back of a magic closet. It was two A.M. Overhead, the canopy of palms was full of night.

At Broadway, he took a left where the old Victorian houses loomed over the curbs, spiney with turrets and buttresses and high-hipped roofs. In the night, and the quiet, it was as though they were passing back into the web of the past, through each island of streetlight into further distant time. Lindy thought that could be Orrin's wish come true from when he was a little boy, traveling through space and time, and that wish itself was somehow doing the traveling in her stead. She felt ghostly. She followed him into the darkness and was safe in the lap of her movement, one foot in front of the other.

At the Bishop's Palace, he unlocked the wide front doors with the key he'd given her to keep.

"You gave me a palace," she said.

"We do the grounds here," he whispered. "Sometimes we have to get inside." He took her hand gently, for balance, and led her through the etched-glass doors.

It was something that had stayed with her from when she was a child, that Galveston was a place on earth where they built palaces like those in books. Even in the shadowy light, the rooms they passed were lavish with antique beds and crocheted coverlets, brass-footed bathtubs, portraits, petticoats, little archives of the people who had lived here fifty years ago and farther back, back a hundred years, to the men who had built these very walls. Back all that way into the past, Lindy held Orrin's hand and let herself be led up the winding stairs to the high floors, to the attic window, out onto the slate roof, where they were above the streetlights, where she could see the moon shining all the way into the Gulf.

He showed her where Venus was, shining green. Lindy could pick out Orion and the Big Dipper, the dog star, the trick star, the Seven Sisters.

"Make a wish," he said, although she could see no reason in the sky to do so.

But if she could have had a wish at that moment, it would have held Orrin and Little Man here in Galveston, living with her in this big house, or Esther's, with the baby she carried. They would spend whole days on the ocean. When they came inside, Orrin would wash her feet with kerosene to take off the tar that came up from seeps in Mexico, heavy on the beaches in the springtime, and they would play cards or eat fruit or drink wine. That was as far as wishing would take her. She thought Orrin had asked because he wanted to be part of her imaginary future, or maybe she wanted to tell him that when she wished, she wished for him too. But when she opened her mouth, he told her to keep it to herself or it wouldn't come true. They lay back and watched the stars.

Orrin said, "The trip to Mars, taking a year or two each way, would leave you unable to walk once you got back."

"You know that from when you wanted to be an astronaut."

He shook his head, but she prodded him, and he told her what he knew about time travel and life on other planets, about a soul going at the speed of light even as the body couldn't make such a trip. He laughed at himself and said he'd tried it once when he was small, leaving his body.

"So did you get anywhere?" she said.

"Did not move."

He was fourteen and had been scientific about it. He wanted to go somewhere he'd never been before but could check on later. So he chose Esther's bedroom. He relaxed, piece by piece, on his bed at home and instantly fell asleep.

"But maybe that's how it works," she said. "You go in your sleep."

"That's what I thought. But I snuck inside and checked. No dice. I'd never even dreamed about that place."

Lindy wanted to say something smart, not so much because she believed what he was talking about, but because she wanted to say something he would remember. But she couldn't think. She had to confess, she had a clean feeling with Orrin from time to time, a first-kiss feeling, first love. He'd been so familiar when they were children, and, in truth, she knew that boy better than she knew this man.

"Makes sense, though," he said. "All that about being in different places at once. Look at you."

"I didn't close my eyes and wish."

"No. But there are people at your home in Charlotte who think about it like you did. They figure they'll wake up and find they'd only dreamed you gone, that you were with them all the time. Like Alice down the rabbit hole."

"You make me feel bad, Orrin."

"Oh, now." He whispered, "Don't you think I wish it was different? Don't you think I wish you didn't have a fiancé any-place at all?"

"Do you?"

"I figure nobody wants to think of the women they knew as girls being with anybody. Anybody but them, maybe, and maybe not even that. I don't like to think you might get hurt."

"Well, you're too late."

"It's just the way it is, Lindy. It has nothing to do with early or late."

If she could have her wish back, she thought, she'd wish he hadn't said those things. Not that they hadn't been true, but that he hadn't brought them up. He had taken her feet out from under her, clean and fast.

"You know how it is for me?" she asked. "In my head, it's as if Cott has evaporated, and someday he'll come back as rain."

"I'm sure he'd like to hear that."

"No. Not bad. Just natural. I don't think about him, because he's stored up inside me, growing. Today, I felt his baby moving. How amazing is that?"

It was amazing. Orrin brought her fingers to his lips, a kiss like a father might make.

"Yeah, but when I think about it," he said, "I wouldn't want to be in his shoes."

He said he couldn't picture her as a wife, a bride, in white. He didn't want to hear about it, wouldn't want to be that man, and he thought she deserved better than marriage. He wanted her to have even those things he couldn't give her himself. And anybody, after all, could get married.

"But, too," he said, "how could I count on you to show up?"

He let go of her hand and stretched back on the roof, his face haloed in the starlight. Her cheeks went hot and she touched them lightly, kept touching, as if that would bring her back to herself from the outside, like a knocking at the door. Her fingernails were long enough to drum a tabletop. Like the dead, she thought; the things that keep growing when we're dead.

"Do you talk to the baby inside you?" Orrin asked.

"It's not talk," she said. "It's like prayer."

He smiled. "That's what I thought it'd be."

She was grateful that she didn't have to explain, but the taste in her mouth was as salty as if she'd been crying, and the weight in her chest was like iron. She knew how dangerous she was being with herself and with others.

"I have to get back," she said.

He walked her home, left her with only a good night on the front porch. But on the nightstand in her mother's room she found a silver stick for her hair, wrapped in a yellow ribbon. The windows had been opened to the balcony, the shutters turned back to the night air. It was as if Orrin was just now leaving her, and she was so confused.

She sat on the edge of the bed and watched Little Man sleep, gathered her hair back and twirled it round the stick, and sat until she heard the neighbors readying themselves for another drive to Houston or elsewhere, until she saw the pink of the sunrise. Her head was full of what it once was like to be inside another person, to be in love, a lover. It was loose and easy, not at all what she'd left behind with Cott, not at all real or whole or breathing.

She went to her mother's writing desk, dug out stationery and an old fountain pen that still flowed its ink. She wanted a record of what she was feeling, something written down to flip back over like a chart, so that she could know what to do next. She wrote:

Dear Joy,

You know me from the other afternoon at Orrin's house. We met only briefly on the stairs, and then you left. You seemed to know about me, however, so I do not feel strange writing to you now. I can only tell you that there is no one else for me to write to: my grandmother has grown impatient with me, I am lost from my family, and Orrin cannot answer the questions I have to ask.

What I want to know is this. What is he to you? I sense that you two had a past together and are separated now, and I imagine that you know things about him that I never knew that I knew when we were children but have now forgotten. It is not my business, and you are free to tell me so.

In exchange, I will tell you what he is to me.

She sealed the letter, turned it over in her hands. She remembered Esther's words to her in the parlor: *Do what it is here that you set out to do.*

She found Joy's address in the phone book, delivered the letter herself, during the night, to a grand old house on Avenue O. It was a tiny action on her own behalf, a step off or in front of this thing that was barreling through her days, taking up her days, this thing of Orrin that had come to be her days. She had always found that small steps served her well.

✺

Then came the month of June and Lindy's wedding day, but her waking thoughts were not church-bound or white or borrowed or blue. They were not of her wedding at all, but of Orrin. He was waiting at her window when she woke up.

The curandera's baubles and ornaments sparkled in the leaded glass like stars around his knees. She thought not that it was June already, or that she had missed her wedding, but that Orrin was at her window and it seemed a long time since she'd seen him.

She rolled over, and Little Man whispered in her ear that he wanted a drink and a cookie, now. She was convinced that she was still dreaming, or that he was. His talk did come mostly in his sleep, and, from what she could tell, he dreamed of food. She stroked his face and he smiled at her.

"What do you want?" she asked, but he giggled and turned away.

Orrin shouldered open the window and came inside, easing over the trinkets on the sill. Lindy couldn't get her bearings. She told him he had come to her that way in a dream the night before, a dream with sprinklers and lawn chairs and people playing tennis that were funny in a way she didn't understand.

"You licked my fingers," she said. "You gave me something that looked like orange juice, but tasted altogether different."

He considered her long and she knew he had no idea what to say. She ducked his eyes, felt length growing in her neck, in her spine. She hadn't expected a response. What she said was something her mind had turned over while she was asleep. It was like stretching or touching her toes, not meant to be studied. She could say it out loud. She could say *I dreamed about you* more easily than *I think about you all the time*.

She stood up, drawing the bedsheet after her, slipped a sundress over her head, and let the sheet fall away. Quickly, she put in her contacts, and touched her hair with her fingers. She didn't preen in front of Orrin, but she liked the way her clothes drifted over her roundness, her swelling body. She was beginning to look like a pregnant woman, carrying something delicate and rare, and she was beginning to feel worthy of the task.

She changed Little Man, got him a banana and some juice from downstairs, asked if that was all he wanted. Again, he grinned. His grin was four teeth wide, top and bottom, but his words were stored up for another day.

"Ready," she called, and walked across the threshold back to Orrin.

The action fired in her head and she remembered what she'd forgotten. This day was marked on a hundred and fifty calendars in North Carolina and beyond. It was the day she was to be married, only there was no she, no place to be found.

She sat down hard. What started up inside her was akin to sadness but not sad, akin to longing and wistfulness, but neither of those. Nothing about this day could ever be as it was planned for her and Cott. In one very important sense, her running away was over.

She felt, first of all, relief. At the time of her leaving, she had left a tiny chance of coming back, like the twinning of opposites. Now that chance had passed. Its weight was gone. She was amazed at how different she felt at simply the turning of a day. Would she have felt that different had she just been married?

Orrin slid the toe of his boot under her backside.

"What?" she said.

"What, yourself," he said.

His gaze was drawn tight on her face, and she knew she was being judged for the significance of her movements. She wasn't sure whether it was only Orrin watching her, or whether she was accountable to something else, seen in Orrin's face. It's the same feeling, she thought, as when you do something right. It's complete, cleaned out, empty. In a way, good.

She took a deep breath. "Weren't you taking me away somewhere?"

"I hadn't thought about it."

She stood. "Fine, then. Think fast. I don't keep well."

"Where would you like to go?"

But she was quiet, and Orrin didn't offer suggestions. It was noon or later. Somewhere else for Lindy, this day would have been mostly over, a blur of white and pink, heavy with lilies, with hugs and kisses and smiles and thanks. She would have held her father's arm, danced with him, caught him crying at some point. But she'd seen that before and did not want to see it again for as long as she lived, let alone be the cause. She would have had too much to drink. She would have forgotten people's names. She would have said something sharp to her mother or to Cott and tried to apologize, not meaning to spoil such a day, such a fat, portentous day. And she wouldn't have spoiled it, couldn't have. It would have gathered enough along its course to bear its weight; a helium event, a hot-air day. It would have lifted into the sky, taking what it promised who knows where.

"It's my wedding day," she said to Orrin.

"Well, congratulations."

"But all of that's spoiled now."

"I do imagine you're in the wrong place at the right time." He sighed. "But it's been spoiled since June died."

What went through Lindy's mind was not June, alive or dead, but Orrin's face, weeks ago, in the curandera's yard, when she told him that June had been murdered. She could feel again, in her shoulders and stomach, the force of his swinging the air, of the cement flying, the strength of his reaction, the weakness of her own.

"Orrin." She sighed, and sat down.

He folded himself beside her on the step.

"Now," he said, "I was under the impression you knew this was coming."

"I did."

"And it's not what you expected?"

"No, it's not. This was supposed to be the day, the day when it all came flying apart and I was reduced to nothing. I'd have been a speck of nothing on the front porch. I was going to spend the rest of my life pushing off this day. It was supposed to be my emptiest."

"And it's not."

"No."

Inside her, the baby fluttered and turned. Her hands went to her stomach, and Orrin's eyes followed, drawn to what she touched. The air in the house shifted for the first time in weeks, and Lindy shivered.

"Well," he said, "I think I know what your problem is, Lindy."

Whatever he was thinking, she wanted him to be right. She wanted him to know her and fix her and, most of all, stay with her now. He looked at his watch.

"Not everything is an event," he said. "Sometimes, something happens, and then it's over with. You can't hang your hat on everything."

He scooped up Little Man and settled him on his shoulders, took Lindy's hand and led her down the steps, through the front door, to the porch, the heat, the garden path. He swept aside the tresses of some hanging vine and let her pass into Esther's garden. When the gate swung closed, Orrin locked it behind them.

The sun struck green at her feet and rose upward like slow lightning through the palms. Sweat filmed her brow, her back; it was a mantle laid across her shoulders. The paths led everywhere, doubled back on themselves, twisted and turned and ran off. Lindy lost her ideas of space; it was as though she could wander forever and never find a fence or a wall to make her stop. She felt the heat of the day held down, the breath of leaves on her cheeks, Orrin and Little Man close behind her, Orrin whispering the names of plants as though he could not keep himself from doing so if he tried.

He leaned Little Man close to touch leaf and flower, and told him that one is a sweet olive and they are fragrant; that's a Texas sage with a purple bloom; this a pineapple guava and you can eat its fruit; a scarlet bottle bush; a Texas mountain laurel, Confederate jasmine, butterfly vine, true myrtle, sweet pea and yarrow.

Lindy said, "Do you remember how June used to tell you about the garden?"

Orrin's face was flushed. "I remember you all let me hang around a good bit."

"No. She used to do exactly that. She'd show you things exactly that way. You must remember."

Orrin shrugged, looked away. In a knife of light, the air was thick with tiny insects.

"It must have meant a lot to you," she said.

She let Orrin take her by the elbow, his steps tucking in next to hers as he led her deeper into the garden.

There were rooms. They passed through an opening in an arching cypress hedge and down a gallery of gated doorways, then wooden, then willow, some still living, vine and flower, and opening each into the next, into hedged rooms furnished with ivy-covered tables, bentwood chairs, beds made of growing grass. There was the fountain bubbling out of a ginger jar into the pond of koi. There was the small grove of fruit trees, and topiary in the shapes of animals.

They came upon the puzzle trees, whose limbs hinged and pivoted against themselves like broken bones, spliced and grafted and spliced again in their trunks. They grew in knots. They made windows. They were trees like sculpture, trees like ideas that took on shape and took up air, as strangely beautiful to Lindy as a body used for art. She thought of henna painting, fine tattoos, a shaved head on a pretty girl.

"What are these?" she asked.

"Linden, birch."

"But what are they?"

"Oh, I didn't make them. I just keep them alive. They belong to Daddy."

Little Man called his ghostly baby call, and Lindy took him in her arms. He reached out and spun an axis branch in the center of a tree trunk the way you might spin a pinwheel. Lindy put her hand over his. The bark felt as much a part of the tree as she expected, yet she would not have been surprised to feel it move, to feel a pulse, or, if she squeezed hard, to hear it call out.

She was as much an outsider here as she would have been on another planet.

Orrin kept pushing ahead into what Lindy had never seen before, and something like fear was making its way up her spine, chilling and sharp. It was as if he were leading her off the face of the earth, into a place where everything was as he understood it to be, and she was lost. Little Man tucked his head onto her shoulder quietly, lay still. Lindy leaned against Orrin's guiding arm. Leaves caught her face like spider webs, leaving evidence of their touch. She knew she was about to step off the edge of whatever they were walking and fall. She had only to allow it.

"Look here," Orrin said. "Look what we've found."

The last and smallest hedge box opened before them, narrow and green and dark. Spread on the ground was a rattle of things: a two-olive martini, a bag of pistachios, a gull feather, an oil lamp, and a glow-in-the-dark Virgin. It was an offering, a spirit house in Esther's garden, like the ones she had admired in the Far East. Lindy dropped to her knees. There was liquid in the martini glass. The lamp was lit. She turned to Orrin.

"Do you keep this for her?" she whispered.

"It started as a joke," he said. "We both kind of threw God out of the house a while back."

"Does she even know this is here?"

Orrin didn't think so. "I owe her a lot more than this."

"Do you?"

Orrin nodded.

"She saved your life," Lindy said. "I think she's saved everyone's at one time or another."

He sighed, sat. Lindy spread Little Man on a mossy carpet at the foot of the shrine and tickled his feet with the gull feather.

When Orrin looked at her, he wore that shined-up expression he'd had around Esther the day in the sauna. He really did believe he owed her everything.

"The fact is," he said, "I took my daddy's wife from him. Even if I didn't do it myself, directly, I made it so she died. You can see how that works?"

Lindy nodded.

"My daddy raised me because he had to and there was no place else he could have sent me. He'd had trouble with the law before I was born. I don't even know his true name to tell it to you."

"Orrin Cordray," Lindy whispered.

"Esther named me. Caroline Cordray was my mama, but the rest, that was Esther."

Lindy knew there were things people did to one another there was no turning back from. Sometimes they were good, strong, honest things, like naming a child. Sometimes they had nothing to do with goodness at all. Her disappearance was like that, and Esther had done all she could to try and help her anyway.

"I've disappointed her," she said. "I've disappointed everyone."

"Not me."

"But I'm here with you."

"You don't get me."

"It's different, Orrin. I'm here, you're here, and they're not. You'd have a hard time staying disappointed every day."

Orrin closed his mouth and looked away.

Mosquitoes clustered in the dusk, and Lindy beat at the air with her skirt, blood on her ankles and calves where she'd scratched. Little Man chattered in his baby play, his voice light and happy, and she pressed her hands to her belly to feel if her other baby was happy, too, as if she could tell by touching. Orrin's hand followed hers, his eyes still somewhere else, and when he touched her, she sensed all of him come through that touch. The whole afternoon had been leading up to this moment, the cool breeze on her face, electricity in her limbs, the thin lightning in the distance, and his fingertips hot on her skin through the fabric of her dress.

"Orrin," she said, "don't you like our being friends?"

He whispered, "Yes. I like it."

"I can't make you any promises. Not about anything. My promises are worthless."

His fingers became light on her belly, spreading like a breath, a change of heart. She could not tell whether she was pushing forward or he was, but she knew she was moving, slightly, like the movement of the stars across the sky.

"But, gosh," she said finally, stupidly, "I'd like to kiss you. I can't remember the last true kiss I had."

He pulled her up then, came up on his knees and knelt in front of her, his face sun-dark, foreign. She reached out and skinned off his T-shirt, and she could see the dimples in his shoulders, the edges of his broad-winged back. She remembered the dimples from when she was a girl and it was raining and they'd ridden on the bus to Houston with Esther. She remembered a stranger's fingers on Orrin's skin to say what a fine and good and pretty child, a doll with dimpled shoulders. Lindy had been jealous.

Seeing him now, she just wanted to be in love again.

So that was where she touched him first, his shoulders, and his skin was warm as if it held the day's sun against the shade and closeness of the garden. But she didn't kiss him, after all. She let her fingers play over the tops of his shoulders and he stayed just at the end of her reach; and deep inside them both all sorts of things came not to matter anymore.

Then there was Little Man, resting his head on Lindy's back, his little arms around her neck. She leaned her cheek to his skin, still baby skin, so soft as to be barely there at all.

"We should get home," she said to Orrin, and he agreed.

He took her arm, but Lindy would not say he led her anywhere, and they walked away from Esther's house, down 17th Street to the Strand.

Orrin's apartment was loud with the prattle of birds. They took Little Man to the kitchen, where he sat on Lindy's lap, and Orrin emptied his refrigerator before him. He ate ice cream and green beans and apples cut from their skins, gooseberry pie, cool cups of milk, hard-boiled eggs, and toast. He ate until Orrin had fed him everything he had that was suited to a little boy, and then he high-stepped his way off Lindy's lap and into the butter-colored room with the bird cages, into the fall of feathers. Orrin made a nest of blankets on the floor. Little Man circled down and began growling at the parrots, and Lindy patted his back until he fell asleep.

In the time it took for Little Man to sleep, Lindy thought of what she was about to do. There had been no question, as she walked with Orrin to his apartment. Her mind was huge with whatever was to follow. She watched Orrin pace the hallway from the narrow kitchen to her and back again, always moving, always on the balls of his feet.

She met him in the hallway and heard his breath catch, as if she'd caught him unawares.

He led her to his bedroom, where in place of a bed was a hammock, strung from a teakwood frame and piled with pillows and crisp white sheets. All Lindy wanted was to lie down.

And then Orrin had her fingers in his mouth, his hands at the swell of her belly. It was late afternoon, early evening. Lindy felt riffs and runs and trills inside her skin and out, felt whole plots of her mind shut off. She wanted to lie down with this man and not get up, not ever, not for anything.

But still, she was not prepared when he pulled her dress over her head. She lifted her arms like a child, tucked her chin, and there she was, pale and pearled with veins, nearly polished to a shine. She realized how long she had been keeping this body to herself, how long since she had put her bare skin before a mirror, let alone another's eyes. Everything about her was changed. She could not sense her edges anymore, and she stood there an endless time, naked before him, as strange and otherworldly as if she'd arrived on the lip of a seashell.

He left the room, and that was good, to be alone for a few moments.

She spun on her heel and folded herself into a wide red chair, tucked her feet beneath her thighs. She could hear Orrin clattering in the cabinets, the birds beating their wings in the cages. She let her wrists break from the chair's scrolled arms, let her head arch back. She decided she was tight and ripe and pretty in her pregnancy, and she put her body out in front of herself to prove it.

When Orrin returned, he knelt before her.

He had a handful of cotton, a bottle of rubbing alcohol. He daubed at the mosquito bites on her legs, the places she'd scratched open. He touched the back of her knee, and her heart came through her chest like something hot and pointed. The feeling of surprise, being touched by someone who had not touched her before, nearly hurt. She wanted him to touch her again so that she could think of that feeling and its sweet, sharp pang, only the most right feeling for now.

He said, "I was fine. And then you took up in my head and wouldn't go away. I knew how this would happen, you and me."

"Shhh."

"I had high hopes," he said, and there was more, but she covered his lips with the back of her hand.

She did not say that she'd had the same hopes, a hundred different times since she first saw him in Esther's yard, because at that moment she was turned around in herself, lost and moving toward light, toward heat, toward what she could name. She was cool at the skin but not inside, so hot inside. She took his head between her hands, turned him this way and that, took his earlobe in her teeth, his neck, his mouth to hers, and then they were inside each other and she could think only of that. For hours, when she did not know what to do, she went to him.

They rocked in his hammock as if they were in the bottom of a boat. Where his chest and back had seen the sun, he was the color of old pennies, and Lindy's nails across that skin left bright marks; her tongue at the hollow of his neck tasted sweat; her voice in his ear made sound in his throat. What a privilege it is to touch another's body, she thought; always a privilege. Where her body was awkward to be with Orrin's, she moved slowly, carefully, the hammock at sway beneath them. Her motions became fluid, without time, and her head became without words. She spoke to Orrin when she touched him, when he touched her, and it was not about making love as much as it was an endless conversation of skin.

They grew tired. They slowed to stopping, to embrace. They lay crossways and almost atop each other, her knee across his legs, his elbow tucked beneath her head. It was natural for both of them to keep all tangled up, and so they lay still and spoke when necessary, turned when some part became uncomfortable, and she let her hands dally over skin where it was smoothest — the tuck of his shoulder, crease of his elbow, top of his lily-white feet.

The sun set; light bodied up the room.

He said, "I lied. I was not expecting you. I hoped, is all. Sometimes I prayed. Maybe I prayed to that baby of yours, too."

"You prayed for me? How nice."

"Oh, Lindy. I prayed for you, cast spells for you, whispered to you in your sleep."

"Why, Orrin? Why, even after you know the trouble I have caused?"

"Alls I wanted was a chance."

"A chance? Like in rummy."

"No. A chance, because you're the sort of woman who only gives a chance. From the moment I came across you on Esther's porch, I planned on giving you everything I've got. What I was praying for was the chance to prove it."

Lindy closed her eyes and felt his skin beneath her cheek, beneath her hand, his leg tucked between hers, and she knew her wants to be so simple. How was it that Orrin had seen her as such a particular woman? She believed, in this moment, that she had always been his, and she floated away from everything else she had ever been on a long tether, the way she and June had floated on the raft across the lake, millions of years ago. She was no more wife, mother, daughter, nurse, sister. In this moment, she was purely the part of herself that belonged to Orrin.

"I'm touched," she said. "I am honored."

He laughed. "I once heard that was the only polite way to respond to somebody's saying he loved you. You're supposed to say you're honored."

"Is that what you're telling me, then?"

He rested his lips on her forehead. He would not have answered had she not pressed him.

"You take it how you please," he said, and so she did.

✑

Sometime in the earliest morning they rolled away from each other, and when they woke, their backs were pressed together and their limbs keeled off the edges of the hammock. Lindy was starving, and Orrin said he'd fetch pastries from the bakery on the corner, but she wouldn't let him go.

"Stay," she said. "We can eat dirt."

He laughed. "I'll be right back."

She caught his hand. "Please. See what's in the kitchen."

She did not want to be alone with her thoughts. She rolled out of the hammock and slipped on her dress, flushed Little Man from his blankets, and followed Orrin into the kitchen. Even those small movements made her buoyant, and she hooked a finger in the back loop of Orrin's jeans to hold herself down.

Side by side on the kitchen floor, they ate toast with honey, Little Man on a stack of old newspapers, opening and closing the cupboard doors, stuffing as much of himself into a kettle as would fit. Orrin downed a glass of milk and pulled her to his lap. She fit well against him, easily and naturally, and that was as far as she let her mind take her.

For days they stayed tucked away in Orrin's apartment, hiding the way Lindy had when she first came to Galveston. When she wanted food, Orrin cooked for her, made dishes out of what was in his cupboard, his freezer, out of thin air. When she wanted touch, he was at arm's reach. She liked the length of his body beside hers, his weight against her, the way she figured some people must like the weight of a knife in their pocket.

"You're happy, aren't you?" he asked.

"Yes."

"This is what you want, isn't it?"

"Yes. It is."

Lindy knew it was, that she had asked for him, the way you ask for absolution, salvation — vague things you knew you'd need, though not how you'd use them, or where, or when. But now she was sure they could hide away forever. It became a strange confidence, the kind you summon up when your back's against the wall.

He waited on her, lingered over her pregnancy, her belly, her sore bones and tired legs. He rubbed her skin with oil. He wanted to know how this felt, whether that helped. He wanted to know what was happening inside her.

"What makes you so curious?" she asked him.

"Extravagant recall of detail is most attractive, and all that."

"It doesn't make you uncomfortable?"

"Not unless you draw attention to that possibility."

"I'm sorry; I didn't understand —"

"I don't understand myself. I just want to know."

She told him how the baby grew a millimeter and a half every day now, how his inner ear was formed, his heart and his fingerprints. In his skeleton, connective tissue made cartilage made bone. She told him she was certain her baby was a boy, and Orrin nodded, as if it could be no other way.

She was surprised at the surge of affection she felt for him, as sudden and terrifying as a shove into traffic.

"It would all be different if that baby was mine," he said.

"Oh, you talk big."

"No, really. You're like the mother of god, or something just as . . . I don't know. Private. If I was that man and that was my baby, imagine how alone I'd feel about now? Even right next to you, I would be sore alone."

"I'm not such a hard woman."

"It doesn't have anything to do with hard. I'm glad to be somebody you still have to talk to in the morning."

Lindy couldn't help it. She thought of the last time she'd spoken to Cott, actually said words to him, not imagined a conversation in her head. It was the night before she left, in her kitchen. The last thing she said aloud to him had been insignificant, and she regretted that now as much as she had on the train to Mobile. The regret had not softened or lessened with time, with distance, with these new days of Orrin, and maybe it never would. Somehow, that was being honest to the baby she carried, and for that spoonful of honesty, right now, she was grateful.

Days, they took cool baths and arranged themselves before the air conditioner. Nights, Orrin took them driving to put Little Man to sleep. They saw the island from tip to tip and crossed the bridge to the mainland, the countryside beyond. In the little town of Hitchcock, where he grew up, they saw the rosy light in the sky as they passed his daddy's farm.

"Come on," Orrin said. "Daddy's playing a movie."

He parked beside a pasture and pulled a flashlight from the glove box. Lindy gathered up Little Man, and they took off running, Orrin's beam jerking over the creek and the willow trees, tall grass and fencepost and forgotten machine. They found another field, lumbered with cows, lit to the sky. A drive-in movie screen rose out of the grass, a single truck parked to view it.

"He won it in a poker game," Orrin said.

Orrin's daddy was reclined in his truck bed, spun around to face the screen, a lawn chair folded out, a cooler at his side. Lindy saw the red tip of his smoke, heard him clear his throat, the way men do in church. Orrin was silent, but his lips worked at the darkness. The movie was *Grand Hotel*, in which Greta

Garbo was a ballerina fallen in love with a thief, and a doctor said smart things at the front desk. Lindy had never seen the movie, but Orrin knew it by heart. They sat against some fenceposts, spread Little Man across their laps. They watched until Lindy fell asleep, and Orrin, even after that.

Orrin told her later how he'd let her sleep, listened to her breathing lengthen and stretch, felt her body go soft beside him, and reached to her face and tipped her head to his shoulder. He whispered the words of the movie he'd memorized and she couldn't hear, how a man without a woman is a dead man, how people come and people go, but nothing really changes in a grand hotel. When it was over, he carried Little Man through the pastures to the truck and came back to carry her.

He crossed her arms over her chest and cupped her jointed parts in his hands to feel her weight full against him, not as when they made love, but all of her, close. He would tell her later that this marked the way he would think about her ever after.

Her eyes opened, but she did not try to get down, and he pretended not to notice; carried her all the way back. She had the keenest sense exactly how far apart their bodies were, and it was down to the breadth of hairs. She wanted him to carry her in his pocket, and that thought stuck with her for days. It is my pregnant mind, she told herself. I think something, and it settles down to grow.

Back at his apartment, they made slow, careful love, their skin so loud as to seem the only sound for miles and miles. Time stretched long for them to be together, as if it were a complicitous force; they were never hurried, never preoccupied; Little Man slept soundly for nights on end, nights that stretched out like long, black cats.

Lindy didn't go back to Esther's house, even for clothes. Orrin didn't go to work; the heat burned lawns all across the island. They didn't visit Esther at the retirement home, and they bought no papers, watched no television. They were pinned together in that apartment with the birds and the boy and the bare cupboards. That was how Lindy thought of it; they were pinned together, a needle through her chest that sewed her to him. When he left the room, she followed; when he showered, she went with him; when he spoke, she took the words and turned them over and over so as to remember them from every angle, to think of here and now and Orrin, instead of what she'd left behind.

This is what she learned, those first days of their being lovers: Orrin had marks on his tongue they couldn't figure out even at the medical center in Galveston. He remembered his baby thoughts. His mind was arranged in great lists of details about plants and animals and features of the land. He had never in his life been outside Texas, save his trips to Mexico, but Mexico had taught him plenty about a game of cards he had yet to show her.

He and Little Man could play endlessly with cards, hiding cards, stacking cards, houses of cards, and card tricks Orrin wouldn't explain to Lindy no matter if she begged. The kitchen was cool in the mornings, and after Orrin had cleaned the bird cages, he and Little Man stretched out on the floor with a deck, just the way Lindy and Orrin did at Esther's after Little Man had gone to bed.

Little Man took the ace of diamonds, patted it to his face, to the floor, slipped it under his belly, and gave a satisfied, single laugh. Orrin handed him the ace of spades, and he did the same.

Lindy found herself wanting to give Orrin something to match the trinkets and little things he'd given her, something small that he could keep close to his skin, hold in his hand. She'd left everything she had at Esther's.

Instead, she knelt beside him in the narrow kitchen, the way you'd kneel to ask forgiveness. "Here," she said. "Take something from me."

He reached behind her ear and drew the jack of hearts from the tangle of her hair. He folded it into the deck he was shuffling. "Pick a card," he said. "Any one."

Later, Lindy cracked ice from a tray in the freezer, let it flake on her skin, melt at her wrists as she held them over the sink. She was so hot. It was the hottest summer in Texas since the war. Train tracks warped, animals baked in the bellies of airplanes, people held contests to see what food cooked fastest on the blacktop. Orrin would have to go back to work soon, and she would return to Esther's house, and their idyll would be ended. What would she do with herself then?

∂∫∫∂

Sometime in the late night hours, Lindy dreamed of June lifting the baby in her arms, changing him, laying him back in his crib, and stepping away to ready herself. Little Man was smaller in the dream, quieter, and it was January all over again, but Lindy was there, in June's house, before everything went wrong. June said something to her that she couldn't hear; then she stepped from the nursery into the hallway, the stairway, down the stairs, and away. Lindy tried to run after her, but her legs wouldn't carry her in that direction. She waited, an interminable, bone-chilling wait. She picked up the tinier Little Man from his crib and found herself back at the hospital, where blood fairly ran from the table.

Orrin woke her from this sleep, brushing her hair from her forehead. Her face was wet.

"Lindy," he said. "Poor Lindy Jain."

She wanted to explain that it wasn't he who made her sad, but the moment she thought it, it wasn't true. He did make her sad, and overwhelmed and giddy and nervous. She turned her face away, but he turned her back to him.

"You can cry in front of me," he said.

"I'm not crying. Not really."

"I won't tell nobody, not one thing."

He kept his hands at her face, brushed her tears with his cheeks, and she stopped trying to think of what to say to him. What did she need to say to him?

He whispered in her ear, "I am yours. You are mine. Everything else, let's make it simple."

She woke again with the sunrise. Orrin was dressing, and she lingered her eyes at the flats of his hips, the rise of his stomach to his chest. It was still new, strange skin, first thing in the morning. Before long, she had to look away. This was what it was to love two people at once, Orrin and Cott. One couldn't replace the other, not entirely, not enough, not ever, and it was foolish to imagine they could.

"Lindy," Orrin whispered, "I have something for you."

He reached into his dresser drawer and pulled out a fold of bills.

"It's a thousand dollars," he said. "It's from what Wolfie and I did in Laredo, not the cleanest, but unmarked. Safe. I have more, plenty, all you'll need until your baby comes. I want you to have it."

He let the bills fall from his hand, to the sheets, to the floor. She stared at them.

"I can't," she said.

"You need it. I know you do, and I need to give it away."

"Can't you spend it yourself?"

Orrin looked bothered, as if he'd tried this moment a thousand times in his head and couldn't make it come out differently.

"I can do as I please," he said. "I want you to have it."

"No, Orrin," she said.

"You make me feel like a fool," he said.

And he was gone. His money lay on the floor like something left for dead. It wasn't how he'd made it that bothered her; it was that she had had nothing to do with it, hadn't known him during that whole part of his life. The money should stay with its own past. It was a trail of bills out the door, like the money that got June killed, but how could he have known that?

She and Little Man couldn't stay in his apartment; she didn't trust herself to wait quietly for him to return. She got up to collect her clothes, a sandal here, another there, her sundress on the closet floor, where she'd tossed it the night before. The dress was snagged. She pulled, and a stack of photographs slid into the room.

Only they weren't photographs. They were posters. They were her posters, the ones about her and Little Man, all torn clear through the top and bottom, as if torn from their staples to be hidden in Orrin's closet, where no one who cared would be likely to see them. She counted twelve.

She rocked back on her heels and remembered something Esther had said to her, how we almost need to make our lives complicated. She felt stupid, exposed. Even though she hadn't felt the chase of home in weeks, there it was, as it always had been, black and white, all around her.

She had no idea how long she crouched there, but when she looked up, Orrin was back, standing over her and shaking his head.

"It's hard to be your champ," he said. He toed the posters aside with his boot. "Busy as I've been this week, these here haven't made it to the mulcher yet."

"You did this for me?" she said.

"More for me, I think. When you leave, I want it to be for someplace other than jail."

"I'm not leaving," she said. Her voice shook.

He shoved the posters back into his closet. "Anyway, it's done."

He reached his arms beneath her and drew her tight to his chest, made his long-stepping way to the bathroom, turned on the water, and set her in the tub.

"You won't take my money, you can take my job," he said.

"Yes," she said. "Anything."

"You come with me. You take that money, and you can help me out on the job for exchange. I don't care."

Lindy pressed her cheek on the cool tile. She felt flattened, weak, relieved. She clung to his hand.

"Where'd you go before?" she asked.

"You're such a little thing, Lindy. I could carry you around all day."

"Orrin. Where'd you go when you left here? Were you mad at me?"

He didn't answer, but passed a long, sweet silence cupping water over her hip with his hands.

"One time," he said, "when I was a little man myself, a Galveston sea turtle showed up in France, two whole years after it left here. Like one of those balloons with a message inside. They'd marked it, lost track of it, and two years later, there it was."

He took her hand and squeezed it. She pulled herself up and out of the water, curling into his lap and letting his arms come around her, letting his blue jeans and his T-shirt dry her off. She would have let him do anything at that moment, would have been powerless to deny him.

"You ever been to France, Lindy?" Orrin whispered.

She shook her head.

"I imagine that's where us lost things go when we have the opportunity. Everything seems to turn up in France."

He shook out a towel and wrapped it around her, pushed her up on her feet. She looked at him, and his face was kind, warm. He would take good care of her, she thought. He had already.

Little Man nudged open the bathroom door. His parrot winged over his head like a bird over a garden scarecrow, but he hardly seemed to notice. He was such a determined boy. He stopped. He pondered. He began tugging Lindy and Orrin this way and that, arranging their bodies by the set of their feet on the tiles. When he was done, he sat on his behind and brushed his hands against each other, the way he'd seen Lindy brush hers, back and forth, quick and satisfied. He lay back on the floor to see their faces, his grin as wide and white as Orrin's, as doubtless as the sun.

Outside, the heat had already kicked up. It would continue to rise through the days of broken records, broken air conditioners, overheated cars, and water rationing. Outside, Galveston was baking in its skin, but there were gardens to be tended.

Lindy slathered Little Man with sunscreen and borrowed a baseball cap for herself. She took Little Man's hand and stood by the door.

"We're ready," she said. "Take us to the sprinklers."

Orrin laughed. "That's my girl. She's a peach."

"Yeah?"

"Sure."

He looked at her sidelong. There was something in her throat, and suddenly Lindy realized that she was close to tears. She wanted to hear something harder, something she could believe, something he believed about her that was true and true only of her.

"No," she said. "Something else, Orrin. Tell me something else you love about me."

He put a hand to her face.

"That's my girl," he said. "She's all her own."

✿

Lindy had to slide the bench seat of Orrin's truck so far forward to reach the pedals that her belly pressed against the steering wheel, but she'd been walking for months and now the prospect of fast travel was satisfying. She gunned it out of curves while Little Man made his motor sounds and Orrin held the dash.

"I fear we may have to stop," Orrin said. "Clean out my shorts."

"Don't be ridiculous."

"We left a pile of tire back there if I'm a day over born."

"It's early," Lindy said. "You're lucky I'm available for chauffeur."

They'd been able to cover most of his yards in the week or so that Lindy and Little Man had been tagging along, because there was so little to be done in each; the gardens had been burned almost beyond their help. They brought trimmers and

185

pruners and flats of flowers in the truckbed and did what they could in the latening dawn. They'd spend an hour looking busy and then move on, the rest of the crew and the big machines necessary only for the houses with irrigation systems.

Little Man kept his parrot tethered to his wrist with a length of string. He carried on rambling conversations with it, jabbering and calling out, sharing his saltines. Some days, he and the parrot would play in a sprinkler, or nap in the truck, or ride Orrin's shoulders for hours on end. Little Man was always busy, and sometimes not ready to leave a place when Orrin's work was done.

In the truck, Orrin set to opening and closing, turning on and off. He was not accustomed to being a passenger, and saw his world differently from that seat. He rolled the window up and down and watched where it disappeared into the door. Lindy had always known men who knew about things — why the sky was blue, how a trailer towed behind a car, what sort of engine went in an airplane — men who knew the measure of things by sight. Orrin knew that, but also he had a fascination with what he didn't know. She leaned over and ran a pointed finger along his thigh. She thought, How sweet he is, and she kept that thought all day.

As she followed Orrin's directions to the Avenue O villa district, she drove past Kempner Park and the grand round Garten Verein pavilion where Esther used to take them picnicking when they were children.

"Do you remember those afternoons?" Lindy asked.

"Turn here."

Lindy pulled the truck curbside and parked.

"You used to draw flowers on our feet when we fell asleep. With marker pens. They'd last for days."

"You have such pretty feet," he said.

He leaned close and kissed her collarbone, scooped up Little Man, and slammed out of the truck. Lindy's thoughts went like film coming off a reel. She could see herself and June and Orrin lazing in the green grass, three children, whole and polished and perfect, their limbs piled each atop the other, their shoes off, the wreaths of ink on her feet faded from her baths but not gone, like a suntan that lasted until October.

Lindy put her hand to the door to follow Orrin, and then she saw which house he'd made her destination.

Joy stood at the edge of her lush green lawn, with muffins and coffee and a cooler of water for the arriving crew. Her blond hair was caught up high on her head, and her face held the flush of exercise, as if she'd been running or pedaling a bike. She pulled at the neck of her T-shirt in the morning's heavy air.

Lindy remembered her letter to Joy and wished she hadn't written it. It had slipped back into the gulfing parts of her mind, the before-Orrin parts, and here, in the light of day, it seemed a silly endeavor to have started. She knew what Joy had been to Orrin; she had known the day she heard them talking in Orrin's stairwell. She pressed at her temples just to concentrate on where she was walking.

Joy smiled, and Lindy tried to smile back, hoping that would be the end of it.

Her gaze trailed Orrin, the distance between them like a formula inside her head. She depended on keeping him close; when she heard his voice, she turned; when he walked past her, she reached out; when he spent too long where she couldn't see him, she got up, brushed herself off, and went looking.

He handed her a flat of sweet peas. She went where she was told, knelt in the bed, and let her fingers dig at the earth. She listened to the crew, the Spanish, the whack and spit of lawn tractors and weed eaters and shears. The crew were all brothers and cousins of Wolfie's up from Mexico, and they knew one another, were never quiet, even when the roar of machinery was too loud for them to hear what was said. Slowly, Lindy's tenseness was replaced with the smell of cut grass, the sound of mowing, the salt taste of her lips in the heat.

Then Joy's sneakers appeared in front of her. "Come inside," she said. "They'll get along without you for a while."

But Lindy did not want to be alone with her. She reached to her skirts for Little Man, looked around her feet and the path she'd traveled, as if she'd dropped him somewhere. Across the lawn, beneath a palm tree, he pulled fistfuls of grass, as happy as could be.

"It's okay," Joy said, and she had no choice but to follow. Joy held open the door for her to pass.

They sat in a wide stainless kitchen, white-tiled and clean of any evidence of food or dish, and watched the men in the yard, their bent, tan backs at the machines. Lindy's eye sought Orrin, and she wondered whether he knew she was here with Joy. She wondered whether that would make him nervous or angry or neither one.

"I got your letter," Joy said.

"I guess I'd rather we dealt in letters," Lindy said.

"But here you are instead."

Joy's fingers turned a silver spoon on the table. Although she didn't meet Lindy's eyes, Lindy recognized the obvious weight of a talk long in coming. Each was in a position she would rather have avoided.

"Are you close to God?" Joy asked.

"I have that kind of faith."

"It's not my business," Joy said, "but I think it makes some things easier to understand."

"I'm sure it does."

"I've had the feeling, for weeks now, that I should tell you Orrin and I were in love."

"I guess I knew that. I figured it out."

"And I became pregnant."

Lindy let out a slow breath.

Joy's head dipped, and she went on. "When I lost the baby, I didn't want anything to do with him. I turned inward. I turned to the church, and it broke his heart."

Lindy looked down at her swelling belly, suddenly wishing it was less apparent. "I'm sure it did."

"I'm not saying that he can't fend for himself. He's a thoughtful person, and he's come to terms with me, I think. I have confidence. I have a great deal of confidence in him."

She trailed off, tucked her chin to her shoulder, and stared out the window. She seemed mired down in this, unable to move forward or take back what she'd said. Their conversation could find no natural way to end.

"How long ago was it?" Lindy said.

"Years, it seems. I don't know. Does it matter?"

"You're okay, now, though."

"I can't have children. Most people never knew I was pregnant."

"But you and Orrin, you're friends. He knows you're telling me this."

"No. But he asked me to help you, to be your friend, so how could he mind?"

She laughed an unhappy laugh, which pierced the air. She said, "I've been trying to be honest about my life, to walk the better path. I want to be honest with you. That was my idea, that we were adults and could be open about what's past."

"Do you think it's important that I know this?"

"It's not about Orrin, Lindy. I'm telling you about myself. I don't know if it's important or not, and I know it's not what you asked for in your letter . . ."

It was as if she didn't completely understand herself. They both gave up and turned toward the window, not to see the lawn or the men or Orrin, but to avoid looking at each other. Lindy wanted to say she wasn't angry, but wasn't sure whether it was her place to be angry. She wasn't jealous so much as grateful, or, at least, her jealousy had conceded to gratitude. There'd been another woman to watch over Orrin before she'd got there, and, in a sense, she owed Joy something for her time.

Joy's breath came low across the tabletop. "Now," she asked, "what is he to you?"

Lindy looked at her. "He keeps me here."

"He's your reason for coming to Galveston." Joy sighed. "You've loved him since you were children."

"No. He makes it so that I don't have to think about what I've done since we were children."

"I know the feeling," Joy said. "I know that feeling well."

She nodded, as though she'd heard Lindy but hadn't changed her mind; she believed Lindy and Orrin had loved each other all their lives.

"We'll always want what we can't have," she said. "It's as old as that, isn't it?"

Lindy guessed it was. And when she looked at Joy again, she saw what Orrin must have loved about her. How pure she seemed, how clear-hearted, her face carved cleanly from her sadness, as if from whitest stone.

♏

Later, the afternoon rose up thick and humid. Lindy found a spot beneath a live oak for some shade. She felt the span of the day in her steps and her shoulders; she'd been awake since dawn. Orrin came to be near her and brought a cushion from the truck, a sip of water, a handful of figs. She had tied up the skirt of her sundress to fall short across her thighs, half for coolness and half for ease of movement. He slipped a finger along the bend of her knee, leaving a trail of earth in the wetness there. He bent to her ear then and said she was free to go inside and lie down if she was tired or too hot. Joy had left a pillow on the sofa in the parlor for her. Lindy thanked him, but said she'd be okay.

And for the rest of the afternoon, she worked hard. She thought, you go looking at things that are none of your business, and you have to deal with what you find on your own. She'd written to Joy for details of Orrin's life; she couldn't now hold against him what she'd learned.

But once they were alone, she couldn't keep it to herself.

In his apartment, sunk to the wrists in soapy water doing the dinner dishes, her gaze trained out the tiny window, she whispered, "I spoke with Joy today."

She glanced at him, could see a throbbing in his neck, his temple. She wanted to say how generous Joy had been, how selfless and unashamed in talking with Lindy. She wanted to say Joy loved him, and how uncommon that love was, how complicated, the way women love brothers and sons. Suds dripped from her hands across their feet, drifts of it, like snow.

"What do you mean by that?" he said.

"That it's okay," she said, and she tried to mean it. "That it must have been so hard for you and her to go through. I can understand."

He took a long survey of her, head to toe, his face a half smile, his hands twisting the dish towel.

"Oh," he said, "I'll bet you can."

And he walked away.

That night, he drove them back to Esther's house. They entered as if it were a church, a holy place, and maybe they were uninvited. They stepped quietly and left the lights out, closed the door gently behind them, Little Man sleeping against the curve of Lindy's belly.

She sensed a change in the house, and first thought it was of her doing; her conflicted, swelling feelings had taken up extra room. She turned to ask Orrin if he felt it too, but he'd slipped back outside already and left her all alone.

He stayed outside and worked in Esther's garden. Lindy could hear him through the open window like a blade in the brush, cutting and carrying and crashing through. In the early morning, when he came upstairs, she could smell the greenness on him as he stood over her and Little Man to watch them sleep. Her eyes were closed. Her breath was deep. She let him think he saw what he was looking at, and then she stretched and rolled away.

❧

Lindy wished she'd kept Joy's confession to herself; it's what Orrin would have done for her. She tried to apologize to him, and he said he didn't understand what for, but he was lying to be nice. He'd never once held her to task over Cott, yet she'd brought this piece of his past to sit between them like a stone. In the morning, when he left for work, he said it was a small job and he wouldn't need her help, that he'd be back early.

"You've never needed my help," Lindy said. "That wasn't what it was about, my coming with you."

Orrin didn't say anything.

"You just want to be alone."

He shrugged, looked at his hands.

"That doesn't bother me," she said. "You can do whatever you like."

Orrin laughed. "Would it were that simple, Lindy."

He broke off, slung his hand in her direction, but couldn't make it mean anything. He left. Lindy followed him to the front porch, but couldn't think of what to say to keep him there, couldn't think of what to do except follow him like a puppy.

But after he was gone, she knew she had to make it right.

Upstairs, Little Man was moving furniture. He had all of Esther's slender cane chairs configured against the grand piano, was starting in on the footstools, the coffee table books. When Lindy walked into the room, he bounced up and down on the balls of his feet, as if to say *Finally. Someone is here to see.* His parrot carved the air around his shoulders, wanting his perch, but Little Man was sweating with the heat and his baby work, and paid no attention to the bird. His knees were black with what he'd picked up from the floors.

Lindy carried him to the bathroom and wiped him down with a cool, damp washcloth. He watched the water at his feet turn black and drain away. Now the parrot found his shoulder, and Little Man smiled up at Lindy, and she knew he needed her. He needed lunch and a clean diaper, and those things would delay her going to find Orrin. Was that right? It was impossible to say who was more important to her now.

After a peanut butter sandwich, Little Man wanted to take the parrot with him on their walk. Orrin was always the one to catch the bird, because Lindy was afraid to put her hands on it. And she was in a hurry. She told him no, took his hand to lead him out the door, but he went foot-dragging limp. She had to pull him down the porch steps and into the street.

Where had he learned to pout? There were no examples here — no TV, no other children — but his face went red like that of every baby in a temper tantrum since the beginning of time. His eyes were dark and his breath heavy. His cheeks puffed. In a matter of minutes, he'd become a stubborn child. Lindy tickled him in the ribs, but he didn't giggle, didn't even squirm away.

"Quit pestering the kiddo," Orrin said.

His truck was pulled up to the curb not a block from Esther's house, the engine killed, the windows rolled down. His boot was propped up on the dash as if he had no intention of driving anyplace ever again.

"Why?" Lindy said, dragging Little Man to the truck window. "Why should he be allowed to sulk like that?"

"Swoll up like a toad," Orrin said.

"Yes."

"Because he's a kid. It's what they do. Especially the boys."

Orrin pushed his cheeks out, let his lower lip droop; then he laughed and took a pull from a bottle between his knees. He'd been at it for a while, Lindy could tell.

She let go of Little Man's hand, and he beat against the door of the truck to be let inside. Orrin unfurled one long arm to scoop him up and haul him through the window.

"My Man Friday," Orrin said. "My little man."

Lindy leaned on the doorframe and sniffed. Rum.

"What have you been doing?" she asked.

"I saw you pass in front of that window there." He squinted, pointed with the neck of his bottle. "Must have been about an hour ago. You were carrying Little Man, and he'd got his hands snarled up in your hair, and it didn't seem to bother you."

He took another long swallow. "I don't think anything really bothers you, Lindy."

"That's not so."

"But I don't see it weigh on you. Just a couple of times, but you're pretty damn collected."

"Do I seem that way?"

"You do." He laughed. "You just answered your own question."

"You say it as if I should be ashamed of myself."

He shifted up in his seat, drained the last out of the bottle, and contemplated the paper bag it had come in. He tore a strip from the bag's edge the way you'd pluck a petal from a flower, handed it to Little Man, and tore himself another. Lindy wanted him to be angry and have it over with.

"What do you suppose makes people want to spill their secrets?" he said.

"I'm sorry, Orrin. I tried to tell you earlier. I don't care who else you've been with. I should never have brought it up."

He smiled into his lap, shook a finger at her.

"That's the thing, baby," he said. "That's the thing. I went over there today and Joy said you'd written her a letter, asking what she knew about me. I was all set to give her hell for meddling in my business, but I didn't have a leg to stand on. And saying you don't care? Well, my God."

Still smiling, he looked at her. "You're lying to my face."

She studied what she could of her feet. "I guess I am."

Orrin took her jaw in his hand and made her look at him, look at his smile still there, for her, not against her.

"You are such a strange, strange woman."

"Kiss me, Orrin."

He came out of his seat and slipped his fingers from her face into her hair, pulling her toward him, his mouth over hers, wet and sweet with what he'd been drinking and what was inside him. She kissed him back just as wholly and well, and when his lips came away, he'd won something from her she had not expected to lose.

"You'll remember that one," he said. "You'll remember that for the rest of your life."

"Yes. I will."

"Then take me home. Put me to bed. Let's make it all up right."

She opened the cab door and pushed him aside. At Esther's, she had him take a chair and then poured him coffee, knelt at his feet, and took his boots. At dusk, they went to bed. Orrin came up on his hands over her body, his eyes full of something she could not yet read, would someday only half be able to, and he made his way over her not so much as if it was something he enjoyed but as if it was something he was good at and could do well. There was the drive of talent at work in him, and the distance such a drive afforded; Lindy could taste it when his mouth reached hers, distance and the afternoon's rum and the rush of getting at something, getting at her. He wanted her to come, and she did, but it seemed more his action than her own, and when he drifted off to sleep in her arms, she could not follow. She lay awake for hours.

Past midnight, she crept downstairs to the kitchen and the sticky yellow light, the broad breakfast table. Orrin's shirt at her shoulders smelled like cashews. She poured a glass of tea and sat down to write to Joy, as if she were casting a coin into a well.

Dear Joy,

I was a good nurse at the hospital. I saw peoples' hearts beating in their open chests. I felt their blood on my skin. I held their babies even before they did, and I stayed with their dead after they'd gone home. Someone died every day, every single damn day. Sometimes it was an old person, but more often a young one, often a child, and the child's parents were waiting in the hallway. At some point even the doctor would turn up his hands and walk away, and I was the one who said the words, who apologized.

When I worked at the clinic, I used to call the patients who hadn't called me first. It started out with the sadder ones, who welcomed somebody to talk to, and then it was anyone I didn't know much about. I'd ask them embarrassing personal questions, and they would answer me, just because I was a nurse.

And so when you ask whether I am close to God, that is what I think about.

She'd never told anyone about those phone calls, the things confided in her, and she told Joy now with relief, for her soul's sake, although it was barely the edge of that. She would not ask Joy about Orrin again. Joy would be like Esther's pen pal in Sweden, who learned of all Esther's secrets even though she couldn't understand them. Lindy needed that.

She pushed up from the table and stepped outside, gathering the tails of Orrin's shirt against the cooling night. His keys were in his truck. She drove to Joy's house and ran to her mailbox, barefoot, light, but not so secret as she once had been. Her belly preceded her; the words on the paper she delivered spilled out. She was running, and something was lifting off her shoulders into this night air, something she no longer needed. Inside, she could feel the baby, she could feel warmth, she could feel Orrin slick on her thighs.

Still, someone was coming for her; she had never been more certain of it nor less afraid.

ॐ

Summer gathered more heat, and fireworks marked the Fourth in the Garten Verein. Lindy and Orrin sat on blankets in the park, kept at the corners with a slip of sandal, one of Orrin's sneakers, a rock. Little Man dug a trench around their blanket with a stick he'd brought from home, and then he rolled in the sandy dirt, like a dog looking for a cool spot.

From the picnic basket, Orrin took pimiento cheese sandwiches wrapped in wax paper, shelled peanuts, celery sticks, wedges of cantaloupe, a salt shaker, a thermos of coffee, and a jug of lemonade.

His body cocked around Lindy's in the darkness, braced on his elbows. He pulled her down to lie beside him. He showed her constellations again, told her how the trip to Mars would take away your power to walk, how force fields ate up space, how black matter made the world go round. He'd told it all before, but she listened as if it were new. She let him go on because he wanted to. In the distance, she heard music scratching from a loudspeaker. Little Man laid his dusty body across their legs.

"Hold on here, baby," Orrin whispered. "Something is about to happen."

The summer became fixed in her mind in this moment. There was the feeling that something was coming, a gentle pressing at her back. There was the dark night in the grass on a blanket, the shallow light of fireworks across her face and Orrin's face and Little Man's sleeping body, sand falling from his fingertips, his little mouth earthy and wet on her lap. There was the feeling that she had laid her table and was waiting to see the trick where the cloth gets whipped away without even a broken glass.

✧

When they returned to Esther's house, Lindy could tell something was not right. She didn't say anything until they were inside, but she could feel another presence there.

"Orrin," she said. "Something's off."

"You show me the way, and I'll put it back on."

He let his hand slip down her chest, and she made a small sound in her throat. It seemed so long since he'd touched her, though they'd walked the whole way back from the park holding hands.

"Let me put Little Man to bed," he said, and disappeared upstairs.

Waiting for him to return, Lindy became more certain they were not alone. Maybe Esther was back, come to warn her of something. She wandered through the downstairs rooms, found nothing out of place, no cause for her discomfort. When Orrin came up behind her, she nearly jumped out of her skin.

"Hey." He stroked her hair out of her face. "Hey, nothing to worry about. We'll take a look-see. Right now."

They searched the house, weaving in and out of rooms like children playing, but it wasn't a game, and when they'd been all through the house, Lindy made them take flashlights into the garden to search there.

She was nervous, moving faster than her body could allow; she lost her breath quickly. She came to the grotto and took a seat inside.

She saw his shadow first, a shadow cast in darkness, and for a moment she let herself believe it was the real estate agent with a reprimand for the other afternoon.

Jimmy White sat on the stone bench in the grotto, a shadow of himself in dark clothing, days of beard, smudges beneath his eyes dark as tarnish.

He said, "If it isn't the outlaw herself."

Then Orrin stepped around the corner. He saw Jimmy White and pummeled him to the ground.

"What are you doing?" Lindy said.

Orrin looked at her with big sheepish eyes, snapped his hand in the air.

"I don't know," he said. "I just . . . did."

"This is bad," Lindy said. "This is June's husband."

"Christ."

"Yes. Well."

They stood over Jimmy White's crumpled body on the easing vegetation, the wild red bloom of a hibiscus already moving in with the slow motion of a plant. Lindy felt her vision honing, becoming razor sharp. *What am I looking for?* she thought.

"This man's bleeding," she said.

Orrin raised his hands before himself. "I just hit him a couple three times."

"No," she said. "He's really bleeding."

She opened Jimmy White's shirt, with care, to a weeping wound between his last ribs, septic, purpling with fluid. He had been stabbed.

"I need linen, a tablecloth, and some tape. Soap. The saline solution I use with my contacts."

She touched back Jimmy White's eyelids with her fingertips.

"Blankets, too," she said. "And my purse."

Orrin's hands clenched and unclenched at his sides.

"Go, Orrin," she said gently. "I don't want to move him."

She went to the fountain in the grotto and scrubbed her hands as best she could, went back and knelt over Jimmy White, meaning to touch his chest, meaning to apply pressure to the wound and stop the bleeding, but she knelt there beside him, with her hands over his body, thinking that no one had been there to do this for June, and she was paralyzed.

The night was coming on fast; the breeze from the ocean, sweet and cooling, lifted her hair from her neck. The sky was clear. There were stars by the thousand.

"You're awfully pregnant," Jimmy White said.

Lindy put her hand to his wound and felt its heat.

"I wasn't going to stop here," he said. "But I can't seem to shake off a knife like I used to."

He licked his lips. She applied pressure.

"Don't talk to me," she said. "I don't want to hear your voice."

He closed his eyes once again.

Orrin had torn the tablecloth into strips. She told him how to fold and hold the bandage to Jimmy White, and she emptied her purse on the grass. Tucked in her checkbook were two packets of Vicodin samples, a couple of Fioricet tablets in a zippered pocket. She held them in front of Jimmy White's face and he opened his eyes.

"See there," Orrin said. "He's up and at 'em."

"You need antibiotics," Lindy said. "I can't get them for you."

Jimmy White took the pills and swallowed. "I'll get 'em in Mexico."

"If you make it there."

Lindy went back to his wound. The bleeding had stopped,

but it was too old and dirty to stitch closed, even if she had the instruments. She told Orrin to tie his arms and legs with strips from the tablecloth.

"You'll still have to hold him down," she said, "but restraints should make it easier."

"Goddamnit, Lindy." Jimmy White spat, and she snapped around to him.

"This is going to hurt," she said.

She straddled him, tucked her knees into his hips to hold herself steady. She pressed open the edges of his skin with the fingertips of one hand, took the bottle of saline, and flushed out the wound. Jimmy White reared up once and then passed out. It made Lindy's work that much easier.

Orrin carried him into the house and tied him to the kitchen table. Lindy filled a basin with warm, soapy water, stripped off his shirt, and sponged him down. She irrigated the wound again, wrapped it tightly, and taped up everything. She hated doing a makeshift job, even if it was only on Jimmy White. From what she could tell, the wound was nearly three inches deep; it had bled well but missed everything major. Unless an infection took over, this would hold him up only a few days.

"So," Orrin said, "did you always hate him, or is this a recent development?"

Lindy sat in the chair opposite Jimmy White. She was tired. Her back shot pain through her hips, and her skin was tight, tired. Jimmy White's chin was slack against his face.

"We were never friends," she answered.

Orrin, leaning in the crook of the kitchen cabinets, studied the floor. He pulled at his lower lip with his teeth, seemed wound tight, charged up. When he spoke, his voice was tense.

"Do you want me to take Little Man to my place?"

Lindy didn't answer.

"I could run him over really quick, be right back. You could come with me, even, and then you wouldn't have to be alone with him."

"Do you think that would stop him?"

"I don't know. I don't know the guy."

"Well. What are we going to do with him until you do?"

They kept watch, Lindy in her chair, Orrin at the cabinets, until Jimmy White came awake. They didn't speak to each other; their fears were separate, discrete, their own. And when Jimmy White reached consciousness, he behaved the same.

Orrin was the first to speak. "Water?"

Jimmy White nodded.

"Can he have water?"

Lindy nodded.

Orrin filled a glass at the tap, untied Jimmy White from the table, and extended his hand.

"Orrin Cordray."

Jimmy White shook his hand.

"What can we do for you?"

Jimmy White laughed. His voice was like steam.

"You all got my son, right?" He looked at Lindy. "You must have known I'd get here."

Jimmy White struggled to sit up. He seemed to lack the joints for it, like a fish trying to sit at a table, but no one moved to help him. He tipped over the glass, and Lindy watched the water puddle on the floor. Orrin was standing between her and Jimmy White like a shield.

"Why did you wait so long to come for us?" she asked.

"I had something else I was doing." He looked at her belly. "Guess you had something else to do, too."

"Shut up," she snapped.

"All right. Let me tell you this. I know who did the thing to June, and I'm taking care of it."

"That isn't going to bring her back."

"Don't you sound uppity, then. I don't think your leaving town with my son is going to bring her back either, but you sure did that. What's done is done, right, Lindy? I'm about moving on."

"I don't believe you," Lindy said. "You once told me you

could never leave June because she'd keep your baby. You told me you couldn't live with that."

"There's a whole lot of things in this life won't be the way I thought they were. I think *you* told me that."

She stepped back. "How'd you get stabbed?"

"How'd you get pregnant?"

"Fuck you."

"Yeah? Me, too?"

He'd been carjacked in Birmingham, he said; a couple of kids with a hunting knife. They'd taken the car, so he caught a bus down here for the medical attention and to see his boy.

"You should just go to a hospital. They can clean that out and prescribe some antibiotics. Have you had a tetanus shot lately?"

"Can't go to a hospital. Can't go back to Charlotte. The cops are still pawing through my stuff. They tap the phone and read the mail and spread the trash over the lawn like a pack of goddamn dogs. When I left, I knew that'd make me their number one man. But you and me have had this discussion before."

"They don't know anything else?" Orrin asked. "Other than you?"

"They got a guy I used to run with in the can on separate charges. They keep thinking he'll roll me over."

There was a long silence.

"But he won't," Jimmy White said.

Lindy was tired; it was nearly three in the morning. She wanted to melt from her chair and stretch out on the floor, and just let everyone walk around her for a few days until she understood what would happen next.

"Are you staying here?" she asked.

Both men answered yes. She pushed herself up from the table.

"I'll get sheets."

Near dawn, she woke in dampness. It was muggy, and she was sweating and being pressed by the baby inside her. Her tiredness had spoiled like a berry. She could hear Jimmy White downstairs getting water from the tap, rummaging in the fridge. He smoked a cigarette. He opened the front door, and she thought maybe he was going, but when it shut, she heard him walking the floors again.

She ducked from Orrin's arms and pulled on a T-shirt. When she crept downstairs, she found Jimmy White at the kitchen table, shuffling Orrin's deck of cards. She sat across from him and he dealt her a hand of something.

"How's Cott?" she whispered.

"He and I aren't real tight, Lindy."

"I know that. But surely you've seen him."

"At first, we'd come across each other in the bars. He told me he drove around all day, looking for you; sometimes he'd drive around at night too. He was real determined. But I get the feeling his thinking has changed. As I understand it, you're not the first woman to burn him."

"What do you know about that?"

"It got to be awful clear that you weren't as dead as you were run off. That can get under a guy's skin. He goes in circles only so long."

Lindy could imagine what Jimmy White wasn't telling her.

"You've seen him other places than bars," she said. "You've seen him when he wasn't alone."

Jimmy White lowered his eyebrows and shot a finger at the ceiling. "Look," he said, low in his throat, "I don't think you're in a position to be raising Cain here, are you? If you were my woman, I'd beat you in the head."

Lindy's stare was enough to start a fire. "Would you?"

"Figure of speech," he said, his hands in front of his chest. "Figure of speech."

Lindy threw her cards at him, pushed herself up from the table. "I was right before. I don't even want to hear your voice, let alone what you've got to say."

As she was leaving the kitchen, he said, "I didn't tell your parents where you are."

Lindy stopped, listened.

He said he didn't tell them what he knew because her flight had thrown the hunt off him. They included him in the midnight phone calls, the plans, the parceling out of information, instead of making him the object of them. Her parents had extended sympathy for a few days, and he was grateful like a dog off the street. He planned to fetch Lindy and the baby himself. He planned to be a hero.

And then they'd stopped their calling, and he realized again how much he hated them. He began to take a mild, numb pleasure in their tripled misery. He remembered what Lindy had told him, how they'd take his son from him first chance they got, and he promised himself it would never happen.

"So anyway. I know he's safe down here with you. And as long as he's here, I know I can find him. These lips are sealed, darlin'. Just this — I need a day before I can get on with it, and I'll be wanting to spend a few hours with my son."

"Oh, just go on and get to Mexico."

"I intend to see my son. Without you around. You hear me?"

"Do you think I'm stupid?" Lindy said.

He took his wallet out of his hip pocket and placed it on the table. He toed off his shoes and kicked them under the table to her feet. The movement made him wince.

He said, "I know what I'm capable of and what I'm not. I'll be right here waiting when you get back."

"The days when our promises meant anything are over."

"So that's the boat we're in, right, Lindy?"

"What if I don't go?"

"I call it on all of us. Right now. What the fuck do I care?"

And she knew he didn't, and that she had no choice. Little Man was his son, and she'd stolen him away. If Jimmy White wanted to have her arrested, he could; if he wanted to have her killed, he could do that, too. They were both outside right and wrong now, and Jimmy White knew that territory better than anyone, which made his command all the more imperative, all the more black.

"Were you calling Esther at the retirement home, looking for me?" she asked.

Jimmy White leaned his chair back on two legs and flipped an unlit cigarette to his mouth.

"I wouldn't have thought to do that," he said. "Wouldn't have needed to, would I."

And somehow that lifted her heart. There was someone, somewhere, looking for her because he loved her still, and not because he wanted what she'd taken away. It didn't have to be Cott. It didn't have to be her father. Anyone other than Jimmy White was almost a compliment. She took the wallet and reached for the shoes from under the table. She turned off the light switch when she left the kitchen, giving Jimmy White the dark.

∿

She and Orrin sat in the cab of his truck across the street from Esther's house. The windows were rolled down, and the breeze moved across their faces, but Lindy had already sweated through parts of her dress and her hair clung to the back of her neck. There was this to comfort her: she knew that Jimmy White, what with the inflammation and the dwindling stash of pain pills, could no way manage to lift and carry Little Man more than a few feet. She had his wallet and his shoes beside her on the seat. She tried to tell herself that was collateral enough, but she knew it was just something to say.

She hated Jimmy White at that moment as much as she ever had, and it was bad for a pregnant woman to spend too much energy on hatred. She wondered about the times during June's pregnancy that she'd been angry with Jimmy White, wondered whether that had passed from her to Little Man. Maybe things weren't going so well at Esther's house because of it. Maybe Little Man had hard feelings toward Jimmy White that went all the way back to the womb.

Orrin started the engine. "Come with me," he said.

"Where are we going?"

"Oh, out of town a ways. I got to get something."

"What is it?"

"Something off the farm," he said. "We can't do much from here."

"We can watch. We can make sure he doesn't leave."

"Lindy," Orrin said, "how far's he going to get with Little Man, the shape he's in?"

"I don't know. How do men escape from prison, survive war? If I had to walk through fire for Little Man, I would. I think I'd be able to get by without my shoes."

"If he's really on the run from the law, Lindy, he's not going to take Little Man. That was what I thought when you showed up. If you've got to move fast, you leave the kids at home."

Lindy shrugged. She didn't speak as they drove across the loops of bridges to the mainland, not because of anger, but because she was preoccupied. There were so many other things a man could find to say when there was something that needed talking about, something like their worry over Little Man, and she was grateful for Orrin's silence. She wished for pureness, directness, or no sound at all.

She looked out at the passing bayous, the canal shacks up on stilts, the topless bars with still-empty parking lots. After Hitchcock, they turned down a highway toward Lake Jackson where the pavement opened out into miles and miles of pasture. The sky was overcast, and the land took on its grayness, reached up for it, and suddenly Lindy wanted a sweater wrapped around her, wanted something between her skin and the moving air. She rolled up her window. Orrin drew his breath.

He turned into a horseshoe drive in front of a long, rambling clapboard house, faded as gray as the coming rain. A passel of dogs circled in the dust, and Orrin whispered at them from inside the truck. "Hey, babies," he said. "Hey, hey."

He sat still, stared ahead of him for a stretch of time that seemed preparatory, important. Lindy was quiet, too. She suspected they'd not be welcome here, at his daddy's house. Orrin looked burdened, and she was sorry for that.

She raised her hand and stretched it toward his arm, but he was moving, leaving, already gone.

He came around her side of the truck, opened the door, and helped her down, but for all his fine manners, they didn't go inside the house and say hello to anyone. The house was quiet, the shades pulled down, the porches swept clean. A wind came up behind Lindy carrying the smell of a barn to her, hay and wet and animals. Around them, so much green and growing, so much earth being put to use. It was a strong place, a weary one.

Orrin's back came straighter out of his belt. He walked a step or two ahead of Lindy, his chin raised, his fingers fooling with something she couldn't see.

"Orrin," she said. "Wait."

She said it mostly to say something, and he nodded, stopped, waited, the dogs nipping at his heels. An Airedale pup came from the pack and tugged at her sundress, causing a strap to slip from her shoulder, and her skin poured out of her clothes, more skin lately than she'd ever thought she had. She watched with a kind of wonder, how she spilled over as if she'd been dammed up, and it was long seconds before she thought to cover herself.

If Orrin had seen it, he made no show.

He led her through his farm, his animals. There were guinea hens in packs, chickens in pens — pens made of tin, tar paper, old license plates, bundles of sticks, lengths of baling wire, chicken wire, railroad ties, stones — pens unfolding one into the other, some open and large, some small and dark as caves. There were peacocks, goats, llamas in a pasture by the barn, horses in the paddock, cats at every turn, and an aviary full of the parrots that had been the first to growl like dogs.

Lindy was taken with the horses, their sleek flesh, the roll of forequarters. Most of them were chestnut, and Orrin leaned his shoulder to the paddock gate and gave out their kind, said paint, quarterhorse, appaloosa, and palomino mare. It was like what he'd done with Little Man in Esther's garden, Lindy thought, and her heart bobbed on a string. It had been months since she'd been anyplace without Little Man, and she missed him now the way you'd miss a limb.

"Wait here for me," Orrin said. "I'll be right back."

She watched him disappear into the barn, but she couldn't be still with her thoughts. She turned into the breeze, felt the sureness of a thunderstorm in it, and she wanted food. She stepped away from the paddock and into a stand of sweet olive, stepped through the olive into an orchard of pawpaw trees, the fruit just beginning to show green on the branches. She knew pawpaw trees from Esther's backyard and the preserves her mother used to put up, and the cream biscuits she'd make to go with the preserves. And now Lindy was so hungry, she thought she might be sick.

In the north distance, she could hear a man's whistling, tuneless, like a call to dogs. She walked toward the sound through the trees and down an embankment, till she stood on the sandy edges of a pond.

There was a man. Leaning against an old dock post, with his knees cocked, his feet braced in the black earth, he was striking kitchen matches on a box and flicking them into the wind. In the pond was a woman. Her head and shoulders, rising from the water, had a slickness that was more than wet, heavier than wet, her skin so thick with it as to look like pelt. She dipped her head back to let her hair into the water, and the hair ran black past her shoulders when she stood. Her skin was iridescent.

She threw a gooosenecked can to the shore, and a bolt of lightning lit the sky.

"Wolfie," the man said, "get on out."

He toed the pile of matchsticks at the water's edge, looked at the rumbling sky as if he were reading a map, a passage from the Bible, something he absorbed more than considered. Farther out in the shallows was a high-poster bed with a blue-ticked mattress, and his eyes fell to that. He did not watch the woman. He did not speak to her again. The woman said something at him, turned away, and saw Lindy on the banks. She smiled.

"Throw me that blanket, old man," she called.

He swung a blanket off a post and into the air, and she caught it above the water by a corner, the rest of it sailing out on the wind. She waded toward Lindy, wrapping her hair first and slowly twining the blanket around herself. Her skin glowed, her belly full and high with a baby of her own.

"Wolfie," the woman said, extending her hand. "Orrin and I used to run to Mexico on the side."

"Lindy." She took the offered hand. "I knew Orrin when we were small."

Up close, Lindy could see the pearled sheen where her skin crossed her bones and could smell the gasoline or kerosene, that mechanical thing in the air around her. She looked out over the pond and the bed in its middle; farther out, a pontoon boat; even farther, a dock. Another flash of lightning showed her pools of the same sheen floating on the water, and on the blanket Wolfie held around her streaks of it were wiped away.

Wolfie stared at her with wide green eyes. "Old man," she called back, "this is her?"

"Yes," he said, "it's her."

And Lindy knew then the man was Orrin's daddy. She'd heard him speak probably a thousand times, but still his voice traveled along her spine like ice, and again she wanted the sweater on her shoulders. She crossed her arms and gave off a tiny shiver.

Wolfie reached a hand to her forearm, left a slick touch, and inclined her head to Orrin's daddy, now ankle deep in the water and raising his arms to test the wind.

"Don't you worry," she said.

"I'm not worried."

"Oh, honey. You should have seen him try to walk on water."

The thunder came, and Wolfie turned to Orrin's daddy and told him he'd better get on with it. He told her she ought to hush her mouth, let him think. Wolfie rolled her eyes, but not at Lindy, and up the bank came a crashing of bodies through the cane, the yipping of dogs. Lindy could hear her name being called, or was that more thunder? She felt faint. She was hungry, and she wanted to be home with Little Man. She sat down in the mud with suddenness, and Wolfie sat beside her just the same, and down from the bank came Orrin, dogs at his feet. He bent to drop a kiss on Wolfie's cheek. In another clap of thunder, every single body became still.

"Daddy," Orrin said.

"Son."

Then Orrin's daddy struck a match, lit a rag-tied torch between his knees. The wind kicked up to help him. Soon there was fire, and he skipped that torch out onto the water as if it were a stone; it flew low and flat to the surface, and its flame trailed back toward the bank, where they all watched; trailed out on the wind with blue and orange and clear, hot color.

The torch hit.

The bed caught; then the surface of the pond around it.

They heard the rush in the air, a great surging sound of fire, and they moved back into the trees to wait for the rain.

Orrin's daddy gazed out at the sky, and Orrin watched him. Lindy wondered what it was like, having to have a father who's a mystery. She suspected it was a pestering thing, a thought on the tip of your tongue, and she could see the loose fit of anger to Orrin's shoulders. She thought that men must receive their tempers early in life, when they had more room inside, and so their tempers grew to be bigger than what women had, harder to rein in, easier to see.

At a clap of thunder, Orrin took her hand and pulled her away. "Thunder like that will sour milk," he said.

He led her through the overflowing gullies by the barn, through the chinaberry and the bramble, past the edges of green, unmowed, unfarmed, unfenced, till they reached the truck. He set her up on the seat and brushed her hair back, tucking its tail over her shoulder.

"You look pretty like that," he said. "You look like June." And he stood, stretched, and walked around to the driver's side.

The truck windows were gray and cast over with splashwater and rain, but Lindy could see the fans of the peacocks, the scatter of hens and chicks in the yard. Daddy and Wolfie were coming up from the pond, Wolfie wrapped in her blanket and her face still sharp to Daddy. She was saying something that called for her to bite off her words. Bending at the hip and the knee, she unknotted a hose to rinse her hair, letting the soaked blanket fall across her back. When she tossed her head back up, Orrin's daddy had disappeared.

"What was your father doing, with the fire and the bed?"

"Miracle-working," Orrin said.

"What miracle was that?"

"Some version of quieting the storm, I think. He likes to bring in a household object when he can."

"Hence the bed?"

"Hence the bed. 'And there arose a great storm of wind, and the waves beat into the ship.' But Jesus was asleep on a pillow. O ye of little faith, and all of that. He thinks he'll bring something about if he keeps at it long enough."

"What's Wolfie's part in it?"

"Oh. She likes to watch."

"Is that your father's child?"

"No." He laughed, but nothing was funny.

"I'm sorry," Lindy said. "I've forgotten to be polite."

"It's her child. Her husband's gone."

But Lindy didn't know whether he meant dead or run off. Gone. That was how she'd described herself, from the first step off the train in Mobile. Gone people were everywhere.

Orrin put his hand to her nape and pulled her toward him. "Something to eat?" He wiped rain from her brow.

"When can we go back?" she said.

He looked at his watch. "We'll get something to eat. Are you hungry?"

"I'm starved."

"I got one more little thing to take care of," he said. "You wait here. Don't go off."

She watched him disappear into the barn and return with a tiny, squirming, liver-spotted puppy under his arm.

"Boy needs a dog," he said. "Hell of a bird dog. This dog's mother could shoot them herself, if you gave her a gun."

He reached out with the puppy, and Lindy saw, tucked into his waistband, what they'd really come out here to get: a small black gun between his T-shirt and his jeans.

Orrin let the bundle of dog into Lindy's lap, let the flat of his hand linger on her stomach, her thigh. The sun came out. It was afternoon, and Lindy thought this trial was almost over.

Orrin took her farther up the road toward Hitchcock, to a little oyster shack, where they ordered bucket after bucket on the half shell, with saltines and cocktail sauce and horseradish. Their knees touched underneath the table, and every once in a while Orrin reached over and fed her a bite of something, as if her hands were too delicate to use for food, and it crossed her mind that they could spend the day in this oyster shack or in the truck, parked across the street from Esther's house; it didn't matter. She would still feel the same patter in her gut, still want Little Man back in her sights, safe and sound. And maybe it would always be like that, some part of her mind turned over completely to the child. Maybe that's what it was to be a mother.

The door opened and let in a cut of late afternoon light. Men filtered from the parking lot with long black instrument cases, and set themselves up on a stage in the corner; loops of Christmas lights blinked on over their heads. A man in a Hawaiian shirt leaned into a microphone and began to sing.

Lindy closed her eyes to listen to his voice, old-fashioned and full of whiskey, a crawl-in-bed voice, a cry-over-a-fool voice. She'd want him to sing for her baby, and it was fast like that she wanted the baby to be his, in a way, wanted to walk down the hallway of some airy white house and hear his voice going at her children like the softest train in the far-off distance.

She looked at Orrin, ringed all around her, and realized she'd thought such about him for a while, since he'd picked up Little Man and began to call him that. She thought how fathers could be found as well as made, and then she stopped her brain, drew her hand across Orrin's knee, and whispered in his ear the best she could.

She said, "All I've been able to think about is my hands on your bare back."

He stood, stripped his shirt over his head, and there was that stretch of skin from his hips, the rise of his stomach to his chest. Orrin would do anything for her; she had only to say the words. He pulled her to her feet and she wrapped her arms around him, and inside was still the thrumming of her nerves, the need to get back to Esther's as fast as they could, but she was held by a promise that was the latest in a long line of scrambling promises she'd made to keep herself on course. She rested her cheek on Orrin's chest. They could have danced, but, instead, they stood beside the buckets and shells and crumple of their meal and held each other. It was as if they'd survived a disaster — a crash, a fire. The man in the Hawaiian shirt sang about all the days he'd been gone away, and Lindy wanted to tell Orrin she would never go away from him, but that was just a wish, so she kept it to herself.

*

Orrin drove with the windows down and the air loud in their ears, the land a blur. He drove fast. They were quiet.

At Esther's house, all the lights were out.

Orrin drew the gun from his waistband, and Lindy slammed out of the truck as fast as she could, her heart racing, the weight of her belly such that she had to hold herself to run. She would not do this again. She would never allow her choices to become this narrow, this desperate. She tore open the screen door, and Orrin grabbed her wrist.

Little Man was on the front porch in a rocker, his parrot perched next to him, as tattered as Little Man, as tired, but untethered and there by his own choosing. Little Man was asleep. His bow mouth was parted and wet, his breathing deep and even. Maybe Jimmy White had tried to take him and failed; maybe Little Man refused to stay inside the house without Lindy. She had no idea how it had gone. Little Man, again, as in his mother's death, was the only witness.

Lindy knelt beside the rocker and stroked his cheek, his hair off his forehead. Orrin appeared with the liver-spotted puppy and placed it in the chair with Little Man, and they watched as the puppy curled itself against his stomach, rested its head on his hip, as if they'd been keeping each other company all their little lives. The parrot lighted, drifted, settled down, and Lindy had all her thoughts about how this was the last, the last, the last. When it was time to go to bed, she didn't want to disturb them. Orrin lifted up the rocking chair, the parrot beat its wings, and Lindy held the door for everyone to pass inside. Their menagerie was safe, and she turned the bolt behind them.

MADE THINGS

L INDY SAT IN ESTHER'S wingback chair at the retirement home and watched the phone ring. She had become unaccustomed to phones in her days in Galveston, so she didn't pick it up. She couldn't imagine how she used to make a living with a phone in her hand. She didn't feel like talking even to the people she could see in person.

Her ankles had swelled up in the heat. She tried not to walk places in the afternoon, when it was hottest, because she'd come to think of her feet as parts of herself she'd rather carry than use, but she needed to see Esther. It was important enough to walk. Orrin had taken Little Man with him and she came down here, had been waiting in Esther's room for nearly an hour. She needed guidance, and Esther was the only person she knew to give that kind of general advice, but she didn't have the energy to go looking for her.

The ringing telephone seemed to conjure her up. Esther strolled into the room on the arm of an orderly. "What did you think, dearie?" She pointed to the phone with Luther's ivory-handled walking stick. "It would answer itself? However in demand I am, it doesn't ring that much."

Lindy passed the receiver to Esther without speaking. It was her mother on the phone; Lindy could tell from Esther's voice, the careful footing, the way the air stopped moving in the room.

Esther said, "No, dear. Well, I don't know anything about that. I don't know why she would say so. It strikes me as cruel."

She turned her back to Lindy, cradled the receiver to her neck. "Well, the woman is a fool; I told you that. I don't think she knows how to sell ice cream in July, let alone an old empty house, and I wouldn't believe her if she came in here and told me the earth was round."

Lindy's breath shuddered in her chest. She tried to remember the day she'd found the real estate agent looking at the house and was certain she hadn't been seen. Maybe the house looked lived in; maybe the agent had been back in the weeks she and Little Man were with Orrin, found food moldering in the fridge, clothes stashed away, slept-in beds. Lindy hadn't left that afternoon expecting to be away.

Esther sighed into the phone. "Now, that doesn't sound like you . . . Because you're my daughter, and I know the manner of your thoughts. You would never in a million years be so . . . negative."

Her voice dropped. She whispered soothingly, and Lindy began to cry.

What was keeping her from taking the phone from Esther's hand, telling her mother hello, that she was safe, that she was pregnant? Her mother would understand. Her mother had run away herself. She'd probably never imagined, in her worst nightmare, that her children would do the same.

Lindy wiped at her face and heaved herself up from her chair. She put her hand on Esther's shoulder and reached for the phone just as Esther was returning it to the cradle.

"Oh," Esther said, "a change of heart?"

Lindy began to cry all over again.

"Oh, now, you can't do that. I can't watch a pregnant woman cry. It makes me want to tear my hair."

"I'm sorry," Lindy pressed out. "I can't help it."

"Another phrase I loathe."

Esther *tsked* her tongue, eased herself into the wingback chair, and continued. "That was uncalled for. I apologize. It's just that I blame you for your mother's sadness, or at least the compound nature of it, and it's become so difficult to talk to her on the phone. Even I feel guilty, and that's a foreign thing to me. Makes me testy."

She smiled at Lindy. "Long time no see," she said.

"I felt a little cast out." Lindy cleared her throat. "I didn't want to bother you here."

"But now you have a worthwhile cause. You've done something, decided . . . what? My clairvoyance is fading with age. What can I do for you?"

"June's husband came to your house."

"Oh, goodness. I imagine that was uncomfortable. Was Orrin there? I assume you and he have progressed beyond the detail."

Lindy nodded to everything.

"So Jimmy White has gone?"

"Yes, but I don't trust him. I worry he'll be back."

"And what would happen then? It sounds to me as if he has no intention of hurting your cause or taking the boy with him. Why would he return?"

"He made a mistake. It happens all the time."

She bit off another sob, and Esther threw up her hands. A wheelchair lurched across the open doorway.

"Arnaud!" Esther called. "Something must be done."

Arnaud wheeled at speed into the room, crashing knee to knee with Lindy. He assessed the situation and gently took her hands in his.

"Oh, now. Now," he said, "let me see. See. How 'bout this, sweetheart? Your grandmother, believe it or not . . ."

"I've heard that one," Lindy said.

"Okay. Okay, your grandmother was the one to lure the

infamous John Dillinger into the alleyway of the Biograph Theater. How 'bout them apples? She was the woman in yellow, who got there before the woman in red. Probably responsible for saving civilization as we know it today."

Esther straightened her back, smoothed her hand across her tired eyes. Lindy sniffed.

"What did you say to him?" Lindy asked her.

"Something wicked, I'm sure. He was a handsome man and I had to lure him away from the stimulating prospect of a movie. I had lovely hair then. Black. Long. I must have said something like, How about you take me to a hotel room and let me lay my hair all over you."

Arnaud's breath left his chest like wind from a jet engine.

"And then he was shot to pieces," he said.

"Well, after he'd agreed to take me any place my heart desired."

"But he was shot to pieces," Arnaud said.

"Millions," Esther said. "The shell casings rattled like keys on the pavement."

Arnaud stared at Esther, and Esther let her gaze wander the distance in her memory, however that memory gauged distance, and Lindy was left with the ghost of her mother's voice to grapple with. She stared at the telephone. Who would she call first, if she started calling?

The baby buffeted at her bottom rib. She had always known he was Cott's baby, but she was coming to recognize a strength in that biology, a pull like the one that brought Jimmy White to Little Man, even as it put him in jeopardy once he left Charlotte. Cott didn't even know she was expecting, but maybe the more pregnant she got, the stronger that pull would become, and soon, for reasons he himself wouldn't fully understand, he'd come and find her.

She excused herself from Esther and Arnaud, saying she was sorry for her little scene, and perhaps she should make her way back to the house and take a nap. She kissed Esther's cheek and left. She was loose inside her own skin, and it would make her sad for days to come.

∾

In those long, doggish afternoons when it was too hot to work, Orrin assigned himself to cheer her up. He insisted they all go into Houston, and he bought the newspaper to look for something they might want to do together there. He read her bits and pieces of things while she watched Little Man levitate a feather in Esther's kitchen. His puppy did not like the parrot. His parrot did not like the puppy. Something would have to give.

Orrin told her the paper said the heat was cresting. As they entered the hurricane season, it would cool off, but personally, he'd rather sweat than worry about his life blowing away. There was a sale on at Buchanan's Nursery in honor of fall planting. There was a rodeo in Alta Loma. Lindy kept thinking he would come across her name or Little Man's, and maybe he'd tell her or maybe he wouldn't, but the experience of listening to Orrin report on the newspaper was like waiting to get bad news through the mail.

He announced they'd found the Evers woman. She'd been someplace in Idaho, saying her name was Mary Poppins.

The story had been front-page news when Lindy first came to Galveston. She'd picked up bits and pieces of it when she was checking the papers, and then it was on everybody's lips in the line at the grocery store. The Evers woman had disappeared back in the spring, leaving a husband, a house, and two kids, and the thinking was that she'd been kidnapped or killed. Why would anyone leave a husband, a house, and two kids? Lindy paid attention to the speculation, because she could imagine her story reading the same way, but here it was, all turned out so different.

"Does she say she had amnesia?" she asked Orrin. "Amnesia is actually quite rare."

Orrin let the paper fold and rolled his eyes in Lindy's direction. "Amnesia, my ass. I say that woman was beat at home and doesn't want to go back. There's nobody who could tell me any different."

"You sound so cynical."

"I'm not. I just know what I've seen. Jesus, Lindy, think of June and that son of a bitch she was married to."

Lindy's brain went like a traffic light. "You knew about that?"

"Hell, you could tell it from the first second you were with him."

He shook the paper back out in front of himself, and Lindy settled back into her silence. If Orrin could spot a beating kind of man right off, why couldn't June? It wouldn't have made any difference; Lindy knew that. You fall in love, you may as well not have eyes to see with. Now who sounded cynical, she thought.

She stretched out across two kitchen chairs and folded up the edges of her T-shirt so that her belly got the fan. She was so hot in these days, she couldn't wear little enough, couldn't sit still enough. Little Man handed his way around the edges of her chairs, around and around, as if she was a wall at the skating rink.

"I don't want to do anything," she said, "where you have to wear special shoes."

Orrin decided. They'd go see the manatee that hung around at the water-treatment plant in Houston. They'd stop at the grocery and buy a sack of romaine lettuce. It was in all the papers how the manatee loved his greens.

"I guess I don't read the papers anymore," Lindy said.

"That's right, Miss Priss. What's the purpose of the newspaper," Orrin said, casting his aside, "if your name's not in it?"

He took her hand and kissed her wrist and pulled her to him to his lap. He said it would be a treat. The next morning, they'd take the truck and roll down the windows and go for the day. She needed the air to be faster around her, needed a change of scenery. Before she knew it, she'd be having a big time.

On the highway into Houston, they passed site after site of road crews. Construction equipment hulked across the road, the earth movers and bulldozers and trucks full of sand. Little Man pressed his forehead against the window and growled. He growled when Orrin pulled the truck beside a building going up. He growled at the asphalt truck laying down the highway. Soon he and Orrin were both growling, and Lindy pressed her fingers to her temples. This wasn't what she needed to lift her spirits.

Suddenly, Orrin swerved into the breakdown lane and jammed on his brakes. Something was in the bed of his truck, he said, but Lindy'd had enough of the horsing around.

"Oh, stop it," she snapped. "Like the psychotic with the pickaxe. Orrin, I'm not up for playing."

"No. I'm serious. Something's moving underneath the tarp."

Lindy glared at him and shouldered open her door. She was out and around the back of the truck, Orrin still telling her how it happened all the time, some creature crawling away to die, and she probably wouldn't want to look, probably wasn't up for that, either. She lifted a corner of the blue tarp he kept over his tools when they weren't locked up. She tugged, tore it free, and flung it behind her, letting it drift over the highway like a kite.

"There's nothing here," she said.

"That was a perfectly good tarp," he said.

Lindy turned and watched it get whisked away on the grill of an eighteen-wheeler. "Well, it's gone now," she said.

"There's a reason I check." Orrin spoke into her ear over the rush of trucks going past. "You want to hear about it?"

He told her there had been an occasion last fall that convinced Esther to put her house up for sale and move to the retirement home. He'd been transplanting seedlings for her all afternoon, and when the time came for him to head back out to the farm, he couldn't find Esther to say goodbye. It was late. The sun had set. He left a note on her kitchen table, telling her when he'd be back to finish up the job, got in his truck, and took off for the evening.

He heard a knocking in the truck bed, but he went to the grocery, stopped by to see a friend, and when he started the truck again, there was the knocking. He drove to the seawall and took a walk, and as he headed back to his apartment, the knocking got louder. He pulled to the curb two blocks from home, took a flashlight from his glove box, and there was Esther. In the bed of his truck, bent and dusty, she lay huddled under his blue tarp with his tools, holding on for dear life, her lips pattering to the sound of traffic.

He touched her back. He said her name. She didn't recognize Orrin, but she seemed relieved to see him just the same. "Good Lord. This is a most uncomfortable mode of travel," she'd said.

It had scared the daylights out of him, and he sat right down on the curb and cried like a toddler.

"I took her home. Stayed with her all night. In the morning, she didn't remember anything about it. She even had me thinking maybe it never happened, but then she put the house up for sale, and that was that."

Lindy looked at him. "Are you trying to be mean to me?"

"No. But you're acting like I'm all joker here. Your nerves are kind of underfoot, you know?"

He shrugged, and Lindy felt like a fool. She was the one turned around inside, and she was taking it out on Orrin. She got back into the cab and dropped her face into Little Man's hair, rich as a rabbit's coat. She needed that advice she hadn't got the other day, something to set her back on her feet, and she could think of no place else to turn. "Orrin," she said, "I think you should drop me back at the retirement home."

"Another half hour, and we'll be to Houston."

"I'd really like to see Esther," she said, and he turned the truck around.

He and Little Man would go to feed the manatee and pick her up on their way back home. Orrin pulled up to the front doors of the retirement home, left the truck at idle, came around to help Lindy down.

She stared over the nose of the truck at the Gulf, high with caps and tide. Orrin stood before her with his hands in his pockets.

"Let me know what you're thinking," he said. "I need a string to follow." He made a tripping motion with his hands and then let them fall to his pockets again. He seemed to want to touch her but not know how.

"I'm being difficult company, aren't I?" she said. "I'm sorry."

"You be the Queen of Sheba if you want to, baby."

Lindy smiled thinly. She felt as if she'd just robbed a bank and had no place safe to go.

"Little Man needs lunch," she said.

"What about you?"

Lindy sighed. "I don't know."

She stood and then wasn't sure what she was standing to do. She leaned into Orrin's shoulders to hold her balance. It was hot; she felt the sweat run over the cusp of her belly, the insides of her thighs.

"The heat's getting to you," he said.

He lifted the hem of her skirt and blew on her legs, sent chills along the skin there. She smiled. He lifted her hem a little higher.

"You enjoy this," she said. "You like my being pregnant and confused, all hot and hungry and sleepy."

"I spoil you."

"Yes."

"I'd be you if I could."

Lindy touched his face. "I think you would, Orrin. I really think you would."

She kissed Little Man's forehead, and watched them drive away.

Inside, the retirement home was mobbed. Old people lined the hallways and spilled into the reception area. The carpets were thick with a scatter of metal transportation: wheelchair and walker and three-pronged cane. Lindy fought her way to the desk, but the nurse, frazzled, was yelling into an intercom system. Lindy was just part of the crowd she was unable to control.

Lindy found Arnaud and grabbed his shoulder.

"Thank goodness you're here, sweetheart," he said. "She's locked herself in and won't come out. Not for all the tea in China."

Esther had been scheduled to give a recital the evening before, but had backed out at the last moment. It was to be her first concert since she'd come to live at the home, and her celebrity was more intact than she realized. In the few short days of planning, the event had built up quite a bit of steam; the seats were sold out, in fact. When people began lining up, both residents and nonresidents alike, Esther locked herself in the conservatory. Arnaud figured she'd just chickened out.

"Not Esther," Lindy said, taking the handles of his wheelchair.

"Well, she says not only is she not playing, but she's not coming out unless we all agree never to mention the incident again."

Lindy told Arnaud to lead the way, and his wheelchair cut through the crowd to the conservatory doors. Through the windows, she could see Esther seated at the grand piano. She was misting with her spray bottle and gazing at nothing in particular. When Lindy knocked, she looked up and came to let her in.

"Did you know," Esther told her, leaning against the door to bolt it, "they've done these experiments where flats of metal get coated with sand? When they play music at the metal, the sand arranges itself in shapes, for goodness' sake. You can make sand dance."

"Really?" Lindy said.

"Yes. It doesn't take much these days to find an audience."

They both sat at the piano and stared at the keys; the banks of velvet seats were perfectly empty. Esther was pensive, and

Lindy was content to sit beside her. She could see the crowd gathered at the door, one angry face after another.

Esther reached over and aimlessly nicked a fingernail along Lindy's forearm, enough to raise a whiteness.

She sighed. "If I had my choice, I wouldn't stay here till the water got hot."

Lindy knew what she meant. It was draining to keep at arm's length the people who wanted you. She leaned over and kissed Esther's cheek.

"I love you," she said, but Esther laughed.

"Don't bother just yet. I seem to have plenty of fight left in me." She lifted her long, trembling hand to Lindy's face, cupped her jaw, and stroked the skin beneath her cheekbone.

"You know," she said, "the natives that settled this island first, they believed in constant sorrow. When a child died, the parents woke at dawn and began weeping; they wept all day, all year long. If you wanted something or didn't like something, you cried about it first. A visit began with an hour of weeping and your host giving over all his possessions. I have always admired that custom. It would make us much more comfortable with tears."

She touched her own face then, followed on her skin the touches she gave Lindy. She seemed disappointed with what she found and let her hands fall away.

"But then," she said, "the Spanish raised their hounds on Indian flesh, as it made for better hunters. The natives had ample reason for sorrow, worried as they must have been about their babies going to the dogs."

Lindy bent her head to Esther's shoulder. They sat for a time like that, and then Lindy whispered, "I love you, Esther."

"Yes, you said that. And I know something that will help you. Learn this, dear. Learn that eventually we grow bored with what makes us uncomfortable. Eventually, we have no choice but to make ourselves content."

Lindy wasn't sure whether she'd done that or needed to. She

wasn't even sure that Esther was talking about her, but she thanked her grandmother and committed the words to heart. Words like those were what she had come looking for.

ഇ

When Orrin came to pick her up, Lindy was exhausted. Back at Esther's house, he insisted that she nap. He took her upstairs and tucked her into bed with Little Man and sat at her bedside until she fell asleep.

"Why are you so good to me?" she whispered.

"Oh, Lindy," he said, and he seemed embarrassed by her question. She drifted in and out; the tease of sleep was heavy. Maybe it was a silly thing to ask.

Then Orrin said, "I don't know that I've even tried." And she was dreaming.

She dreamed she was swimming. She was sinking, then stroking, breathing through the water like a fish. Her legs beat behind her, and she was fast, sure, diving deep, the water losing its color to blackness and her eyes closing, closed, tight. She did not need her eyes. The water on her skin got cooler, the rush in her ears grew louder, the pulse of the water matching the pulse of her blood, and her body going deeper and deeper and deeper.

Later, she tried to open her eyes, but the bright light of the room hurt, as if a flashlight was shining on her face. She fought to see, but it hurt to fight, and then she was dreaming again.

Later still, the front door banged. She brought her hand to her eyes, but the hand was prickly with sleep and fell hard across the bridge of her nose. There was a burning in her stomach, and when she turned her head, a catch in her neck shot pain into her skull. Someone was at the door. Someone calling her name, and banging.

In the bed beside her, Little Man cried with no sound. His face was dark red, his eyes were wet, his mouth was open but silent as a yawn.

She scooped him to her with her good arm, scrambled down the stairs to stop the noise, stop whoever it was at the door, make him stop. Little Man was heavy. The hair on the back of her neck was wet. Her sleep-needled hand spiked hot and she flicked her fingers to make them take the knob.

Joy stood on the porch steps. Orrin's truck idled at the curb, but there was no Orrin inside it.

"Come with me," Joy said, and it was plain that she'd been crying.

Lindy's hand stung with the blood coming back to it. Little Man would not breathe, would not cry; he hung somewhere between, red-faced and hot. Lindy knew Orrin must be hurt — or worse than that. How were she and Joy linked other than by Orrin? She turned, looked to the floor around her feet for some seed of confidence to gather.

"What's happened?" she said.

"It's Wolfie." Joy's voice trembled. "She's losing her baby."

The joints between Lindy and the world shifted, and she had the same sense of disaster as before, but for different reasons.

Joy said Wolfie had called Orrin in the late afternoon. She wasn't feeling right, and she didn't know where his daddy was. She needed a ride to the doctor. By the time Orrin got to the farm, she was hemorrhaging.

Joy could not bring herself to say any more, only that Orrin was at the hospital now, and she was sorry he'd had no other way to get in touch with Lindy. Lindy was already slipping past her toward the idling truck.

Joy drove. Lindy held Little Man on her lap, and he still held his breath. She wanted to shake him into breathing. She wanted to make something go the way it should, and it took determination to keep her hands to herself. Stubbornness, she thought. People could be very stubborn, and sometimes that was to their advantage.

She saw the stained towels in the floorboards.

"Fetal heartbeat?" she asked.

"I don't know."

"Transfusions?"

"They didn't say."

"Who's with her now?"

"Only Orrin. And he's real upset."

An abruption could kill a woman, as fast as a pint a minute. It could kill a child, a mother, as it had killed Orrin's. Joy's face in profile looked almost painted white; her grip was white on the steering wheel. Lindy thought Orrin must be coming apart.

They made the hospital. Lindy put Little Man down to run beside her, held his wrist in her hand, and half-dragged him behind her across the parking lot. She couldn't pick him up and run too. But he stumbled, foundered, and went limp. He'd held his breath so long he'd fainted.

She got him through the emergency room doors and found Orrin leaning against a block wall. There was blood; it was on his T-shirt. He held two cups of coffee. Lindy pushed Little Man into his legs and went on to find the nurses' station.

It was a teaching hospital, like the one where Lindy had worked in Charlotte, and the nurses were accustomed to requests, to questions. The nurse Lindy spoke to said something about the time to choose sides, and Lindy didn't have to ask what she meant.

"May I go back with you?" she asked.

In the ICU, she touched Wolfie's forehead. She was pale and muddled, her lips dry, her hair matted to her skin. They'd put her under for a cesarean delivery when she arrived, and now monitors flashed, tubes and catheters spilled from her. She was still bleeding. She would bleed for days.

"You'll be okay," Lindy said, but there was no sign that Wolfie heard.

The nurse touched her arm. The baby was dying, she said. Was there someone who would want to hold her?

In the hallway, Lindy asked.

"I do," Orrin said. "I will."

He slid his back down the wall, his elbows coming to his knees. Lindy knelt beside him. It was a motion she'd gone through a thousand times before with strangers about to take on something difficult, and in that moment, touching Orrin was like touching a stranger. She let her hand slip from his shoulder.

"I'm going to stay with Wolfie if they'll let me," she whispered.

"That's fine," he said.

He stood and picked up Little Man, started down the hallway toward the nurses' station, and then stopped and called Lindy's name. His face was prooflessly sad, Little Man's head resting against the bank of his shoulder, the two of them like foundlings in a black-and-white photograph. Orrin held her there a long time, frozen in the hallway, yards away from him.

"I'm sorry," he said finally.

"There's no reason," she said.

"Yeah."

But he was not done with her. "I'm sorry that this baby isn't mine," he said, and Lindy's breath clutched in her chest.

He meant the dying baby, down the hall. He meant he was sorry he hadn't had the chance to hold his own baby, the way he would hold this one, but Lindy thought, *What if?* Her hands went to her belly. She felt a turn, a pressing out, a life beneath her touch. She could not take her hands away.

Orrin put Little Man on the ground, still holding Lindy's face with his eyes, and Little Man set off tottering the space between them, slow and roundabout, a step in every direction. They could have stood there for days; who could tell her differently?

Then Orrin was following another nurse out of sight. Lindy walked past Little Man, past Joy, out the doors of the hospital. The sea air was heavy, like a pillow to the face. She took long draws to get her breath. When she heard her name being called she could not find her voice to answer.

Little Man's arms locked around her knees. His mouth was wet on her leg.

"I'm here," she said. "I'm fine."

Her hand went to his hair, curling at his neck, nearly white. She crouched on her heels to hold him and stroked her hands along him, toe to tip.

His knees were skinned from being dragged in the parking lot.

"Oh, Little Man," she said. "Does that hurt? Did I hurt you?"

He batted his eyes up at her, and she bent her lips to his scraped knees and blew an airy kiss. It made him laugh, so she blew again. His body was so soft, so snug against her. It would have been easy to stay right there, nestled at the entrance to the emergency room, for days and days on end.

♪

Joy took her home to Avenue O and made herbal tea. They sat in the parlor and watched Little Man arrange the pettipoint footstools by height and then by color. In such a pleasant setting, Lindy found herself at a loss to understand the afternoon. She'd been asleep, then at the hospital, and now was in Joy's parlor, a different person from the one she'd been that morning. It was enough to make her numb.

She watched the steam rise from her cup. Joy looked sympathetic, but numb herself.

"Well," Joy said. "Do you know Wolfie?"

"I met her. A few weeks ago, at the farm. She's Orrin's boss?"

"She was his boss's wife. For a time, she and Orrin did something illegal in Mexico. Drugs, I think. I never wanted to know."

"Sometimes it's worse to know."

"Sometimes."

The words were light, but Joy's voice trembled in the air. Lindy could see her mind roll back to the hospital, maybe Wolfie's trip to the hospital, maybe hers before that. She needed to keep talking, and Lindy listened.

"Wolfie's husband left her," Joy said, "and she was devastated.

Orrin was still living out at the farm, but he and I were out of touch. I think it was very painful for him to see Wolfie mourning. He's an empathetic man."

"Of course," Lindy said, and Joy went on.

"Wolfie wanted a baby very much, and I guess Jack . . . well, who knows the workings of a marriage. After he left, she discovered she was pregnant, and it became her lifeline. She threw out all Jack's clothes. She sold his car and his house, but she wanted that baby."

Lindy rested her head on the back of the overstuffed sofa. She knew, for Orrin, the desire to grant someone's wishes was overwhelming. Anything she wanted from him, she had only to ask for. She thought of the day she'd met Wolfie out at the farm, the kiss Orrin had dropped on her cheek, a sweet kiss, a kiss for someone he cared about. Maybe he'd cared enough to give her a child, if that was what she'd asked for.

"Joy," Lindy said, "Orrin was so torn up at the hospital; he said he wished the baby was his own."

"I heard what he said." Joy's teacup rattled on her knees. She stared at it, as if it might solve the problem. "The child was Jack's, of course. Wolfie and Orrin have always and ever been only friends."

Somehow that made Lindy sadder. She was sad for Orrin, because he grieved for another lost baby and for the baby he had lost. His life before she came into it was as long and complicated as her own, and as full of regrets.

"There are things we do from pain," Joy said. "Surely you can understand that." She looked at Lindy's belly and then to her face.

Yes, Lindy said. She could understand that. She understood, too, that nothing Orrin might have done would turn her away from him, nothing she might hear would make her think she did not love him anymore.

She reached an open hand across the coffee table, and Joy took it. Lindy knew that sometimes it was so difficult to just be offered sympathy. When Joy spoke, her voice was just above a whisper.

"Twice a year, I'm desperate for him again. My chest hurts as if the life is being squeezed from it. I think it will never pass, but it does. And some months go by before it happens again."

"Do you think it was a mistake to leave him?" Lindy asked.

Joy was silent. Finally, she spoke. "I know there hasn't been a single morning when I don't feel all that for my lost child."

Little Man came over to Lindy and settled his head on her knees. She wanted to bend to him and smell his hair, breathe him in, but her belly blocked the way. With one hand, she smoothed his curls back from his forehead. He seemed so content, so compassionate of her knees, that it broke her heart.

Joy could not look away herself. The tea grew cool in their cups, and then Lindy let go of Joy's hand, took Little Man, and left.

✑

When she got back to Esther's house, it was past midnight, and Orrin was waiting for her on the porch. He seemed not to know what to do with himself, so she made decisions for him. She led him to a chair and made him sit, and went upstairs to put Little Man to bed. When she returned, she sat down next to Orrin, and that night they rocked away on Esther's porch once again, not touching, not lovers. He rubbed his palms clean on his thighs, stared off into the night sky. His jaw was set hard; his face was wet from the heat, the salt air, his heavy regrets.

"There's a meteor shower tonight," he told her. "If we're patient, we'll see the sky filled with falling stars."

"They've always made me sad," she said.

"A soul gone up to heaven," he said. "What could be sad about that?"

She reached her hand to the back of his neck, and he bowed his head under her touch, as if she'd granted him a favor.

"'Earth's the right place for love,'" he said. "'I don't know where it's likely to go better.'"

"That's pretty."

"A piece of poetry I remember."

"And you remember lots of poetry."

"It's a poem by Mr. Robert Frost."

"Say it again," she said.

"I love you, Lindy. Here on earth. That's what I was saying."

Lindy knew it was true, that they loved each other even though doing so wasn't pretty or neat or proper. She pulled his mouth to hers. To kiss him made her head go light, made her feel that he was drawing her out, the way you'd salt a piece of fruit for its juice. She could kiss him all night long.

She had come to see how loving someone took away from her, split and turned inside her, took parts of her wherever it went. A part of this love she had for Orrin went to Joy, a part to the baby they'd lost. And so what: she'd gone away from Cott and fallen in love with Orrin. One didn't cancel the other. The child she carried would send her heart in another direction, and there was what June had taken, what Little Man had, what her parents kept. She did not know how each love could accompany the others. She knew only that it was happening, and she did not want to think about it too hard lest it not happen anymore.

They went to bed, and in the morning, Orrin wanted to tell Wolfie where she could find her husband.

He sat on the edge of Lindy's mother's bed, Little Man's sleeping body curled around his hips. It was early and they whispered.

"You know where he is?" Lindy asked. "Have you always known?"

"It was last winter. I came across him in Cuernavaca. He passed me on the street. I don't even think he saw me. He was whistling that song about the chestnuts roasting."

"It was Christmas," Lindy said.

"Yeah, Christmas, and this man I've known since I was knee high, he walked right past me. Just like anybody else."

"Did you tell him Wolfie was pregnant?"

"I didn't even tell him hello."

"Really?"

"Really. Weigh it out," he said. "It's what you'd have done in my shoes, what you'd want me to do."

His words flipped on her, and it was a long cool moment before she spoke.

"Orrin, I was going by a whole different set of rules."

"Like what?"

She shrugged. "I guess I don't know."

He tipped her back into the pillows so that she had to look him in the face. "I'd like to know," he said. "I'd like to know what you think is going to happen. Because there's some guy out there who's going to find out about his kid you've got, someday, by some fluke. Maybe a friend of yours will pass him on a street and not be able to keep quiet. He'll find out. And he'll want his share."

"I'm sure you're right."

"So what are you going to do about it?"

"I hate a question like that."

"It's the only kind I got."

"Then don't talk to me."

Orrin sighed heavily and let himself back on the bed. He was frustrated with her and with not knowing what to do about it.

"My hands are tied," he said finally.

Soon after, he left for work. When he came back to Esther's in the evening, he said he hadn't spoken to Wolfie. All night long, Lindy felt the press of his confession, a constant fluttering weight within her. They did not speak of it, and had little else to say.

Days passed. Orrin left for work in the morning and returned at sundown. They were quiet with each other, not distant, but not talking. Lindy asked again.

"No," he said. "I haven't seen her yet."

"Have you gone looking?"

Orrin didn't answer.

"Are you sitting this fence," Lindy asked, "for my sake? Because I didn't ask you —"

"For Christ's sake, Lindy. You didn't ask. You just are. There's what you are, sitting out there like a blinking red light. What do you think I'd do if somebody turned you in right now? You think I'd care whether they were telling the truth?"

"You're angry," she said. "At me."

"No, I'm not." He sighed. His voice was tired.

He was sad for Wolfie. He wanted to give her something she could use, now, when her life must seem useless. Lindy could understand that. When she spoke, she felt the heat of the conversation drain away.

"When I was a nurse, patients told me things because they thought they were dying. They figured it might make a difference in how they died, as if whether or not they loved their husband might save their life."

"Did it?"

"I have no idea. I think people believe in last-minute salvation. I think people believe the truth is a good thing and will help us if we need the help."

"But you don't."

Lindy raised her shoulders, crossed her arms atop her belly.

"No. It's not good. It's neither here nor there."

Orrin started to speak, but she brought her fingers to his lips.

"There was a time," she said, "I'd have thought you needed more reason to track that man down than it's the right thing to do. I'd have thought about myself and how I'd hate that to happen to me. But my thinking about what's fair is changing. Maybe Jack had reason to be gone. Maybe he has reason to come back now."

Orrin kissed her fingertips, her lips, her cheek. He didn't say anything else, and neither did she.

Moments after he left, it began to rain.

⁂

Piece by piece, Little Man's puppy ate his Big Wheel. Lindy could hear the chewing and thumping as the dog finished one part and began on another. It had been raining for days, and the ceiling leaked in a dozen places in her mother's room alone, but rain was just the edge of it. A hurricane was coming.

The water had risen and was lulling at the gutters in the street, coming up to saturate the lawns, flush the sidewalks, lap at the edges of the porch. For days, the storm had been building off the coast, drawing warmth into itself at eighty miles an hour. Twice it dashed at the coastline and backed away, at Corpus Christi, Port Aransas, moving north, allowing its wind and wave and strength to swell. Twice it had risen, choosing neither to strike nor to wear itself thin over land.

Upstairs, Lindy listened to the radio, which called for the hurricane to break up and become a tropical storm by morning, a good deal more rain, some high winds, a few downed trees at the worst of it. The station was broadcasting from Houston, and it played soothing music, Brahms, a lullaby.

But at the seawall, the waves were growing, ten feet, twelve feet, then over the seawall onto the boulevard, down the alphabet streets into driveways and carports and garages. Most of the island had been evacuated already. Orrin was to pick up Lindy and Little Man in an hour, and they'd make for higher ground.

Little Man took his puppy by the tail and slid down the steps on his behind, one by one, to the mullions, to the screen door. He could reach the knob on his tiptoes. The door was light if he leaned against it. The wind outside blew his curls off his forehead; the rain made his face wet; the ocean came all the way up the street with its white waves, and Little Man laughed. The puppy wrapped around his legs in his scamper to get outside, and Little Man followed right along after him.

It took Lindy only seconds to recognize the sound of the door opening, the slap of it caught on the wind and thrown against the house, and she was surprised less at the sound than at the force of weather outside. She pressed her fists to the small of her back and made her way down the stairs carefully so as not to slip on what she couldn't see. The rain came scattering into the foyer from the open door, sheets of it, then waves, the rain rising off the floor as if it were coming from the wood itself.

With a yip, Little Man's puppy was right there on the oriental carpet, but no Little Man was attached to him. No Little Man at all.

Lindy jumped the last few steps and ran out the open door.

Little Man turned from where he stood on the curb, the water at his knees and getting higher, turned and saw Lindy and started to cry. He took a step in her direction, lost his balance, and slipped, his head going under, his footing lost. He pushed himself back above the water and called her name.

He was in the street now, farther away by the minute.

"Don't move, Little Man," Lindy yelled. "You stay right where you are. You keep both feet down."

He brought his hands to his face, but a swell caught him from behind and pushed him farther away. The water was up to his thighs, or maybe he wasn't standing anymore. Lindy thought she heard his crying, but it could have been her own breath, could have been the wind. She was moving as quickly as she could.

"Hold still!" she yelled. "Hold still." She stretched for his hands, but Little Man was cupping his face with them.

A branch in the current struck her legs and pitched her down. She rolled and caught herself on her hip, her elbow, but she'd struck asphalt and she could feel her skin rasping away. She knew they were in real danger.

To get Little Man, she'd have to pull him down with her.

She snatched him by his shirttail, then into her arms and up to her chest in spite of her belly, held his legs across her body and his head in the palm of her hand. He was coughing. It was raining to beat the band.

"It's just water," she whispered. "It's just water. Just water," but she couldn't even hear herself.

It was water in waves, breaking around Lindy's stomach and bent knees where she sat, washing her face in sheets. She struggled up and dragged them to the house.

Inside, the floorboards were seeping. It was coming on much faster than had been anticipated. Little Man squirmed in her arms to get more flesh to her flesh, more of him touching her, not to get away. She reached up to wipe her eyes and wiped away a contact lens.

Her vision shifted, became wavy, dim. Pain shot through her right leg, a pinched nerve, and she held very still for it to pass. She found herself humming and then Little Man hummed with her. They stayed by the front door with the puppy and watched the streets fill up with rain.

Lindy thought of Esther's favorite hurricane, the Great Storm, a hurricane before the time when hurricanes were given names. It was the worst natural disaster in North America, even to this day. The Gulf and the Galveston Bay met over town, and whole buildings got swept away, wind a hundred miles an hour, water twenty-five feet and more. In the streets, shingles cut people in half. Esther's father drilled holes in the floor of the house so that the floodwaters would weigh it to the ground.

If Esther was nearly a hundred years old, then she would have been younger than Little Man in that storm, maybe even a baby in her mother's belly. Lindy knew hurricanes could bring on a woman's labor, the extremes of pressure, the fear for your life. She was frightened now, as she imagined her great-grandmother must have been.

Then there was Orrin's truck, cutting a wake at the curb, his cages of birds tied and tarped down in the back. He leaned across the seat to open the door for her, and she and Little Man ran.

Bridges were closing, gullies flooded with rainwater and wind water. Any time now, the roads would begin washing out. Orrin's hands were tense on the wheel; Lindy could feel his tension. The baby inside her had the hiccups, an even rhythm at her ribcage. By the time they got to Hitchcock, the truck was crawling through a foot of hurricane washing across the blacktop.

At the farm, Orrin's daddy was building an ark.

"We're going to have to run for it," Orrin said. "Give me Little Man."

"I've got him."

"For Christ's sake, Lindy, let me help you."

"It's okay," she said, but he gathered her and Little Man into his arms and carried them through the rain to the barn.

Inside, it was cool and smelled of close bodies. The building had been an icehouse at the turn of the century and held coolness by nature, had survived dozens of hurricanes. Underneath a trapdoor was a reservoir once used for saltwater refrigerant. It was now filling up with the rain, so they would be kept dry a little longer than the rest of the world. After the reservoir was full, they would have the ark.

Wolfie's brothers and cousins, stripped to their waists, used chainsaws and hasps and nails held between their teeth. They'd pulled the pontoon boat up from the pond, built a platform on the floats, and were now at the business of loading it with blankets and water and Sterno and supplies. They'd been at the building since first rainfall. Lindy grabbed at Orrin's sleeve, but he was already loosing himself from his shirt, climbing up the wood and splinters to take a hammer, to help.

Lindy held Little Man in her arms as though she would never put him down.

The dogs were corralled in the hayloft, threatening the rails. The guinea hens and chickens and peacocks and parrots roosted high in the rafters, up above the stacks of cats. The horses and goats paced in their stalls. Lindy, sore and heavy, stayed on the ground and held tightly to Little Man until a cheer went up in Spanish.

It was done.

Orrin lifted Little Man, took Lindy's hands and helped her foot the pontoons, the ladderboards, over the railings to the deck, then left to fetch his cages of birds and Little Man's puppy.

On the foremost part of the ark, the men stretched their languid bodies in scattered hay, pillowed themselves on the backs of llamas, and opened bottles of beer. From overhead rained the luminescent feathers of birds: the parrots and peacocks, hens and chicks. Someplace, there was the yipping of dogs, the beat of the storm on the outside, the light of lanterns within. There was the smell of the horses, the cant of Spanish. Little Man moved from beast to beast, stroking their heads like a nursemaid in a war.

Wolfie lay curled in a corner on a stack of pillows. She turned, rolled, squinted into the lantern light. Her face had changed since she lost the baby, turned colorless as paper, her body slowly sinking back into itself. She was a beautiful woman in her loss; Lindy had begun to appreciate that kind of beauty.

"How is she?" Lindy asked, and Orrin shrugged.

"Did you tell her?"

"Not yet."

He stretched out beside her with a hand of cards fanned against his chest. He wavered in and out of sleep, his breath changing, fluttering. Lindy had no idea what time it was, whether it was time to sleep or not. There were no windows in the barn, nor was there light outside to tell time by. Her eyes ached from the strain of her gone contact lens.

"I love to sleep in the rain," Orrin said. "There's nothing more relaxing than a nap in the rain."

He pulled at her hand and she moved closer but did not lie beside him. When she stroked his hair, it was as though she'd done so every day of her life. How was it they had not always been together? She must have carried Orrin in her head since she was a child. Suddenly, she knew she would carry him still, long after today, no matter what happened. She imagined that such thoughts accompanied death and the saddest of love affairs. She did not want either. She lay back in the wake of hay and prayed that neither would be hers.

The wind howled and beat itself against the barn. The floodwaters were rising, lifting the ark to float on the pontoons. Wolfie's brothers and cousins called out to one another and crossed the deck, carrying their lanterns as if they were walking with balls of light. The smells of the animals clung to the air, making it as thick as cotton. Lindy felt as if she were the only one who knew there was a hurricane outside. She knew she was the only one who felt it in her bones.

Little Man reclined among feather and fur and flesh, fastened around the neck of a kneeling llama, his baby parrot on his shoulder, peacocks fanned before him, the liver-spotted puppy at his feet. He'd all but forgotten the scare in the water, and Lindy wished her mind could be so forgiving, her heart that clear. Perhaps all children were resilient like that, their fears rolling off them.

When she held out her hands to Little Man, he came running.

"Where's Little Man?" she asked, and he pointed to his head.

"Where's Lindy?" she asked, and he pointed to his heart, his chest, where she had pointed to herself to show what she meant.

She asked for a kiss, and he leaned his mouth close to hers, blew some air on her cheek, and ran away.

Wolfie came over and crouched at Lindy's shoulder, her elbows braced on her knees. "You're lucky," she said.

"I hope so."

"I'm a big believer in luck."

She told Lindy how she used to go to work wearing ribbons holding amulets and talismans and milagros pinned to her underwear. Miss Clotilde, the curandera, gave her massages, sometimes with eggs for divination, fed her pomegranates and saffron, cinnamon, aloe, sweet flag, valerian. She herself was from Oaxaca; when the Zapoteca women gave birth, they always wore masks, and when she was born, curanderas were in attendance. There were those who sucked in and those who blew away and those who lit candles.

"I could light you a candle if it would make you feel better."

Her gaze never left Lindy's belly.

"I feel okay," Lindy said. "Really, I do."

Wolfie shrugged, as if Lindy could have it her way, but she knew otherwise. Then she rested her hand on Lindy's stomach, her fingers moving slowly, lightly as she spoke, the way one might spin a globe.

Wolfie said, "They told me I need to be looked at every few days, but I don't know. I don't want to go back to that hospital. You're a nurse, Orrin says. You could do it. You could live out here with me until your baby comes."

"Thank you."

"I could make up for what I may have done to your luck."

"The arrangements I've made for myself are delicate."

"I don't need to know any of that. I only thought we might make a deal."

She knelt, swept the cards from Orrin's chest and stacked them on the deckboards to a count of three. She made the motion quickly and easily but then seemed to regret it, seemed ashamed to be so familiar with Orrin. Lindy let it pass.

She still couldn't tell whether it was day or night, or when it had last been those things, so she told time by her body's rhythms, her body which had become bigger than herself, as big as clocks and light and weather. She had to pee every few hours. She was hungry every few hours. She could not sleep for very long, and so time passed in those small increments.

The ark rose and sank on the floodwaters. Lindy heard the hurricane eye passing overhead, its strong, eerie silence, as she and Orrin curled together. She felt the pressure of the weather in her body, remembered how storms and fronts could bring on labor, and again was fearful of the forces outside at work on her insides. She slipped in and out of sleep, waking to the pressure in her ears, the straining of the wind, the banging of the planks in the stalls.

"A storm like this could run you out of town."

Lindy rubbed her eyes, as if rising from out of a dream, not certain what she'd heard, who'd spoken. She closed the eye without the contact lens, then the other. Orrin's daddy stood over her, his hands crammed into his pockets.

"Is it worse?" she asked, thinking he was trying to tell her something he was not.

He stood over her for a long minute, and Lindy wanted to

cover herself with her hands. His eyes were piercing blue, even in the dark, his voice preacher-deep. "I'm not my boy's friend; never have been," he said. "And he don't live under my roof, so his business is his own."

Orrin stirred in his sleep, tucked his face into the back of Lindy's neck. Daddy stiffened, soured, spat on the deckboards. "But I tell you this," he whispered. "He ain't stupid. He knows it ain't worth a dime if you got to beg for it."

"And you think he's had to beg for me?"

"I ain't saying he has or he hasn't. But I wouldn't go expecting it if I was you."

"I don't," she said, but he had disappeared into the darkness, into the sound and scent of animals as instinctual as himself.

She began to feel a change inside her, a tensing, a tightening across her middle that neared pain — and then she wasn't sure. She lay still beside Orrin, listened to his breathing, her own breathing, even and deep. She could hear, feel, a heartbeat and had no idea whose it was, Orrin's, hers, her baby's. She waited. She was patient.

She realized that what she'd made with Orrin was also a living thing. What they had between them was growing its own parts, readying itself to be born away from her, and she had no choice but to let it happen. It was the way these things had gone for centuries, and as natural as the rain.

୬୦

It was all over that next morning. The ark returned to land, and some of Wolfie's brothers threw open the barn doors to a crystalline sky, swept clean and unbelievably blue. All the pens, the wire and siding and sheets of tin that had kept the animals, were now piled at the side of the barn, the plywood had blown loose from some of the windows on the house, and the earth, where you could see it, was scraped raw.

Lindy plucked Little Man from his manger of animals, shook Orrin awake. She hadn't slept since the few streaks of labor in her back and belly. They'd stopped, but she was on the hunt now, listening for everything.

"Let's get out of here," she said, and they did.

The ground was shot through with rivulets and puddles of the receding floodwaters. The bed of Orrin's truck held tree branches, lengths of wire, roofing tiles; the gullies were still high, pasture fence broken, trees down. Livestock wandered along the shoulders of the highway, and the sky was like a brilliant stone. Orrin made her close her eyes as they drove across the bridge to Galveston so that when they got there, she could see full force what had happened while they were gone.

In the aftermath of the Great Storm, a hundred years before, Galveston was a two-story pile of wreckage, six blocks long, the ground as clean as if it had been swept. Six thousand people had died. For nearly a year, men loaded bodies and pieces of bodies into carts for burial at sea, only to find them, later, washed ashore. After that, there were the burnings. The pyres burned for a solid month, and then they built the seawall.

Orrin took her straight there.

He parked the truck and let her open her eyes on the angry, leaping gulf, the waves licking at their tires, a slab of house siding clattering beneath them like a knocking at the door. The whole island was silent, no traffic on the boulevard, no one else on the sidewalks. The streets were empty of anything familiar, only drifts of sand across the blacktop, broken glass, broken boats, the high, wide waves, and Lindy, Orrin, Little Man.

And Lindy's old gold Cadillac, where she'd left it, months ago.

"I'll be damned." Orrin dropped his arm from her shoulders. "A lesser car would have blown away."

The rear window was shattered, the interior soaked with gulf water, swimming with fish and house parts, glass, sand, as if it were an ancient aquarium. Orrin slapped at its fender and laughed.

They would get the car towed out to the farm. He knew a

man in Hitchcock who would know just how to make it right, and the way he saw it, if a thing as mighty as a Cadillac returned to you out of a hurricane, well, it was always yours, forever more, and had been to begin with.

"They say the red eye of Jupiter is a hurricane," he said, taking Lindy full in his arms. "I wonder if they see a red eye when they look at us from space."

"I wonder," Lindy said, and she could think of nothing to add. She and Orrin had said such things to each other for months, big blooming things, but now it was as if she'd lost her place and couldn't remember what came next.

"Will you take me back to Esther's house?" she asked, and he turned the truck in that direction.

The house was gone, nearly whole cloth. Orrin started to drive right past and get Esther from the retirement home, but Lindy made him stop and let her out. She waited on the curb and studied the remains of the foundation, pieces and parts winding into the sky, the staircase to a single room, a single bed, all else dissolved into the strange dark blue wind of the day. She wanted to cover the mess the way you'd cover a body with a sheet.

She thought of Cott. This would have been Cott's dream, to start building the world all over again, from scratch. He would have loved this, and she couldn't help but smile.

Then came the chuff of Orrin's truck behind her, Esther's arm resting on the rolled-down window. Here was a hundred years of her and more, scattered in the trees, across the lot, into the street. Lindy watched her face for high dramatic pain, but there was only a tiny wrinkled brow.

"I never would have sold the place," she said.

"I'm sorry," Lindy said.

"We can clean it up," Orrin said. "You have the lot, and there's insurance."

She laughed. "Insurance. That's for you children. I'm too old for putting my teeth beneath my pillow."

Then her tears came, and Lindy apologized once more.

"Not your doing," Esther said. "Not anything to worry over."

And she was quiet. The whole island was quiet. For many lean minutes, Lindy stood on the curb and Esther wept over what her house had become, and there were no stories to tell about it, nothing to compare it to, no wishes to make in the face of this. Everything was gone, changed, accepting the quiet it deserved.

Lindy moved forward into the wreckage, running her hand over a pile of glass and splinters and wet mess. Someplace, there was the silver hairstick Orrin had given her, the dozen charms of the witch. Someplace, there were the contents of the cedar closet June had found the last time she was here, the toe shoes and hoop skirts and clothes they'd worn as costumes when they were children. Underneath a china cupboard, Lindy found a basket of dirty laundry tossed with shards of cup and dish, soaked with rain. Everything was coated with silt. Everywhere was sheet music. Everywhere was piece and part of a piano.

When she turned around, hours had passed. Little Man was stomping in puddles on the street. Orrin's truck was parked at the curb. He was leaning against the passenger door with his ear bent to Esther's lips. They'd been watching her the whole time, talking between themselves. She let the trinkets she'd collected fall from her hands.

Orrin went to fetch Little Man, and Esther crooked a finger at Lindy. "You know," she said, "sooner or later, I have to call your mother, and I don't think I can keep her from coming here."

"I know. I've known that all day long."

"I leave the choice to you then. You can make the call or I will. Whichever one you want."

Lindy felt the day trail behind her like a lifetime, and she was certain that if she were to look in a mirror, she would be older, grayer, just since the storm. She could sense what was coming, and what was coming after that, the huge release of letting it all come apart. By nightfall, by weekend, but soon; she could end it, or she could let it end.

The longer I wait, she thought, the less is my decision.

ℐℛ

What there was left to say to Orrin was only words.

"I love you," she said. "No matter where I live."

He shook his head. "Oh, Lindy. Don't."

They stood in his kitchen. He was talking out of fear, and her heart went to him. She was scared, too, and she told him that, even as she hated to hear the words out loud. He went to take her in his arms, but she had things to say first, and she backed away.

She told him there was a strength to doing something simply because you promised to. She'd once promised to love Cott. The baby she carried was his. She was changed from the woman she'd been when she left Charlotte — Orrin had changed her — and that meant she wanted to return on her own two feet, the way she'd left, and not be pulled back because she'd been hunted down.

"My life is with this baby," she said. "His baby. It's still possible, I think. I owe him the choice."

Orrin slid his back down the wall, his elbows to his knees, his hands to his face. She thought he would cry, and she wasn't sure she could stand that, but when he looked back to her, the chance was gone.

"I don't want us to be sad," he said finally. "We do that alone. I don't want us to be sad together if we don't have to be."

"Orrin," she said, "you never asked me if I still loved him, if I wanted to go back to him. It was as if that didn't matter to you."

"It didn't."

"And I took that up myself. A whole lot of things didn't matter to me either — whatever happened with you and Joy, and what the two of you had been through. So here we are. All those things that didn't matter are right here on our doorstep."

249

"Is that what you think?" he said.

"That's exactly what I think."

Orrin battled something inside himself. He opened his mouth to speak, and then shut it.

Lindy made herself as plain as she could. "Esther is going to call my family back in Charlotte, and they'll come to help her. They'll find me here, and I have to be ready."

"You could go out to the farm."

Lindy realized, months ago, she would have done exactly that, let him hide her away until the next desperate occasion called her to move on. She drew a long breath, spoke carefully.

"I can't," she said.

"You can't go, Lindy."

And then he told her why.

Nearly two years ago, June had come to Galveston. She'd stumbled on Orrin in Esther's garden — the bend of his tan back at some machine — and she'd recognized him, all grown up. She'd thrown her arms around him and kissed his cheeks, pulled him to Esther's front porch, and let the night whisk away.

They drank their way out of his cooler of beer. Drank their way inside and upstairs and into the sheets. June had been honest with him. She said she'd always wanted a man who would kill for her, a man who'd write a song about her, a man who'd live the rest of his life with the sweetness of her skin a taste in his mouth. She said, in the end, that these were the things she wanted, but she'd gone and got married anyway.

She told him she wanted a child all her own. That was a possibility she wouldn't hide from him, but wouldn't share either, if it came to pass.

He left her in the night, in the bed, slipped out and away from her and did not return to Esther's house for weeks after, so as not to run into June, so that she could be alone with what she wanted.

"Little Man," Orrin said. "I've kept after him, in my mind. And then you all just showed up."

Lindy felt the heat rise in her chest.

"Why now?" she asked. "Why tell me now?"

"Because I need him. Little Man." Orrin raked his hair with his fingers. "I don't know. Because I need *something* from you."

They were quiet, Orrin's words in the air as fragile as glass. Lindy was breathless. She knew that a course was now complete. She found herself thinking, *So this is it. So this is what really brought me all this way to Galveston.* She did not feel angry or hurt. She felt right.

Orrin said, "It's out now, Lindy. Everything is truly told. I want you to be with me, and I want Little Man to be with me, but I won't beg you for it."

"I won't ask you to," she said.

He stepped away, closed the door silently behind him. She listened to his footsteps in the hallway, the soft click of the front door, and his truck engine turning over where he'd parked it in the street — all the sounds of Orrin going away from her. Now she knew that June had heard these things, too, the night he left her, if he'd left her, if any of this was true at all.

"Little Man," she called. "Little Man, come here."

From the kitchen, he came, lit behind by the falling light, his fine white hair, his baby skin, pale in all the places she and June were their darkest. She could have seen it if she'd wanted to. She could have known this months ago.

She took Little Man into her lap, put her lips to his forehead. It had never mattered to her much who his father was. He was the last piece of June here on earth. That she knew, and that was all she cared about.

She carried Little Man down the stairs and out onto the street. She could see Orrin's truck still where he parked it, the engine running, could see him sitting behind the wheel, watching her. She imagined he'd watched June just the same, even as he said he hadn't. She imagined he couldn't have resisted.

She walked barefoot down the sidewalk. He let his arm hang from the window. She walked right up to his ear and whispered,

"When I come asking you for something, it will be as huge as this."

He took her hand and kissed it. He turned off the engine, opened the door, stepped out, and helped Little Man into the truck. Lindy went back inside alone. She left Little Man and Orrin to their business, and not once did she panic, not once was she nervous. She watched them for a time from the front glass of the apartment building doors. Orrin had his arm around the boy. She heard him tell how the red dust on Mars made for pretty sunsets. Up there, the sun was cold and far away, but it set like the devil himself.

His son. As much as Little Man was a piece of June, he was a link to her. Lindy knew sometimes that was how we kept hold of what we'd lost, what we're losing. We tie ourselves together, make what we have bigger and stronger and huge enough to wrap around us, and now, always, Little Man would be a link to June and to Orrin. She watched the boy point his baby fingers to the sky. She knew in her heart it was how June would have wanted it, if June could have made the choice.

❧

Late that night, they drove Orrin's truck out to the center parts of the island, out where the seawall ceased to be and the pastures full of horses ran right up to the water. It was a balmy August night. Lindy's belly was tight against what clothes she wore. They had a plan to go swimming. They had Little Man, drowsing on the seat between them, and they held hands across his lap so that they'd not let each other out of touch.

The beach was white in the moonlight. Orrin drove the truck over the sand, killed the engine. They listened to the rush of water before them, its pounding upon the solid land, force upon stillness. Lindy slipped out her other contact lens and threw it to the wind.

She believed Little Man was Orrin's. She believed Orrin had told the truth, and, too, she thought there were gradations of truth-telling. There's the truth of what you'd do in a situation that may never come to pass. There's the truth of how you feel when you know it won't change a thing.

Orrin asked, "If I up and went to France, would you come with me?"

He told her again of the sea turtle, leaving these shores and ending up there years later, still marked as coming from Galveston. He had suitcases of money; it would be even more when they turned it in for francs. He told her of the Seine and wide boulevards and the long tight skirts he'd buy her, cafés where they would linger, strange clouded drinks they would mix for themselves at the table, like the people in Hemingway's books.

He opened the door and took her hand, helped her down from the truck and out of her clothes. He knelt at her feet, touched her wide, white belly, whispered things she could not hear and believed she wasn't meant to.

She made her way to the water. It was warm with the day's sun, the waves low, the pull light. She let herself walk in slowly, turn and watch for Orrin coming after her. He was not slow, but diving, swimming, past her and out to sea, and then she was taking after him, slicing at the water with her flat fingers, her pointed toes, her fast clean breath upon breath until it was gone.

She stopped. She could feel him treading the water beside her.

He would want her to be a cancan dancer, a fashion model, a whore. He would be a painter or a chef, and for weeks at a time they would live on hearts and brains he had fashioned into food. They would always have wine and live in a white room with high ceilings and curtains that gauzed at the breeze, a white room over a busy street, a street that spat and glittered and hummed all the day and all the night. When they walked that street, they would nestle into each other and he'd hold her arm as if it were something to take into himself and she'd lean into his chest from time to time as if she could not go on without his touch. It would be hot and the air heavy, but above that there would be the way their bodies fell into each other, like latches and meters and time spent close to something necessary. They would never learn to speak French. They would live like strangers to everyone but themselves.

He caught his arms around her shoulders, under her knees, and spun her through the water, letting her hair trail out behind her. She looked at the sky. She could see every star there ever was. Her baby was days from being born.

He said, "So if it was France, you would come?"

She said, yes, of course, and always.

But they weren't talking about his leaving. They were talking about hers.